BETRAYED

BITTER HARVEST, BOOK FOUR

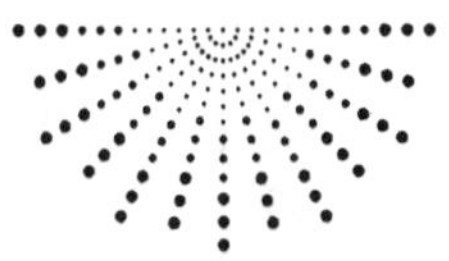

ANN GIMPEL

Edited by

KATE RICHARDS

CONTENTS

BETRAYED

BITTER HARVEST, BOOK FOUR

Dystopian Urban Fantasy
By
Ann Gimpel

BOOK DESCRIPTION: BETRAYED

A runaway spell is the most dangerous weapon of all.

Karin's watched magic ebb and flow over her long life. A healer by nature, as well as a wolf Shifter, she fixes what she can and buries her personal needs deep. In a race against time, she and a small group of Shifters and humans are sailing toward a gateway in the Arctic. If they can't close it, Earth will be doomed.

Daide's a scientist, first and foremost. Once a world-renowned expert on treating cetaceans, his skills are rusty. Ten years as a Vampire altered a whole lot, and he's still analyzing his brand-new Shifter magic. Karin caught his eye before they left Ushuaia, but she seems to be in love with a dolphin Shifter. Immersed in jealousy, Daide considers walking away, but he can't give up. The only woman he's ever loved is worth fighting for. Consequences be damned.

Vampires, Witches, high-handed gods, Kelpies, and a host of others all want either the ship or the Shifters' magic. Even the simplest tasks grow thorny edges, and misunderstandings threaten to destroy everything.

1

DEATH COMES CALLING

Karin Carson had been relieved the lab on Deck Two was empty. It wasn't likely to remain that way, so she hurried up, fussing with the controls on the darkfield microscope. Nothing changed on her slide. Not the way she wanted it to, anyway.

"Yeah, right. Why would it? Sheer wishful thinking on my part," she mumbled.

Dragging herself upright, she moved to a prep area, stabbed her finger with a lancet, and made three more slides. Even though she worked automatically, fatigue dragged at her. A weariness so pervasive it was tough not to curl up in a ball on the floor and close her eyes.

"What did you find?" her wolf asked.

"Not sure," she hedged not bothering with telepathy. Magic of any kind took energy, a commodity she couldn't spare right now.

"What do you think you found?" her bondmate pressed. *"Must be something, or you wouldn't be making more of those glass things."*

Instead of answering, she prepped the new slides with different reagents. She'd suspected something was amiss when she hadn't bounced back from healing the dolphin Shifters' alpha. It had been

1

significantly more than just healing, though. The creature died, and she'd held onto its spirit with her magic, urging it back to this side of the veil. It had drained her resources down to bedrock, so she hadn't thought much about it when she didn't have her usual complement of energy afterward.

Working with Daide, one of two veterinarians aboard *Arkady*, she'd gone on to cure eight more dolphins, feeling slightly worse after each one. The last dolphin had been two days ago, and she'd expected her depleted energy to stage a recovery. It hadn't. If she were honest, she felt worse now than she had after they'd finished the dolphin.

Her bondmate had noticed. How could it not have? Because of its urging, she was here in the lab she'd helped set up on Deck Two, assessing what could possibly be wrong. She tamped back a wry grin. Nagging, wheedling, and cajoling came closer than urging. Her wolf had a relentless streak, one of many things she loved about it.

The slides were as ready as they'd ever be. She walked them over to a normal scope, set one on the stage, and bent over the binocular eyepieces. The same dyscrasia she'd seen earlier was even clearer here. It fit with her white count being off the charts high, but what made no sense was how she'd developed what looked like a precancerous anomaly in her blood over a few weeks' timeframe.

Bodies didn't operate that way.

Apparently mine did.

"Are you going to tell me?" the wolf demanded.

"Something is wrong with my blood." Karin straightened from her hunched position, not bothering with the other two slides. They'd contain the same information.

"Can you fix it?" Her wolf punctuated its question with a howl.

She scrunched her eyes shut to rest them and rubbed her temples to ease the headache that rarely let her be.

"Well, can you?" the wolf persisted.

"I don't know. The dyscrasia—wrongness—has to be a byproduct of magic, but I don't get it. The dolphins are Shifters too.

Their magic should be similar, nothing that would attack me, but it's the only logical explanation."

"What is? I'm your bondmate. Why are you making me dig so hard to get anything out of you?"

"Sorry. I don't mean to. There's this lethargy, and it drags at me. Makes it hard to think, and then I panic. If I don't figure this out damned soon, I fear my capacity to reason things through will desert me."

Yeah, and then I'll be totally screwed. She kept her last thought to herself, but the wolf probably culled it from her mind.

"What's the only logical explanation? I get the lethargy part, but you never answered me from before."

"I absorbed something when I healed the first dolphin shifter. I was far closer to him than the others since I forced his spirit to remain when it would have departed. I patched him back together with magic and cells from my body. It's impossible to do that without cross-contamination."

"Tell Ketha," the wolf urged. *"And Recco and Daide. Working together, maybe you can—"*

"Not yet," she cut in. "I appreciate you're worried, and that you care about me, but we'll be in Invercargill soon. Goddess only knows what we'll face there. My problems are trivial by comparison. I'll dose myself with something and see if I can't fix this on my own."

The wolf's silence was significant. Clearly it saw through her false assurances.

After another glance at the slide, she quickly slotted the next two into place and muttered, "Same story, different verse." Because Ketha, a microbiologist, and the men would recognize what was on the slides, she ditched them in the biohazard waste bin and marched to the cabinet where they stored their limited supply of pharmaceuticals.

Antibiotics weren't the answer. Neither was anything else in the cupboard. Maybe one of Invercargill's hospitals would have a selection of chemotherapy agents or immune modulators. It was possible. Even if the town was in as bad shape as Ushuaia had been, drugs that disappeared from clinics were items like opioids and benzodiazepines. No one wanted chemicals that made you puke and lose your hair.

She bit down hard on her lower lip. A precancerous condition that sprang out of nowhere didn't bode well. Meant it would progress fast and not be particularly amenable to standard treatment approaches. She'd have to engage her immune system to have a prayer of winning this battle, which meant she had to get her magic back online.

When she assessed the reservoir where her power dwelled, it was just as empty as it had been the day before. Why wasn't it bouncing back?

If I could figure it out, I'd be able to fix what's wrong with me.

Ketha trotted into the lab, coffee mug in hand, and stopped abruptly. Dark hair shot with red and gold strands fell in braids to her waist, and her golden eyes—byproduct of her wolf bondmate—narrowed. "Jesus. You look like hell. Are you sick?"

Karin shrugged. "Maybe. I'm sure I'll be right as rain after another night's rest."

Ketha covered the distance between them and splayed the flat of her hand across Karin's forehead. Before she could duck from beneath Ketha's touch, a jolt of power rocked her. The other Shifter's eyes widened. "Holy crap. You're running a fever. Your blood pressure is dangerously high, and your respiration rate—"

"I already know all those things." Karin dropped back a couple of steps to avoid Ketha's questing fingers—or magic.

"If you do, why aren't you doing something about it?" Ketha set her cup in a holder and crossed her arms beneath her breasts.

"Maybe because doing the wrong thing would be worse than doing nothing."

"What have you tried so far?"

Karin shook her head. "How about if you let this go for now? I'm sure it's nothing—"

"Well I'm not. We're never sick. Maybe you should shift. Your wolf heals faster than you do."

"If it comes to that, I will."

Ketha dropped her hands to her sides and angled her head. Her forehead creased into worried lines. "Why haven't you done it already? It's our first line of defense."

Karin turned away and closed the drug cabinet. When she turned back, she pasted a reassuring smile on her face. "I'll take care of it as soon as my magic's done recovering."

"But it's been two days since you and Daide finished with the dolphins," Ketha protested.

"Enough." Karin marshaled what little energy she had into the one word and strode out of the lab. In truth, she didn't have enough magic to shift—at least she was fairly certain she didn't. If Ketha kept picking at things, she'd be bound to discover how depleted Karin was. Once it happened, all bets were off, and everyone aboard the ship would be focused on her instead of what they should be thinking about, which was Invercargill.

What would they find there? It was a reasonable bet the natives would pose problems. If any remained. No one had responded to their radio calls. She dragged herself up one flight of stairs and along the corridor to her cabin, wishing she could lock herself inside. So far, Ketha hadn't followed her, but given time, she would. Hopefully, she wouldn't round up reinforcements.

Of all the times to come down with a mystery ailment, this wasn't a very good one. Not that any occasion existed when it wouldn't be problematic to operate at less than a hundred percent. Karin slumped into the room's single chair, weariness crashing over her in waves.

She steepled her fingers, pressing the tips together to force a point of concentration. Maybe she was onto something with her incompatible magic theory. Zoe had been right there with her, but

Karin had absorbed the dolphin's essence, shielding it so Leif's primary form wouldn't die.

Her wolf was quiet, but she felt it prowling within her. "Do you know when our line diverged from the sea Shifters?"

"What exactly are you asking?"

"Not whatever we argued about that created the schism. It's not important. Do you know when they took to their sea forms while we stuck to the human ones? Also, when did we abandon a social structure where alphas ran things."

"Long ago, your primary form would have been mine. All Shifters were animals first, humans second, until the Romans made it dangerous for wolves and coyotes. They were captured and tossed in pits to fight. Hawks and eagles were trapped and forced to hunt."

Karin frowned. She thought she knew Shifter history, but she'd never heard about this part. "Why wouldn't we have fought back?"

"When we summoned magic to win contests in the pit—and save our lives—it revealed what we were, and many of our ancestors were hanged or burned."

"So someone decided we'd be safer in our human bodies. Makes sense."

The wolf growled. *"Like all solutions, some things improved, but others grew worse. We lost a goodly share of our magic during the tradeoff."*

"Which explains why the sea Shifters are more powerful than we are." Karin mulled it over. "Might also explain why their magic is different. You'd asked what is wrong with me, and I only gave you a partial answer. I'm convinced a disparity between my power and Leif's created the problem. His magic fought mine, and remnants of it are actively sabotaging my power. It's the only explanation that makes sense."

"So, get rid of the remnants. Seems simple enough."

Karin twisted her mouth into a grimace as she recalled the patchwork quilt she'd created where she wove her power with Leif's fading energy. He'd been ill for years with parasitic infections and was nearly at the end of his strength, so she'd borrowed liberally from her own magic and used it to shore up his. If she hadn't, he'd be dead.

But because she had, her own demise stared her in the face. If she couldn't reverse the process eroding her tissue and organ systems—and damned soon—there'd be nothing left to salvage.

"It's not simple," she told her wolf. "This is like an autoimmune disorder where my body is attacking itself. A healthy immune system sorts friend from foe. When I joined with Leif, I confused mine, and it's turned on me."

"Can you fix it?" the wolf asked again.

"I don't know. If I grow much weaker, I won't be able to do anything."

"If you're too depleted to shift, do you want me to break through? I can force a shift."

Karin shook her head. "I thought about it, and it's too dangerous for you. If I'm developing the sea Shifters' pattern, you could end up stuck. Instead of being able to return to the animals' world, you'd die here, and I won't do that to you."

"You don't know that."

"Oh but I do. If those dolphins and whales could have returned to a world like yours when they fell ill, they would have. They were stuck here." She swallowed around a thick spot in her throat. "I love you too much to have you sacrifice yourself."

"How about if I love you too?" the wolf countered. *"This is both our choices, not only yours."*

Karin blinked back tears.

Her door flew open, and Ketha marched inside, face twisted with pain—and anger. She kicked the door shut. "I dug your slides out of the trash. Why didn't you talk with me?"

"We have bigger problems than me right now." Karin kept her words simple, mostly because it was all she was capable of. "We're stopping in Invercargill at least long enough for Recco and Daide to make use of the cetacean institute's pools to work on the five whale Shifters. It will be a miracle if something doesn't attack us while we're there. You need to be planning for contingencies, not worried about me."

"I will not focus on contingencies while you wither and die on us." Ketha plopped onto the bunk nearest Karin. "Christ! You're an MD. I don't have to interpret what I found on those slides for you. Your white count is astronomical. Your body is destroying itself—"

"I know what's wrong. At least I believe I do," Karin protested. "What I'm less certain of is how to neutralize it."

"Maybe we can get hold of some chemotherapy drugs in Invercargill."

"Already thought about that. It might slow things down, but it won't work over the long haul. Immune modulators might, but chances of finding them in Invercargill are almost nil. The parts of Leif I absorbed when I saved him have to stop fighting me. I assumed our physiologies would be compatible, or I'd have made certain to establish a few degrees of separation."

Ketha shook her head. "You were in full savior mode. I know you, and when you go there, the last thing on your mind is your own safety."

"Your point?" Karin spoke stiffly.

"Not sure I had one. Can you shift?"

"No. Not enough magic, and before you suggest having my wolf circumvent the problem, I won't place it at risk."

"At risk, how?"

Breath rattled through Karin's teeth. "I already explained this to my bondmate. Do you think the dolphins and whales remained in a poisoned ocean voluntarily? Hell no, they didn't. They couldn't return to whatever borderworld they live in, or they would have. If I'm correct, and I'm changing into something more like our sea kin, my wolf could be trapped here and die."

I can fight this thing off. I know I can, the wolf chimed in.

Karin wanted to wrap her arms around its lush pelt and hug it, something she'd never be able to do.

"I heard that." Ketha's voice was soft. "Why not give your wolf a chance?" Without waiting for Karin to answer, she continued. "Have you spoken with Leif?"

"Of course not. He was my patient. I took chances that didn't seem risky at the time, and—"

Ketha waved her to silence. "He might know a way to intervene. Those dolphins haven't had their human forms long enough for me to get to know any of them, but there could be a healer in the bunch. Their magic is stronger than ours." She turned her hands palms up. "Worth a shot."

Karin straightened, horrified by how much energy it took. "It is worth a shot. And if it doesn't work, I'll let my wolf shift for us."

A delighted howl ripped through her.

Ketha placed her hand on Karin's leg. "I'm going to find Leif now. If he has any ideas, I'll bring him back here."

Karin swallowed hard. "Thanks. I'll throw some cold water on my face. I'm burning up."

"Take some aspirin or Ibuprofen." Ketha quirked a brow. "Physician heal thyself."

Karin smothered a snort. "Awk! Since when did we stoop to quoting scripture? Christians would just as soon burn us as look at us, or have you forgotten?"

"Nothing holy about it. Only a phrase. Back very soon, I hope." Ketha sprang to her feet and bolted out the door.

Karin struggled upright and tottered to the sink. Cold water on her face and hands helped, and she swallowed three aspirin. She came close to breaking into a litany and telling her wolf how much she loved it, how much its presence and undeviating loyalty had always meant, but it knew. They'd been together for more than two centuries.

Karin rarely told anyone how old she was. In the first place, it didn't matter. In the second, she feared it would insert artificial distance between herself and the other women she'd ended up with in Ushuaia. Rowana had known, but she was the only one.

And now Ro was dead. She'd died a hideous death in Karin's arms, racked with pain but absolutely certain it was her time to go.

"Damn, but I hope I can exit with a tenth her grace and style."

"You are not going anywhere," the wolf said, steel in its voice.

The sound of running footsteps alerted Karin moments before her door swung inward. A worried-looking Leif burst through with Ketha right behind him. The dolphin shifter was naked and still dripping ocean water. The salt scent of the sea clung to him. Blue-gray hair shrouded his tall, broad-shouldered form to knee level, and he trained sea-blue eyes on Karin.

"Apologies," he said. "Finding clothes took a backseat to Ketha's summons." He placed a palm across Karin's forehead, and she felt a jolt of rough magic, glass shards and pepper flakes. He moved his hand from her face to her upper back and then her chest across her collarbones. Each place he touched her tingled unpleasantly, but the crippling inertia eased too.

"Well?" Ketha hovered behind him. The door was shut, so presumably she'd closed it.

Leif drew his brows into a thick line and skewered Karin with eyes shaded to gray. "Why didn't you call me sooner, wolf Shifter?"

"I kept thinking this would improve."

"Mmph. Would have been far easier to intervene a few days ago. I must summon the other dolphins. This will require all of us."

"What are you going to do?" Karin and Ketha asked at almost the same time, their words tripping over each other.

"Reclaim the parts within the Shifter doctor that do not belong," Leif said. "And hope to hell we don't injure her in the process." He blew out a tight breath. "This would have been simpler right after it happened, before my essence put down roots trying to displace land Shifter magic."

"At least it explains why I have no power," Karin muttered.

Leif leveled his gaze at her. "If we do not intercede, nor will you have a life. Sea Shifter enchantment is trying to convert you, except our two types of magic have grown incompatible over the centuries. Left unchecked, there's but one way out of this."

A knock was followed by dolphin shifters filing into the cabin. "We need a bigger space," one of them said.

"Aye, no room to maneuver in here," another voice chimed in.

"What in the hell is going on?" Daide yelled from somewhere in the hall.

Karin tried to tell him it was nothing, but her head whirled crazily. It might have been the three aspirin, since she rarely took anything. It might have been so many people crowded into her cabin. It might have been fear she wasn't going to make it through what lay ahead. Desperate to hang onto a semblance of control, she made a grab for consciousness. Did her damnedest to hang onto it, but it eluded her, and she fell ass over teakettle into a deep, black hole.

2

TOUGH CHOICES

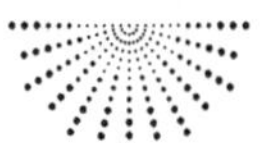

Dr. Diego Vegas—Daide to everyone—stood on *Arkady's* broad deck watching Invercargill draw closer. One of New Zealand's southernmost cities, it sat at forty-six degrees, which placed it eight degrees north of Ushuaia. Eight degrees meant a lot this far south, and it was warmer and wetter by a good, big bunch. He curled his gloved hands around the chilly metal railing. Whereas the tip of South America was nestled amid high, jagged mountains, Invercargill was farm county, stretching along a broad, flat plain.

What would they find there?

He sucked in a lungful of marine air and frowned. He didn't want to jinx their visit by assuming the worst, but they hadn't run across much that didn't want to kill them, or suck their magic dry, since leaving Ushuaia.

The water swooshed in choppy waves as dolphins breached the surface, expelling plumes through their blowholes. Grinning, Daide waved. After an inauspicious beginning where he'd damn near killed one of them, he'd managed to coax the other eight dolphin Shifters back to health with far less fanfare. He and Karin, that is, a wolf Shifter who was also an M.D. and a damn fine healer. Recco, his long-time practice partner, had worked alongside both of them with his usual, unflappable competence.

Bright jets of magic threaded through the spewing water, and the dolphins joined him on deck in their human forms. Wet. Naked. Happy. Hair wound around them in all colors of the rainbow. They left footprints across the cement deck as they darted through a door to a locker set up just for them. It contained clothes and boots, except none of them ever put the boots on.

Five whale Shifters circled *Arkady*, looking like reincarnations of geysers as they exhaled enormous showers of water. Daide wondered what their human forms would look like. Distinct from him, where his coyote's body was secondary, sea Shifters spent most of their time in their animal manifestation.

Leif, the dolphin he'd damn near killed, strode over to him still naked. Apparently, he hadn't joined the rush to the clothes locker. Blue-gray hair shrouded his well-muscled body, and water dripped from his long, straight locks. His deep blue eyes twinkled with anticipation, and he slapped Daide across the back.

"I swear, coyote Shifter. Not a day goes by that I don't feel stronger. I had no idea how feeble I'd grown."

Daide eyed him. "You wouldn't have because it's not a black and white thing. When you fade slowly over time, there's not such a contrast from day to day."

Leif nodded. "Yes. I knew it was bad, but I was in full denial about how serious my condition was."

Another dolphin, Lewis, joined them, clothes tossed on at haphazard angles. Straw-colored hair draped to knee level, and his eyes were smoky holes. He bared squared-off teeth and made a joking pass at Daide's arm. "Care for a rematch, mate?" he asked in a distinct British accent.

"One go-round with your teeth was enough, thank you." Daide put out a hand, and Lewis shook it.

"Will there be people there?" Lynda, another dolphin, pointed at Invercargill.

"People are fine," Daide said. "It's the other things I'd rather not deal with."

She shook wet, black hair over her shoulders and regarded him with deep-violet eyes. "We used to avoid those like you, coyote Shifter, but I remember Vampires and demons. They didn't bother those of us who lived in the sea."

"I can see where they wouldn't have. Not an easy environment for land-dwellers." He hesitated. "This question will demonstrate my ignorance, but why did all of you select names beginning with L?"

A musical trill reminding him of whale song burst from Lynda, followed by a laugh. "That's why. I just told you my sea name. Long ago, we only had sea names, but when we were human, we needed something pronounceable."

"The L names were a stopgap," Leif added. "Depending on which country we were in, we sometimes adopted something different if it fit the culture better."

"Before the Cataclysm, how much time did you spend in the sea?" Daide asked, wanting to know as much as he could about the dolphins.

Lewis shrugged. "Maybe 80 percent. We rarely ventured onto land for obvious reasons." He ticked several off on his fingers. "Clothes. Lodging. Money. Humans are a suspicious lot, and showing up naked and penniless doesn't engender trust."

"Leif!" Ketha called from a doorway. "I need you. Now."

"Sounds urgent," he muttered and trotted to her side. "Give me a moment, and I'll cover myself."

"No." Closing a hand around his forearm, she dragged him inside.

Daide stared after them. "What the dickens was that all about?"

"If it's important, our alpha will inform us," Lynda said, her demeanor turning somber.

Daide was still staring at the door that had closed behind Leif and Ketha. He didn't have a good feeling about her summons. Ketha had a cool head, and she'd sounded rattled. He turned his attention inward to his coyote. *"Do you know anything?"*

Before his bond animal could answer, Lewis spoke up. "There's something else we don't do."

Daide quirked a brow. "What?"

"Hold conversations with our animals when we're human and vice versa."

"But how do you get to know one another?"

"We just do," Lynda said. "We're born in the sea in our sea form. Our parents raise us in the ocean. The human part is far less important. It shows up later." She frowned. "I can't imagine my dolphin not knowing everything there is to know about who I am as a human."

Daide started to comment about how differently the two branches of Shifters had evolved when a startled look washed across Lynda's face. Spinning, she ran for the nearest door leading inside the ship with all the dolphin Shifters crowding close behind her.

After a hurried internal argument where Daide lectured himself whatever was going on was none of his business, he ran after them. They could tell him to get lost, but he didn't believe they would.

Shifters spilled out the door to Karin's cabin and into the corridor. No way to force a way through them, so he yelled, "What the hell is going on?"

The crowd parted. Leif strode through them, an unconscious Karin clasped in his arms. Ketha walked right behind him, and Daide fell in next to her. "Talk to me."

"It's a long story," Ketha muttered. "Follow us to the second dining room. We need a place Leif and the others can work on her."

"What are they going to do?"

Ketha trained her unnerving gaze on him. "I don't have access to their magic, so I have no idea. All I know is healing her was beyond my ability. And hers, which is how she ended up like this."

"But she was all right a couple days ago," he protested, followed by, "Never mind."

A tight place formed behind his breastbone as he went down a flight of stairs. Concern radiated through every nerve ending, and his muscles tightened into unyielding lumps. He cared about Karin. She had sharp edges, but they were tempered by compassion. She'd done plenty to ensure his connection with his coyote was strong and healthy. And she'd seen all the way to the bottom of his soul, ferreting out secrets that caused him shame.

Dragged into the light of day, those secrets hadn't been so bad after all.

The expression on Ketha's face told him how serious Karin's condition was. What had happened? She'd seemed subdued when they'd worked on the last two dolphins, but she'd never complained. Nor had she asked him to do more. He strode into the smaller of the two dining rooms. Leif had arranged Karin over one of the long tables. Lewis and three of the other male dolphin Shifters stood at her sides, hands extended over her prone form.

"What's going on here?" Viktor demanded as he bolted into the room. A raven Shifter, and captain of *Arkady*, he was also Ketha's husband. He'd been a vampire when they met, but she'd fallen in love with him anyway. Tawny hair spilled past his shoulders, and his green eyes were pinched at their corners.

"Silence!" Leif didn't turn around. "Better yet, shut the door and seal it with magic so we're not disturbed."

"I'll take care of it," Ketha said and covered the short distance to Viktor. "In or out?" she asked.

"Depends. Is this as critical as it looks?" He lowered his voice to a whisper, but Daide employed his acute coyote hearing to listen.

Ketha nodded and bent so her mouth was right over his ear. "The sea Shifters' magic is incompatible with ours. Incompatible enough, apparently they can't coexist in the same vessel."

Viktor's eyes widened in understanding. "This happened when she kept their alpha from dying, didn't it?"

"Good a guess as any." Ketha thinned her mouth into a harsh line. "Damn it. That woman never asks for anything for herself. I caught her in the lab. She was running tests, but do you think she told me anything?"

"I'm guessing no."

Daide edged closer, not wanting to miss anything. A sinking feeling twisted his stomach into a knot. Karin had stepped in because of his screw up. If he hadn't been so goddamned certain what the dolphin shifter needed— He hacked his line of thought off at the roots. He could feel guilty and responsible later. Right now, the important one was Karin.

She had to survive. If she died because of his misplaced confidence in his rusty veterinary skillset, he'd have a hell of a time living with the fallout.

"Pretended nothing was wrong," Ketha was saying. Daide had missed the first part.

Viktor gave Ketha a quick, hard hug. "Keep me posted. I'm going back to the bridge."

Blue-white jets shot from her fingertips as she sealed the door once he was through it. She sidled next to Daide. "You heard all of that."

"Yes." He didn't bother to deny he'd been eavesdropping.

"Good. Means I don't have to say it again."

A glowing nimbus flashed and flared in blues and greens around Karin. Leif clasped one of her hands; another dolphin Shifter had the other. The lyrical notes of the sea folk's language rose in harmonic cadence, beautiful and enigmatic by turns.

The squeaks, howls, snorts, and grunts blended into a whole far more than the sum of its disparate parts. Daide had listened to dolphins and whales for years, but these notes spanned the scale from high to low and back again. They beckoned to him, invited him to immerse himself in the sea.

He shook himself hard. A sea dragon had used words to entice him to join it in the ocean, but all it wanted was to drain his magic. Even his coyote hadn't seen through the wily creature. Panic engulfed him. Whose side were the sea Shifters on? When they were done, would Karin be one of them?

Ketha caught his gaze and held it. When she was certain she had his attention, she shook her head. "The die is cast. This course was the only one open to us, so we must believe in it."

"We don't know if this was the only way," he hissed. "What else did you try?"

"Nothing. Goddamn stubborn woman wouldn't admit anything was wrong until I dug her slides out of the biohazard waste and confronted her."

Daide leaned closer. Science was his comfort zone. Where he lived. Never mind it had turned into an anachronism. Dolphin song bleated around him, the antithesis of science. Compelling and foreign, it made it harder to think, but he couldn't block it out. "Slides? So she must have known—or at least suspected—how ill she was. What'd you find?"

"Her blood is chewing itself up. Looks like an autoimmune reaction at the eleventh hour."

"Must be some way for us to intervene." Daide sucked in a tight breath as possibilities bounced from one side of his brain to the other. Every potential intervention required drugs they didn't have, though.

She shook her head. "Wish we could, but I don't see how. What's magic-spawned requires magic to fix."

The corona around the sea Shifters grew, forming walls, and the salt smell of the sea intensified as water filled an oblong container around Karin and the Shifters. Breath stuck in Daide's throat. In the space of a minute, flashing lights had transformed into a capsule full of saltwater. He ground his teeth as helplessness pummeled him.

"But she won't be able to breathe," he protested and started forward.

Ketha latched onto his arm. "They're cetacean. They don't have gills, which means they have to drain that contraption sometime soon. Do not disturb them. No matter how alien this seems to us, if we interfere, goddess only knows what might happen."

"Are you certain she was dying?"

A quick, harsh glance answered him without the need for words. He balled his hands into fists. How could something like this happen so fast? He wasn't exactly a virgin where magic was concerned, but the ten years he'd been a Vampire didn't count for much. He'd only been a Shifter for a handful of months, a timespan when they'd fought for their lives almost every day. Of the other three men aboard, who'd been Vamps right along with him, he'd had the most difficult time with their transition.

Maybe because his bond to his coyote had been weak, he'd been targeted first by a sea dragon, and then by demons. He still felt raw and dirty from the dark things that had taken up residence in his body, but Karin had admonished him to move past the personal.

This was about all of them, not his horror and distaste at being chosen by evil.

Karin.

He tried to peer through the wall of sea Shifters to see what was happening, but they'd closed ranks. Maybe on purpose to shield whatever their alpha was doing.

"I don't like this," he muttered.

"How do you think I feel?" Ketha twisted to stare at him. "Quite aside from my long friendship with Karin, she and Rowana stood in as mothers when my own decided I didn't need her anymore."

Something about Ketha's words snagged his attention. "How old were you?"

She made a sour face. "Doesn't matter."

A gurgling gagging sound rose over the chirps and honks from the dolphins.

"Damn it. She's drowning." Daide ripped his arm out of Ketha's grasp and covered the distance to the sea Shifters in two long strides. All of them were inside the translucent wall. He splayed his hands across its rough surface, and a blast of electricity shot him halfway across the room.

One minute he was on his feet. The next, he sprawled on his ass. Every part of his body vibrated from shock and pain. He bellowed his outrage.

Ketha fell to her knees next to him, hands moving over his body and checking for his pulse. "I was afraid something like that would happen if we touched the barrier." She punched a fist into the floor. "I tried to warn you, but you moved too fast."

The strangled gurgling noises grew more frantic. Daide lurched upright and forced his legs, which didn't want to cooperate, to carry him closer. He needed to see. Except the wall of dolphin bodies hadn't budged.

"I trusted you, and you were nearly the death of me." Leif's voice blasted into his head. *"I require the same trust from you. That jolt of current cut both ways. Another like it, and the wolf Shifter won't make it."*

"How can we help?" Ketha asked.

"By not interfering."

"A tad bit of faith wouldn't hurt," the dolphin with the British accent added.

"It would be easier to have faith if we could lay eyes on our friend. May we talk with her wolf?" Ketha raked hair back from her face.

"Best idea you've come up with," Leif replied. *"Now, leave me to this. I must concentrate, and I only have a few more minutes before I'll have to take down my healing dome."*

The wall of Shifters moved, allowing a partial view of Karin. Her body was convulsing, hair fluttering around her in water that danced to its own tune, ebbing and flowing from one edge of the tank to the other.

Ketha dropped a heavy hand on his shoulder. "I'm opening my magic to you, so you can hear this too."

Daide waited, unable to stop staring at Karin. At least she was still twitching, but damn if her movements didn't mimic death throes.

Faith. Leif said I had to have faith.

He swallowed around a bitter taste where bile had splashed the back of his throat. The hard truth was he didn't trust anything magical. His attitude had its roots in his tenure as a Vampire, but it hadn't truly changed over the months fighting alongside Shifters. Chagrin filled him with a creeping, uncomfortable sensation.

Apparently, this stint on *Arkady* was his opportunity to come to terms with himself—in an uncomfortably up-close and personal way. Whether he wished to or not.

"*Well met, old friend,*" Ketha's wolf said.

A gravelly growl reverberated through Daide's skull. "*Scarcely well met, though you and I are indeed compatriots.*"

Daide did what he could to still his racing heart. The second voice had to be Karin's wolf. Deep within him, his coyote yipped once and quieted.

"*How can we help you?*" Ketha's wolf went on, voice liquid with compassion.

"*The alpha is doing everything he can. I tried to tell my bondmate we'd been contaminated by sea Shifter residue, and that it wouldn't end well, but she ignored me. Until she was almost too weak to stand.*"

"*Why didn't you let one of us know?*" Daide asked.

"*Doesn't work that way,*" Karin's wolf replied. "*My first loyalty is to my bondmate. If she'd wanted you to know, she'd have told you herself.*"

"*You're still within Karin,*" Ketha's wolf observed.

The statement was open-ended, so Daide assumed it was significant, but wasn't certain quite how. Would the wolf abandon Karin before she died? It had that option, but might not choose to exercise it.

Ketha's fingers tightened painfully around Daide's shoulder. Her teeth grated together; hot breath grazed his cheek. "Get ready. This next part will happen fast."

Daide pushed his primitive magic outward in an arc. Something monumental bore down on them. Harsh, arcane enchantment sucked the air from the room and left him gasping as if water surrounded him too. His lungs burned, and his vision hazed to gray. A crackling thud battered his ears, and the seawater container fractured down one end. Water rushed across the dining room floor but was absorbed almost as fast as it escaped.

Ketha let go of him and shot forward to the table where Karin lay. She turned her on her side and pushed on her back. Water spewed from Karin's mouth and nose. Seeing something as simple and non-magical as first aid broke into the inertia that had him in its grasp, and Daide leapt toward them.

He and Ketha worked as a team clearing Karin's lungs and starting CPR. At first, he couldn't find a heartbeat, but he kept pushing on her chest, willing her to live while Ketha did rescue breathing. Thirty compressions, followed by two breaths. Over and over.

Leif hovered, but remained silent. Daide met his worried blue eyes. "The thing you did, was it…? Er, were you…?"

"Yes, coyote Shifter. But my success will be moot if—"

Karin choked and gagged. Daide flipped her onto her side, and she vomited seawater onto the floor, followed by a coughing fit. When he looked at Ketha, her eyes shone with tears. She knelt and gathered Karin into her arms. "Thank the goddess you're as tough as you are," she muttered and planted a kiss on Karin's forehead.

"Too mean to die," Karin choked out between coughs. "Jesus, I feel like warmed-over dogshit."

Leif pushed Ketha aside and gathered Karin close, pushing curly white hair out of her face. "Be grateful you feel anything, wolf Shifter," he admonished. "The dead feel nothing."

"Why'd you almost drown me?" She struggled to a sit.

"Not a quick answer for that." Leif sat next to her. When he wrapped an arm tenderly around her to support her, a dart of jealousy stabbed Daide between the eyes. He wanted to shove Leif out of the way, kick his ass across the dining room for making

Karin suffer. And for having the temerity to hold onto her in such a familiar way.

Christ on a fucking crutch, whatever is wrong with me?

Muttering, "Glad you're okay," he stalked across the room before he made a huge mistake. Going after Leif would alienate the sea Shifters forever.

"Where are you going?" Ketha called and withdrew glowing magic flickering around the sealed door.

"To report to Viktor," he replied without turning around. If he did, the expression on his face—desolation mixed with anger— would give him away. As he made his way up endless stairs, truth pounded into him. Somewhere along the line, he'd fallen in love with Karin, but his insight came too late. Plus, it was a bad idea.

Even worse now Leif was in the picture. Leif was old—like Karin. Far better mate material for her. She'd treated Daide like the green, newly hatched Shifter he was. She'd been kind, maternal even, but those were scarcely the elements in a romantic partnership.

"Coyotes fight for our mates," his bond animal spoke up.

Daide didn't bother to reply. He didn't need his coyote reminding him how deficient he was, and it rankled. Fighting for Karin was out of the question. He'd make a bigger fool of himself than he already had.

He stepped onto the bridge. Viktor took one look at him and swore in German. "That rough, eh, mate? Do I need to officiate at another sea burial?"

Daide gazed at him, bleary-eyed. "Oh no. Nothing like that. She'll recover."

Viktor stared hard at him. "They why do you look so trashed?"

"It was a hard road." Daide shrugged. "Mostly, I stopped by here to let you know Karin was all right. If you don't need me, I'll be on my way."

"What the fuck is the matter with you?" Viktor pressed. "You don't seem anything like yourself."

"Just tired. Once you've figured it out, let us know how you want to finesse landfall in Invercargill." Without waiting for Viktor to reply, Daide retraced his steps and ducked into his cabin. Maybe if he stayed there long enough, he wouldn't have to see Leif with his arm around Karin again.

At least not today.

3

WOLVES HAVE NINE LIVES TOO

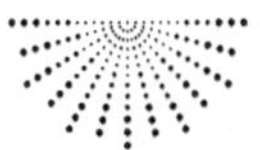

Karin lurched back to awareness as Leif carried her through the corridor. A bizarre, Fellini-esque consciousness where she watched herself from the sidelines through wavy glass that splintered her vision. When she tried to move, she couldn't. Paralysis had set in. Dying was like this. You lost control over your body from the periphery inward.

Dammit! Who fucking cares. This isn't a physiology text. It's my life for chrissakes.

Karin reached for her wolf, relieved by its steady presence. *"You should leave,"* she told it, surprised telepathy was still within her grasp. *"I'm dying, and—"*

"None of that!" The wolf's familiar voice cracked like a bullwhip. *"The sea Shifter will help us."*

Karin was so out of it, she'd nearly forgotten Leif. Stupid of her since he'd just laid her on a table, which meant she had to be in one of the dining rooms. While she struggled to wrap her fading mental processes around what that meant, he ran his hands over her.

Magic flared, skidding through her from top to bottom and side to side. It tingled and burned. A million stinging bees couldn't have been much worse. She groaned and tried to escape his questing fingers, but they were all over her without any regard for propriety.

"Wolf Shifter." Leif's voice buzzed, leaping from one side of her brain to the other in a symphony gone wild. *"Can you hear me?"* He gripped her right hand. *"Squeeze if you can."*

She did her damnedest, but her fingers weren't any more cooperative than the rest of her.

Telepathy. I can use telepathy.

Ridiculously grateful she'd figured even such a small thing out, she said, *"Yes, but I'm paralyzed."*

His blue eyes widened in surprise. At least her vision hadn't given up the ghost, but then it would be one of the last things to go. Controlled by the optic and oculomotor nerves, numbers two and three respectively of the twelve cranial nerves—

Karin would have laughed if a few of her other cranial nerves had been more cooperative. Her med school professors would be proud their lessons transcended death.

I am not dead yet, she lectured herself, punctuated by a growl from her wolf.

"Since you can hear me," Leif said, *"the next things to happen won't be pleasant, yet if I do not proceed, you will die. I must reclaim what is mine. Our magics were never meant to comingle in a single body."* He bent until his head was even with hers and augered his strange eyes into hers. *"You should have said something. This would have been far easier even twenty-four hours ago."*

"I didn't want to bother anyone, and I was certain I'd get better. What are you going to do?" Karin tried to tilt her head, but it didn't work any better than her other efforts at movement.

"Better if you don't know. Trust me. Believe in my magic. It's stronger than yours, and I owe you my life. I will do everything in my power to return the favor." He glanced at the other dolphin Shifters ranged around her impromptu gurney—or bier. *"My pod will assist me."*

As if he'd cued them, the dolphins began to chant. At first, she heard music, but then it shaded to squeaks, squeals, and grunts, not unlike whale song she'd listened to. A booming filled her ears, and water rushed over her, sharp with the tang of the sea.

Panic crushed her, along with the weight of the water. She tried to hold her breath, but it was a lost cause. Water rushed into her lungs, and she cursed herself for a fool. Why had she trusted a sea Shifter? The ones who'd rather spit on their land cousins than say good morning.

I trusted him because I had no choice. I'd lapsed into unconsciousness when he snatched me up.

Her mind spun crazily, latching onto one meaningless thing after another. Was this how her life would end? Drowned by a dolphin?

Her bondmate. Her wolf. *"Are you still here?"* she cried, her mind voice fuzzy with her ebbing energy.

"I am. Hang on, heart of mine. They're nearly done."

Bright lights flared, and Karin felt herself drawn toward them. She understood what was happening. Random neurons were firing in her dying brain. *"You have to go,"* she insisted. *"I will not cause your death. Return to the animals' world, and—"*

"Enough," the wolf snarled. *"The woman I've been linked to for two centuries is not a coward. Believe in us. In your life."*

A snap sharp as a guillotine blade sent shock waves through her, and the water left as quickly as it had come. Hands pushed hard on her back, driving water out through her lungs and nose, but she still couldn't move. Couldn't even blink.

How could she be dead and still sense what was happening around her? Ketha was the one pounding on her back. Daide joined her, and they did a credible job at CPR. Karin wanted to tell them to keep going, Not to give up. She wanted to thank them. She struggled, decided she was making this way too hard, and reached for her magic. A paw closed over her hand, claws raking flesh, and the two of them punched through the shroud that held her prisoner.

The brilliant, beckoning white light exploded into bits of nothingness.

A cough racked her, deep and burning and insistent, followed by several more. Daide flipped her onto her side just in time for bloody vomit to fly from her mouth—probably from her lungs too. More pounding on her back. More coughing, each fit feeling like it ripped cells from every organ within her.

None of that mattered. She was alive. Jubilation careened through her until she felt drunk. And why not? Being drunk and throwing up went together. Another series of heaves rocked her, but they cleared her lungs and airway.

Ketha knelt and gathered her into arms that trembled. "Thank the goddess you're as tough as you are," she muttered and planted a kiss on Karin's forehead.

"Too mean to die," Karin choked out between coughs. "Jesus, I feel like warmed over dogshit."

Leif moved Ketha aside and pushed Karin's wet curly white hair out of her face. "Be grateful you feel anything, wolf Shifter," he admonished. "The dead feel nothing."

"Why'd you almost drown me?" She struggled to a sit.

"Not a quick answer for that." Leif sat next to her. When her uncooperative muscles threatened to dump her onto the floor, he put an arm around her shoulders to stabilize her.

"*See?*" Her wolf sounded insufferably smug. "*Told you. If you're going to pick anyone to believe, it should be me.*"

"*I do believe in you, dear heart,*" Karin said. "*But that belief was sorely tested. I knew I was dying, if not already dead. For you to argue I wasn't felt like wishful thinking on your part.*"

"*I may love you,*" the wolf said, "*but I'd never lie about something as important as our survival.*"

Karin could have hugged it. "*Apologies. Don't mind me.*"

"*For now, I won't.*" A whuffling gurgle that was probably laughter rippled from her belly, finding its way out her mouth.

"Where are you going?" Ketha called.

Karin focused her still-groggy brain and understood the question was aimed at Daide, who was most of the way across the room. She wanted to thank him, but before she could get the words out, he was gone. "Nice job on CPR," she mumbled. "Be sure and let Daide know."

Ketha snorted. "I will. Coming from you, Madam Doctor, that's high praise."

"You asked about your near-drowning experience," Leif said. "I had to immerse you in water to loosen the bits of me that you'd retained. Luckily, there weren't too many of them, and they came to me willingly enough when I called. I'm mostly a creature of the water. Not true for you. You're primarily linked to land. Because sea Shifter magic is stronger, it fought for ascendency, and it wouldn't have stopped until it drove you into the sea."

"A place she couldn't survive," Ketha said.

"Precisely." Leif nodded. He gazed at the other dolphin Shifters, who'd moved into a semicircle around them. "You did well. You may leave to refresh yourselves as you choose."

One of two women inclined her head. Black hair scraped the floor and her violet eyes shone warmly. "We are grateful you survived, wolf Shifter."

A chorus of "yes" and "open waters and wind at your back" rose from the others. They filed from the room chattering in the same honks and squeaks Karin had heard before. "You speak your sea language as humans."

"We do," Leif concurred. "How do you communicate with your bond animals?"

"Telepathy in whatever language is primary for the human. The animals know every language."

Leif made a grunting noise. "You don't want to know what my dolphin thinks about that."

"Probably not." Ketha screwed her face into a thoughtful expression. "I almost hate to ask, but have you been in communication with your lieges?"

Leif furled his brows. "Poseidon and Amphitrite?"

"Who else?" Ketha muttered.

"The answer to that is no." He pressed his mouth into a thin line. "They do not come to my call, and believe me I attempted to reach them over the long years of what you labeled the Cataclysm. Even when they never answered, I continued to try anyway. Informed them how desperate our plight was."

"Surely, they must have known," Karin said. Compassion for the dolphin warmed her, but made her sad too. "Whale song carrying news of each whale dying must have reached them."

"You would think." Bitterness lined his words, and he gazed at Ketha. "Why did you ask about the sea gods?"

"We're nearly in Invercargill. It would be lovely for us to sail in and out of there without incident, but it hasn't happened yet. Every single place we've stopped has held unpleasant surprises."

"You were hoping for a god or two to fight on our side?" He shook his head. "Best of luck to you. If they bypassed us and our plight, it's not likely they'll lift a finger for you and yours." He stood. "My dolphins and I will provide what aid we can. And I'm certain the whales will mount a defense once they're cured of the parasites. You do still plan to treat them?"

"Oh my yes," Karin said.

"Mmph. Then why did the veterinarian run out of here as if a shiver of sharks was after him?"

"He's had a hard go of it," Ketha explained.

"Hopefully, that's all it is," Leif muttered. "He seemed put out about something. Do you feel like eating a little?" he asked Karin.

Her insides felt scoured, raw, but food would help her recover. "Sure. Maybe some soup and tea."

"I was thinking a stiff belt of whiskey," Ketha said.

Karin's stomach rolled over onto itself. "God, no. Not booze. Things are unsettled enough in here." She patted her midsection.

"Good choice." Leif extended a hand and helped her to her feet. "Sea Shifters do not drink anything alcoholic. It interferes with our power. If you come with me, I will warm something nourishing for you in the ship's galley."

Karin leaned against him. "Thank you. That would be appreciated."

"I'll head up to the bridge once you're settled," Ketha said. "I've been expecting Viktor to announce 'land ho' any time. Surprised it hasn't happened yet."

"I can come up there after I'm done eating." Karin smiled gamely.

Ketha shook her head. "I don't think so. Rest up. Save your energy for the whales. In case you have to help Daide and Recco."

Karin tottered toward the door leading across the hall into the other dining room. The larger eating area backed onto the galley. Ketha placed a hand under her elbow and helped Leif keep her upright.

"Damn. I hate feeling this feeble." Karin inhaled deeply. Maybe if she could move more air into her lungs, she wouldn't pitch onto her face. She yelped as the deep breath made her abraded bronchial cells burn like crazy.

"It will pass." Ketha helped her sit at a table, and Leif disappeared into the galley. "I'll wait until your meal arrives."

"You're not fooling me." Karin kept hold of Ketha's steadying hand. "You don't trust me on my own. I wouldn't trust me either at this point."

"Shifters heal fast," Ketha reminded her. "You'll feel ever so much better in a few hours. Have you seen Recco and Zoe lately?"

"Trying to give me something to think about other than my own misery, eh? I recognize that ploy. Used it myself a time or two." She chuckled. "Yes, I've seen them. They're disgustingly immersed in one another. Nothing like getting laid after a long hiatus to bring a glow to your cheeks and a shine to—"

Ketha jabbed her in the ribs. "I'm happy for them. And for Juan and Aura too."

"So am I, sweetie. We had such a miserable decade in Ushuaia, we deserve every single good thing that comes our way. I was being my usual, irascible self."

"I heard some of that." Leif crossed the room balancing a tray.

Karin inhaled hungrily. "Smells wonderful. I didn't think I could choke down more than a bite or two. In truth, I was humoring both of you by coming in here, but I'm about to make a liar out of myself."

"Good." Ketha exchanged a pointed look with Leif and stood. "Take care of her."

"No worries on that subject." Leif set the tray in front of Karin and sat in the seat Ketha had vacated.

Karin picked up a spoon and dipped it into what smelled like a rich chicken broth. "Aren't you going to eat?" she asked Leif.

"Later. In the sea." He smiled broadly. "Now that fish are returning, it's such a pleasure to dine again."

"What did you eat before?" Karin spooned soup into her mouth, following it with a bite of biscuit.

"Whatever we could find. When the seas yielded nothing, we took our human forms and ate vegetation and small mammals." He made a distasteful face. "None of us liked it, but the alternative was starvation."

"We ate plenty of rats in Ushuaia," Karin said. "Never got used to them. They have a bitter taste." She valued directness, and dished it out. No point beating around the bush when you wanted to know something.

"I see a question forming in your mind. You have my permission to ask."

She straightened from her slump and eyed him. "Since when do I require your permission for anything?"

He shook his head, nostrils flaring. "Poor choice of words. When you've been an alpha as long as I have, sometimes things slip out."

"Tell me what you know about how our magics carved out such divergent pathways. Were we ever similar enough to share power?"

"You might be better served asking one of the whales. They're truly ancient, and out of all the sea Shifters, they were the only ones who almost never took their human forms."

"They why be a Shifter at all?" Karin dipped her spoon into her bowl, surprised to find it empty.

Leif steepled his fingers together and rested his chin on them. "Sorry. I'm not being clear. Long ago, maybe as much as two millennia, we were all the same. Obviously, we'd bonded with different types of animals, but our abilities and magic were indistinguishable. We also walked proud in those days. Humans revered us, saw us as gods…"

A shadow crossed his face. "The Christian era brought many changes. Men no longer respected magic or magical beings. Instead, they viewed us as anathema and began burning and hanging us."

"It couldn't have only been Shifters," Karin cut in and polished off the last crumbs of bread on her plate. "Hang onto the answer to that. I'm going to get myself a tiny bit more since what I've eaten seems to be settling."

Ridiculously pleased by how much stronger she felt—anything would have been a striking improvement—she crossed to the galley and plopped another biscuit onto her plate. Instead of eating it plain, she slathered this one with tinned apricot preserves, all the while blessing a food industry that had figured out how to produce products that didn't spoil.

She returned to the table and sat, licking jam off her fingers.

Relief shone from Leif's eyes, a pale blue this time. "You truly are better. I can rest easier now. The first span of time is the most critical. Back to our discussion. Of course it wasn't only Shifters. Mages, Druids, Witches, even Vampires were targeted. The prudent course was to hide our magical ability. It was far easier for land Shifters, since you'd always preferred your human bodies."

"Not so easy for you, though." Karin chewed and swallowed, enjoying the flaky pastry as it broke apart on her tongue.

Sadness rolled from him in waves. "The Selkies came to us for protection. We failed them, but then we could scarcely protect ourselves. At that point, our magic was exactly like yours, and we weren't able to spend long periods in the sea. Our power was unpredictable. We had little warning when it would break apart. If a human saw us shift, that was the end of things. We were killed on the spot, or dragged before a kangaroo court that tried us without benefit of judge or jury."

"What happened?" Karin rested her chin on an upraised hand. Even though Leif's story was hideous, he was easy to listen to.

His gaze skittered away from hers, and his cheeks turned ruddy. "We made a bargain with the Witches. That was when our power changed and was no longer like yours."

Karin's eyes widened. In a spontaneous gesture, she gathered a magical net and draped it around him, testing his magic. Sure enough, Witch power burned behind the scenes. Truncated, it slotted perfectly with Shifter energy, essentially vanishing unless she'd known to look for it.

"That's quite an elegant spell," she said.

He made a sour face. "Sneaky is more like it, but it was the best we could come up with. The price was high, rather akin to selling your soul to the devil."

"No way back, eh?"

"About the size of it. Poseidon and Amphitrite were furious, but we'd begged them to intervene before we sealed the Witch bargain, and they ignored us."

"I'm guessing it's a pattern for them." She shrugged. "Not that I have any right to criticize. The Celtic gods never showed themselves to any of us. Not the Greco-Roman crew, either. Or the Norse batch. It was a clean sweep."

"Have you had enough?" He cast a pointed look at her plate, now empty for the second time."

Karin nodded. "Did you ever ask the Witches to unwind their casting?"

"I have no idea. That's a whale question. My best guess was we grew used to the new normal and spent more and more time in the sea. Our marine nature was a boon after the Cataclysm hit. I'm not sure any of us would have survived if we'd been stuck in a town. Humans are a superstitious lot, even the modern variety. They'd have wanted someone to blame for the disaster, and magic-wielders would have risen to the top of the heap fast."

"Didn't work that way in Ushuaia. Humans were suspicious at first, but then they welcomed our assistance."

"Because they had no choice." Leif leveled his gaze her way.

"True enough. Thank you for taking care of me." Karin laid a hand over his and stood. "I believe I'll find my way to my cabin. Ketha was right to give me hell when I said I'd show up on the bridge."

Leif scrambled to his feet. "I'll ferry your dishes back to the galley and then retire to the sea."

"Thank your pod for me."

"I will."

The PA system crackled, and Karin stopped halfway to the door.

"We'll be dropping anchor in half an hour," Viktor's deep voice with its hint of a German accent rumbled. "Everyone but Karin head to the bridge for a briefing now."

She felt torn, but she'd do a whole lot better if she put her feet up for even half an hour. Nodding to herself, she made for the door.

"Still going to your cabin?" Leif asked.

"Yup." Karin said over one shoulder.

"Good. I will make certain you know the gist of this briefing."

She turned to face him. "I thought you'd be in the sea."

He picked up her small stack of dishes. "My pod will need to know what Viktor has in mind too. I'm the only one left aboard, so I'm the logical choice to respond to his summons."

"Even though you'd prefer it otherwise."

His sadness from earlier shimmered around him in dark blue swirls shot with black spots. "We rarely get to pick our preferences, land Shifter."

"Isn't that the truth." She plodded out the swinging door and dragged herself up one flight, her inertia from earlier back with a vengeance.

Her bunk looked so inviting, she dove into its soft folds and was asleep before she could dissect Leif's story. She'd wanted to analyze it and overlay everything she knew about Witches, but it would have to wait.

4

SOME BARGAINS KEEP ON GIVING

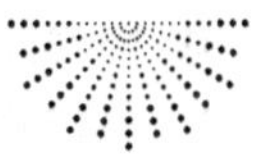

*D*aide hunkered next to Recco in a Zodiac headed for a phalanx of crumbling piers. Viktor manned the helm, having left Juan to watch over *Arkady*. They'd worked together before the Cataclysm, running a polar adventure cruise service. Aura, Juan's mate and a mountain cat shifter, was with them, along with Ketha and Moira, a vulture shifter. Recco's coyote shifter girlfriend, Zoe, sat on Recco's other side. Boris and Ted, two human refugees they'd picked up from the ruins of Arctowski research station on King George Island rounded out their shore team.

"Too bad about the piers," Boris said. "It would have been convenient to make use of them."

Viktor shaded his eyes with a hand, staring shoreward. "Yeah. I considered bringing *Arkady* in anyway. This bay used to be plenty deep enough to accommodate ships with her draft, but I wasn't certain how much debris is littering the harbor. We've been here before, you know. For a couple years, we ran tours from Invercargill to McMurdo."

"Why only a couple years?" Ketha asked.

"The trips ended up being mostly ocean and not enough shore expeditions for most of our clients' tastes. Plus, they tied the boat up for a month. We made more money on twelve- and fourteen-day trips. Out and backs from Ushuaia to the Palmer Peninsula."

"Sure and it always comes down to the bottom line." Zoe smiled and leaned into Recco. He slotted an arm around her.

Daide cast a quick glance their way, trying not to be obvious about it. He was glad they were finding happiness together, and he hoped to hell it would last.

"I wore too many clothes for today." Moira pushed her hood off her black hair. A bevy of curls tumbled in the breeze, and she gathered them at the nape of her neck and stuffed the mass of strands beneath her parka.

"You're quiet, *amigo*," Recco murmured, aiming his words at Daide.

He shrugged, not willing to rip open the can containing his raw emotions. As if to taunt him, dolphin fins cut the wake around them. Viktor killed the engine, and Leif swam close. "We'll be over there"—he aimed a flipper to the east—"checking out the cetacean institute. If enough of the deep pools are left for us to take advantage of, I'll let the whales know."

His speech as a dolphin was garbled but understandable. To avoid thinking about the Shifter with his arm around Karin, Daide recalled the morphology of dolphin vocal chords. The topic was sterile enough, it had a settling effect.

"Make sure the whales keep their distance until we're certain what we face." Viktor shifted his attention to his wife and raised his eyebrows.

Ketha shook her head. "I've scanned and scanned, but if my magic is correct, nothing lives in Invercargill anymore."

"It's odd. I'm not even picking up mice and rats, and they're ubiquitous. I always figured they'd be the last to go in Ushuaia." Zoe scrubbed the heels of her hands down her face and unzipped her parka a few inches. "Damn, but I'm overdressed."

Daide was sweating too. Once they left the Zodiac behind and the ambient wind off the ocean, it would be even warmer. Maybe he'd leave his thick waterproof jacket in the raft—along with his life vest.

Recco leaned closer. "You seem off to me. Is something wrong?"

"Nah. Only tired. That episode with Karin was difficult—and unexpected."

Recco punched him companionably. Straight dark hair blew around his high cheekbones and square chin. His looks reflected his native South American heritage, the same as Daide's own. "Yeah. I heard about it when Ketha told Vik. Why didn't you call me? I'd have helped."

"Everything happened really fast. My telepathy skills aren't all that great." He stopped shy of telling his old friend and practice partner he'd stormed the dolphins' barrier and been tossed halfway across the room, landing on his ass.

"I'm glad she's okay. What a stroke of luck Leif understood how to intervene."

"Yup. Of course. Lucky, indeed." Daide glanced away, feeling small and petty. He'd never cared about a woman before—not enough to let her get under his skin. Why the hell had Karin suddenly blossomed into prominence?

Because someone else wants her.

The thought made him feel even smaller and pettier. He'd never viewed himself as spiteful, and they were so few he had to get over his snit fast.

Viktor rose to his feet as the beach grew closer. "You know the drill, folks," he said and cleared the bow, slogging through water with the anchor rope in hand.

"Who wants the weapons?" Boris asked. He dragged an iron saber off the raft, and Ted carted an old-fashioned Remington. Its main claim to fame was it had come with bullets fashioned from silver and iron, guaranteed to make short work of Vampires. The rest of them exited the raft, and Viktor tied it off to a wooden piling canting at a thirty-degree angle but with solid attachment to a concrete pier block.

"We're nine," Aura noted. "And we have two weapons. Maybe we should split up. We could cover—"

"Nope." Viktor spoke over her. "We remain together. I'll be the first to grant my magic isn't particularly well-honed, but the absence of anything living seems damned odd." He put out a hand for the iron saber.

"It is odd," Aura said. "Also eerie and unsettling." She turned in a circle, scanning the terrain. "Where are the bodies? Or the bones?"

"Maybe we'll find them when we get more into the town proper, but it feels like something powerful masked the town," Ketha said.

"What exactly does that mean?" Boris asked.

"Draped a spell over everything to make it appear nothing is here," Moira replied.

Daide unclipped his life vest and tossed it into the raft. His jacket followed. Other outerwear joined the pile as most of them stripped off at least one layer. Where he'd been too warm with the parka, he felt chilled without it. Or maybe his shivers were more emotional than physical since the air felt heavy and oppressive. "What would be the purpose of such a spell?" he asked.

"To avoid being threatened by anything magical." Ketha chewed her lower lip. "Although, it's hard to imagine why they'd bother."

"We won't discover anything standing here." Daide set off across a rock-strewn beach. Invercargill had been about the same size, population-wise, as Ushuaia. Both towns had around fifty thousand people, but Ushuaia was far more isolated and less sophisticated in terms of architecture and culture. He'd visited Invercargill twice for veterinary conferences and been impressed by the town square that could have passed for a nineteenth century European city with its old-fashioned, well-constructed edifices.

He tuned in his sharp, coyote hearing, but not so much as a chirping bird showed up. How could everything possibly be dead? It made no sense, but at least he had something other than Karin to occupy his thoughts. He reached what had once been a busy wharf area. Piers extended like spokes of a wagon wheel with boats still tied in slips. Cars, trucks, and motorcycles were neatly parked along the curb, covered with a thick layer of dust and dirt. A creeping wrongness pinged the edges of his power.

Where were the bodies? Ushuaia's streets had been clogged first with bodies and then with bones. Hell, Ushuaia still had humans, granted not all that many, but still… How could fifty thousand people have vanished into thin air?

"I don't like this," his coyote said.

"Beyond the obvious, can you put your claws on why not?"

Viktor and Ketha caught up with him. Recco and Zoe chugged up behind them with the others strung out in a loose column. A bright flare of power surged among Ketha, Zoe, Aura, and Moira.

Zoe scrunched her face into a frown. "What if we don't care overmuch for the results?"

"Results from what?" Viktor sounded annoyed. "You can't just hatch a plan and put it into action without—"

"Wasn't going to." Ketha narrowed her eyes. "When did you stop trusting me?"

"Aye, we were simply tossing ideas about," Zoe seconded.

Daide made come-along motions with one hand. "What ideas. Inquiring minds want to know."

"The way I see it," Recco spoke up, "either we march through town, poking through empty buildings until the bogeyman jumps out and snatches us, or we come up with something more elegant."

"Might not be a bogeyman," Moira muttered, "but it's likely wishful thinking on my part. This is damned creepy. If all the people died, who the hell buried them?"

Aura cleared her throat. "The best idea we came up with is joining our power into a sphere and then feeding it until the container can't hold any more. When the ball explodes, it will act like a magnet for anything magical and either expose or destroy it."

"The risk, of course, is what we might uncover." Ketha squared her shoulders. "Maybe it's something we should leave hidden."

"It's enough to make me wish I had something to offer in the magical realm," Boris muttered. Dark hair fluttered around his face, and his black eyes were serious.

"You mean besides a steep learning curve to absorb a world that includes monsters and demons?" Ted countered. As fair as Boris was dark, his white-blond hair had been braided close to his head, and his blue eyes gleamed with a sharp intellect. He and Boris were lovers, but they played their relationship very close to the vest.

"What happens if we do nothing?" Daide asked. "Just wander through town, grab what we need, assuming we find things we could use aboard *Arkady,* and leave."

"We can't leave until we've worked on the whales." Recco cradled the Remington beneath one arm.

"Yes, I haven't forgotten about them," Daide said.

"That approach—the wandering through town one—holds risks too," Zoe muttered. "If magic-wielders live here, and they're choosing to remain hidden, all is well and good. What if we do something to piss them off, and they uncloak themselves?"

"Deal with it then?" Viktor suggested. "I like Daide's suggestion. No reason to whack the beehive unless we're getting stung. If there truly are no humans here, I'm hoping no one's looted the marine supply shops. Two are located at the end of this street. Or they used to be."

"Let's go look," Daide said. His coyote hadn't responded when he'd asked it for details. "Have any of the rest of your bond animals weighed in?"

"Oh hell yes," Ketha said as they headed up a broad, flat street.

The town looked like it had been suspended in time. If it weren't for the dust, grime, and rain-splattered glass, Invercargill could have risen out of Brigadoon's mists, absent the singing Scottish lads and lassies. Daide rolled his eyes at his digression into a world that was no more. Not Brigadoon since it had never existed beyond the minds of Hollywood screenwriters, but a life where he watched movies and wasn't constantly looking over one shoulder, expecting the worst to rear up and swallow him whole.

"Are you going to say more?" he asked Ketha as they trotted smartly past deserted cars, deserted shops, and through a bizarre quiet that gnawed at his innards.

"My wolf is chomping at the bit to shift. It wants to take over since I'm not turning every cobblestone upside down searching for what went wrong here."

"First stop," Viktor announced cheerily and pushed on a glass door blazoned with "South Island Premier Marine Supplies, Ltd." He cursed in German. "Apparently the people who all vanished weren't so distraught they forgot to lock up. Ketha, could you open it?"

"Probably." She stepped close and extended her fingertips. Blue-white light shot from them like mini lightning forks. Rather than the click of a deadbolt giving way, the metal absorbed Ketha's magic, almost as if it were tasting it. She fell back a pace and cut the flow of her power. "Hmmm. That's not good."

"Mayhap a wee alteration in the incantation," Zoe muttered, and power jetted from her hands.

At first, Daide heard metal straining, tumblers groaning, but they quieted, and the tarnished copper key plate developed a dull-gray patina. He bent and picked up a good-sized rock. "How bad do you want inside?" he asked Viktor.

"Not a good idea." Ketha had moved off to one side, but her gaze never left the shopfront.

"Do you suppose all the buildings are booby-trapped?" Viktor glanced to both sides.

"That would be my guess," Ketha muttered.

"But why?" Zoe bent forward, peering through the filthy glass doors.

Aura, who'd turned in a full circle, flipped back to face them. "Clever. They've woven their power in with wood. Since wood is part of the natural world, it lends itself to such projects."

Moira dropped both hands on Aura's shoulders. "Who is 'they'?"

Aura shrugged her off, ducking from beneath her grip. "It sure as hell isn't Vamps. Nothing natural ever danced to their flute."

"Leaves a whole lot of options. Witches. Druids. Mages. Shifters." Moira ticked them off on her fingers. She'd removed her gloves, and they dangled from a metal clip on her bibs.

"Nah. Not Shifters," Zoe said. "They'd welcome us."

"Are you sure about that?" Daide asked. "The sea Shifters are far from our friends."

"Sea Shifters wouldn't have bothered to ward these buildings," Aura replied.

"Aye, 'tis true enough," Zoe cut in. "For centuries, they've had little interest in aught that lives on land."

Viktor squared his shoulders. "You may as well drop that rock," he told Daide. "The question is, what do we do now? Press forward? Or return to *Arkady*?"

"So long as we're here," Daide said, "I'd like to explore a bit more. Invercargill had two universities. Both the Southern Institute of Technology and Otago maintained campuses here. Maybe their science wings won't be as tied up as these buildings on Main Street."

"I'm game," Recco said. "We're missing a whole lot of instrumentation and drugs."

Ketha shivered. "Whatever we're about, we need to be quick. Something's not happy we're here."

Viktor focused his green eyes her way. They'd shaded darker, radiating concern. "What precisely are you homing in on? My raven has been squawking up a storm, but most of its commentary has been in Gaelic, and I've been lucky to pick up one word in three."

"Hard to articulate, but something nasty and prickly is out there. Occasionally, it feints close and stabs me, but it's gone before I get a bead on it. Come on." She took off at a lope along cracked asphalt.

"Turn left in two blocks," Viktor called before he raced after her.

"You still in there?" Daide asked his bond animal.

"Of course. Where would I have gone? You should leave now, while you still can."

Footsteps pounded around him, and he quickened his pace. The farther he moved into the town, the more the creep-factor assailed him. The place felt like a science-fiction movie, but one leading into a dystopian hell. Within him, the coyote prowled, restless and silent. It had tossed its opinion down like a gauntlet, but Daide wasn't complying with its plea to leave.

Why not? What had activated his stubborn streak?

He didn't like the answer when it popped up. He was on a mission to prove himself. The only way he knew how to do it was via medicine, but he was on a fool's errand, one which might get them all killed.

Ahead of him, Ketha careened to a stop. Viktor ran squarely into her and grabbed her so she wouldn't fall. Daide caught up with them. "This was a stupid idea. We should go. My coyote was quite clear about that back at the marine supply store."

Ketha's eyes widened. "Women. To me. Now." Power, indigo blue this time, crackled around her in a widening arc. Zoe added white to the mix. Aura and Moira's colors turned the spinning magical vortex first violet and then deep green.

"Get in the middle." Zoe grabbed Boris and Ted, forcing them through the throbbing magical nimbus.

"At least we're about to find out what has this place in thrall," Ketha growled, followed by, "Vik. Recco. Daide. Join our power circle. The magic flows one way. Out of you. Do not allow any to enter. If you didn't understand, turn this over to your bond animals."

Before Daide could request assistance, his coyote snatched their mutual power, and it fountained from him in a silvery cascade, joining the women's magic. The air thickened around them until breathing became difficult. It reminded him of how the ether had felt on Arctowski, and he girded himself for some hideous mage swathed in black robes to march out of a fissure in the sky. Not that Arctowski's sorcerer had ever shown himself, but it was how Daide had imagined he might look.

"I don't like this," Boris muttered.

"Neither do I," Ted seconded. "Too much like déjà vu."

Lightning flared off to one side followed by a ripping, tearing boom that grew louder and louder until Daide wanted to slap his hands over his ears. Except he couldn't. They were part of maintaining the power flowing from him. His head spun, and his vision first hazed and then splintered as if he'd been looking through a glass that shattered.

The scents of ozone and rotting flowers buffeted him, sickly sweet and cloying until he wished he had a surgical mask to mute it.

"I know that smell," Zoe cried. "Witches! Show yourselves. We mean you no harm."

Cackling laughter rose above the shredding noise, and then abruptly fell silent. The fractured world he'd been viewing dropped away in streamers and chunks of unrelated colors. When the vista around him reformed, it looked a lot like Ushuaia. Rotting bodies and bones littered the formerly tidy thoroughfare. The neat, well-kept aspect of Invercargill had been nothing beyond illusion crafted by magic.

Three tall, thin women stepped out of a lightning bolt. It flickered behind them before vanishing to nothing. Dressed in rags, two of the group had braided black hair. The third's was pure silver and fell to her feet unbound. She raked black eyes over each of them and angled her head appraisingly.

"All Shifters but two humans, eh?" She extended an index finger, jabbing it at Ted and Boris. "Why are you keeping such shoddy company?"

"They saved our lives," Boris said.

"Leave," one of the dark-haired Witches ordered. "We have no need of your magic or your presence."

"Looks as if you've done a fair job covering up something." Ketha took a step nearer the silver-haired Witch. "What I want to know is why? Did you kill everyone? Is that what you've been eating all these years?"

The Witch hissed at her, a long sibilant susurrus that raised the hair on the back of Daide's neck. Magic still flowed from all the Shifters, but the Witches clearly weren't impressed—or the least bit cowed.

"I don't care what you've done." Viktor positioned himself next to Ketha. "We'd be glad to leave, but I need to pick up a few items for my ship. Surely you've no use for tools or lubricants."

"Everything here is ours," the silver-haired Witch informed him.

"Why?" Ketha shot back. "You can't make use of anything manufactured. Your power is linked to nature, exactly like ours."

"Our magic is nothing like yours, Shifter," a dark-haired Witch who'd been silent until now said.

"Oh, come now," Zoe inserted, her brogue in full bloom. "Sure and ye can see the similarities. Now, if we were comparin' Vampire power to yours, then ye might have a leg to stand on."

"Goddess preserve me from the Celts," the Witch muttered. Raising her black eyes to stare squarely at Ketha, she repeated. "You appear to be the leader. Leave now."

"Or?" Ketha countered.

The Witch shrugged. "We'll incorporate you into our spell."

"I'd like to see you try it." Ketha bristled.

"No, you wouldn't." One of the dark-haired Witches narrowed her eyes. "Our magic is locked to the land. You won't be able to defeat our spells. Hell, you weren't able to figure anything out until we showed ourselves."

"Only because we chose a peaceful approach," Aura said. "Are there more of you?"

"What do you think?" the Witch retorted.

Magic circled them and the Witches, turning the air pregnant with menace. Black sparks ignited when the circles ran up against each other. Charm had always been Daide's long suit, so he smiled disarmingly.

"So few of us remain. What's the percentage in not working together?" He looked guilelessly from one Witch to the next.

"Shifters broke the world." The silver-haired Witch drew herself up tall. "We have no interest in linking ourselves to slothful miscalculation. Furthermore—"

"We weren't the ones to craft that ill-conceived spell," Aura snarled indignantly.

"But we are the reason it's receded," Ketha said.

"Receded, but not gone," one of the dark-haired Witches retorted. "If your magic were stronger, you'd feel it like a coiled spring seeking an opportunity to resurface."

Zoe waved a hand, and a bolt of magic arrowed right at the Witch who'd spoken. She evaded it easily and laughed. "Save your power, Shifter, it's—" Her gaze slanted toward the ocean, and something akin to hope frittered across her concave cheekbones.

"Well, I'll be damned if it's not sea Shifters," the silver-haired Witch muttered. She brought one hand crashing down. "The rest of you will keep. We'll return later and decide what to do with you."

The same choking sensation he'd experienced earlier returned. Daide sputtered and gasped, but it didn't create more oxygen.

"Reel in your power," Ketha instructed.

"Aye, 'tis doing naught but making this worse," Zoe said.

Daide cut the flow of his power. The world beyond where the nine of them stood turned into a nightmarish landscape. Partially the pristine world produced by illusion, partially a vista cluttered with bones and decomposing flesh. At least the insects and rodents were back. Birds too. A vulture cawed overhead.

Moira raised her head and cawed back.

Daide turned, intent on returning to the Zodiac, and realized he couldn't move beyond an invisible perimeter. "Really? They trapped us? How the fuck could they do that?"

"If their power is truly linked to the land, it wouldn't take much," Ketha replied, a sour note beneath her voice.

"I don't get it," Zoe said. "Normally, the Earth barely tolerates Witches with their dirty spells and crappy hex bags."

"Apparently, they established détente with it during the Cataclysm," Aura muttered.

"So? We let the land know the Cataclysm is over." Daide dusted his hands together.

"That one Witch said it wasn't, though," Recco spoke up. "Why were they so excited about the sea Shifters?"

"More importantly," Boris cut in, "can you bore a way through their enchantment while they're gone?"

"Not sure, and I have no bloody idea about why sea Shifters would ring their chimes," Ketha said.

More cawing drew his attention skyward. Where before there'd been a single vulture, now half a dozen winged toward them.

"That's our ticket out of here." Moira pointed. "I hope."

"We need more than that," Zoe protested.

"This is only the forward guard," Moira retorted. "Getting the lay of the land so to speak. My vulture asked for help. Be grateful the illusion that kept everything hidden has crashed and burned."

5

WITCHES BE DAMNED

Karin was locked in a dream. She clung to it. Gold and silver runes were morphing into faeries, harp-playing faeries churning out heartbreakingly beautiful music. She did her damnedest to tune Leif out, but his insistent shouting intruded. *"Wake up, Karin."*

"Huh? Leif? Aren't you in the sea?"

"Karin! Pay attention. Please."

She blinked, bleary-eyed, and understood she'd replied out loud, so she repeated her questions using telepathy.

"Yes. It's Leif. Remember what I told you about Witches? A whole coven's worth took over Invercargill. They've set their gunsights on us."

She bolted upright and swallowed nausea. Her head pounded, and her vision wasn't quite right yet, but it edged toward clearer focus. *"Can you swim back to the ship? Or teleport here? Your magic will do that."*

"It would," he corrected her, *"but they netted us with a spell we can't break through."*

"Can the whales help?"

Leif paused before answering. *"Sorry, I had to check. They're still free. If you look outside, you'll see them circling the ship."*

She rubbed her temples. At least she wasn't dizzy anymore. *"What can I do?"*

"Alert everyone. Talk with the whales. They know the whole story."

"Will you and your dolphins be all right?"

A long sigh rattled from him. *"I have no idea. We traded a lot for power. The Witches know it. They want something from us."*

Karin walked to the sink and positioned her cupped hands under a stream of cold water. She sluiced it across her face. *"Don't give anything away if you can help it. Last thing you need is more Witchy residue."*

"I'll be back in touch if I can."

The echo that meant they were connected disengaged abruptly. Karin's clothes were still damp. Presumably her sheets were too since she'd been lying on them, but that problem was at the bottom of her list of priorities. Stripping to skin, she dressed again, stepping into her Wellingtons last.

"Ketha!" Karin called.

"Yup. We're here. How are you?"

"Never mind about me. I'll live." Karin hurriedly sketched out what Leif had told her about Witches and sea Shifters. A startled intake of breath from Ketha told her all she needed to know. Apparently, none of them had the slightest inkling about the unholy alliance their sea kin had forged.

"I fecking hate Witches," Zoe growled.

"Hey, Zoe. Is everyone listening?" Karin asked.

"All of us who can," Viktor concurred.

"And maybe some who shouldn't be," Ketha tossed out. *"We need to watch what we say."*

"Understood. Presumably I didn't tell any nosy Witches anything they didn't already know about our sea kin. I'm headed to the bridge to apprise Juan and whoever else is here about the situation. I presume you're traveling back our way?" Karin sucked in a tense breath. She did not want more bad news. Not as shitty as she still felt.

"Working on it," Ketha replied. *"Over and out for now."*

Karin strode out of her cabin. *Working on it* wasn't a yes, which meant Ketha and the shore team had run into trouble. Witch trouble. Karin doubled up a fist. She could relate to Zoe's comment. Even though they kind of played on the same side, there'd never been any love lost between Shifters and Witches. For one thing, no bond animal had ever warmed to a Witch. Something about their magic felt dirty. Bottom barrel scrapings from the white magic side of the supernatural world.

She hadn't been in very good shape when Leif relayed his humiliation-laden tale of parlaying with Witches when the sea Shifters' backs were up against the wall. If she'd been firing on a few more cylinders, she'd have made more disapproving noises and tried to troubleshoot solutions. Surely, there was a way out of their predicament.

Even if it meant spending more time on land.

Running on instinct, she went outside, grateful the breeze was merely cold, not icy. Karin scanned the ocean, easily locating whale fins, and walked to where the gangway was still deployed. A quick trip down the swaying stairway brought her to the platform with the sea washing over it.

"Whales come close, please." Rather than telepathy, she cupped her hands around her mouth.

Two of the fins headed her way. Amid water spewing out blowholes, they swam close. *"What do you need, land Shifter?"* the nearest whale asked in a deep, rumbling voice.

"Witches are in Invercargill. From the sound of things, they may control it."

"We already know. Leif said as much. Do you have news?" The whale slapped the water with its tail, showering Karin with seawater.

She held onto handgrips as the platform canted from side to side. "The Witches trapped them with magic. Several of us went into Invercargill. Best I can tell, they're trapped as well."

The three other whales formed a circle nearby, and a cacophony of hoots, bleats, and honks filled the air. Karin waited for the outcome of their conversation. Water dripped down her head and face, and she brushed it away. Thank the goddess the crippling inertia was on its way out. She felt far stronger than she had when Leif ripped her from sleep.

A tail slap refocused her. "Yes?" She knelt on the platform, and a whale focused one of its laterally placed eyes right on her.

"We will attempt to shift. At least two of us—maybe three—are probably still strong enough."

Karin perked up a few more notches. Treating whales was well within her ability. "I took part in all the dolphin healings," she told the whale still staring at her. "I can probably determine what amount of the medication mixture you'll need to attack the parasite infestations." A thought snapped her head up. "I can use telepathy and talk with Daide and Recco too. They'll know if my milligrams per kilogram conversion is right."

She closed her teeth over her lower lip. "Do any of you have the slightest idea how much you weigh?"

The whale right next to her burbled laughter. Water erupted from its blowhole, getting her ever wetter.

Karin chortled. "Never mind. It was a stupid question. The vets will know." She straightened. "How about it? Are you game for me to dose you?"

"Yes, but only the two weakest whales. You can treat the rest of us later. I don't want to take any more time than we have to. While you're doing your doctor dance, I'll work on shifting. It's been a long time, and it might take a while to get the magic right."

She straightened. Water sluiced down her, and she wondered why she'd bothered to change clothes. "If you're successful shifting, turn right at the top of the gangway and take the first door inside the ship. You'll see three green metal lockers. When you open them, you'll find an assortment of clothes."

"Clothes," another whale groaned. *"I'd forgotten that part."*

"You'll appreciate them if the wind picks up. I'll be back here as soon as I get your drug cocktail mixed up."

She fairly flew up the gangway. Where would she find an injection point? Would she use the same proportions? Inside *Arkady*, she trotted down one flight to the lab. *"Daide,"* she called, hoping his telepathy would be up to the task.

"Karin?" His reply was almost immediate, but he sounded stiff and subdued. *"How are you?"*

"Fine, but this isn't about me. What dosage and drug mix for the whales? Where's a decent injection point? Do I need to stick with intravenous, or will subcutaneous do? How about time for a response? Anything special I need to be alert for?"

"Hold on." Daide stemmed the flow of her questions. *"Give me a moment to confer with Recco."*

She'd begun gathering chemicals when Daide provided a set of concise instructions. She asked a few questions and then went to work. This wouldn't be as difficult as she'd feared. No need to swim beneath the buggers and find some vessel buried beneath layers of blubber.

As she worked, she replayed the interchange with Daide. It had held a stilted quality. Was he angry with her for keeping her condition hidden? The more she thought about it, the surer she was that had to be it. Her misplaced confidence had nearly been her undoing.

"Not as if I'll make that mistake again." The acerbic note in her words steadied her as she prepared injections. Since they lacked needles long and thick enough to penetrate whale hide, she was planning to inject the drug mixture beneath their tongues. Daide had reassured her they'd scarcely feel it, but she wasn't so certain. Karin said a hasty prayer to the goddess to guide her hand.

She'd just gathered her materials into a leather bag when two large men and one woman marched into the lab. They looked like Neanderthal throwbacks with thick, unruly blonde hair, stocky builds, and close to seven-foot heights. Not exactly heavy, they had barrel-chests and legs like oak trees. Clothing built for smaller people stretched across their girths, and they were barefoot.

Karin inclined her head. "Whale Shifters, I presume."

"At your service, madam healer." One of the men bowed formally.

Juan burst into the lab behind them. "What in the devil is going on? Vik didn't say much, but I believe he fell into some type of snare in Invercargill. I can't raise Leif. I was getting ready to launch another raft when I saw you three"—he jerked his chin at the whales—"trooping up the gangway."

"Sorry," Karin said. "I meant to find you first, but I got tied up with the whales. I'm off to dose the two weaker ones. Once all five have shifted, we'll meet you on the bridge."

"Hurry," Juan said before adding, "Oh yeah. I'm glad you're better, but I'm frantic about the shore team."

"I understand." Karin crossed the room and gave him a hug. "We'll get Aura back. Your mate is tough. Don't underestimate her."

"Never." He grinned wryly. "She'd flay me alive." Turning, he ran out of the lab.

The whales hooted and honked and gestured for her to get moving. "Did you reach the vets?" the man right behind her asked.

"Yes. They told me what to do."

"Will you require our help?" the woman asked in a low, musical voice.

"Maybe. I'm not sure. Recco and Daide are standing by in case I need them. What are your names?"

"Unlike the dolphins, we don't have human names," the woman said, followed by a musical trill. "That is my whale name."

Karin reached the gangway and hurried down to water level with the others lined above her on the stairs. The male who'd spoken with her first joined her on the platform. He sang a few notes and a whale swam close.

Karin knelt and withdrew what she needed from her medical bag. "Open your mouth, please. I'll be injecting this beneath your tongue. Shouldn't hurt at all."

A needle inside my mouth?" The whale stared doubtfully at her.

Bleats and clacks rose around her, mostly from the Shifter on the platform, but also from the whale in the water. After a heated run of honks, it made a pathetic squealing noise and opened its mouth.

Karin bent forward but reached a tipping point fast. The Shifter sharing the platform with her wrapped his huge hands around her waist. "I've got you."

Hoping she wouldn't have the bad luck to hit a nerve and scare the reluctant whale into clamping its jaws around her head, she probed with a gloved finger. When the whale didn't react, she traded her finger for the large syringe and slowly injected the medication.

The man hanging onto her pulled her back onto the platform from where she'd been sprawled half in the whale's mouth. "All done," she said brightly.

The whale shut its mouth and produced a series of chirps.

"Everything all right?" Karin asked.

"Yes," the whale answered in English this time. *"Thank you. I never even felt it."*

Thank god and all the bloody saints for small favors.

The next whale's treatment went off with far less fanfare. She was dropping her used syringes into her bag when Daide's voice rang in her head. *"Well?"*

"You gave me excellent instructions. All is well."

"You have to keep an eye on them for at least the next hour," he cautioned.

"Someone will. Not trying to be short, but I promised Juan we, er, I would meet him on the bridge as soon as I finished here." She stopped shy of telling him about the shifted whales. No reason to give the Witches additional ammunition—assuming any might be listening. *"Any changes on your end?"*

"Not a thing."

Karin stared at the whales in the water. They seemed okay, but she should listen to their hearts, take their pulse—if she could find a pulse point. Both were coughing and blowing. Worms spewed from their blowholes.

"It's all right." The man who'd held onto her patted her shoulder. "I will watch over my kin. If anything appears amiss, I'll summon you."

Karin stuck her hand out, and the sea Shifter shook it.

"Please come to the bridge with me," she told the other two and skirted around them on her way up the gangway. "We're throwing a war council, and all of us must be part of it."

"I'll be along as soon as these two have shifted," the man standing on the platform said.

"Sixth deck—" she began.

"I'll find it. I'm no stranger to ships." The whale Shifter nodded curtly.

Karin ran lightly up several sets of risers with the whales right behind her. She pushed open one of the doors onto the bridge. Everyone was there. Seven humans, four from McMurdo and three from Arctowski, stood in a tight circle looking worried. Six female Shifters she'd spent a decade sitting out the Cataclysm with in Ushuaia were bent over Tarot spreads. Juan stood at the helm.

"Any news?" Juan's tone was casual, but the way he stood wasn't. Tension streamed from his upright posture and white-knuckled grip on the wheel.

Karin gestured to the whales onto the bridge. "Welcome. I'd do introductions, but you'll figure it out."

"We already know who you are," the whale who'd helped her said.

"Could you sketch out the high points of what power the Witches hold over you?" Karin asked.

A muted gasp rose from Tessa and Becca. "Gawk. What power? How come we never knew anything about it?" Tessa made a sour face. "We hate Witches."

The female whale Shifter stepped forward. Color rose to her ruddy face. "Better me than a man for this task. They're still appalled." Her nostrils flared. "You know how the male Witches died out before the Crusades?"

"I didn't realize they'd totally vanished," Karin said.

"Yeah, there were rumors for years about Warlocks running amok. They're even memorialized in some of our Shifter history tomes," Tessa added.

"The rumors had no basis," the female whale muttered, her tone caustic. "The last one died somewhere around 1200, perhaps 1250."

The other whale Shifter blew out a noisy breath. "It was in the Witches' best interest if folks didn't realize how tenuous their grip on survival really was." He sent a pointed glance at the female in a mute plea for help.

She nodded briskly. "Witches are far from immortal," she began. "They don't even live as long as we do. When they breed with humans, most of their magic is lost in the mix. Human-Witch hybrids barely have enough power to light a candle."

"And they lose even a prayer of living past a single century," the male cut in.

"Do you want my help, or no?" The female rounded on him, followed by a few bleats and clacks.

He hooted her way and gestured for her to continue.

"It's easy enough to extrapolate," the female went on. "Within the span of a single generation, Witches would have been a thing of the past if they couldn't unearth a way to pass their power to subsequent generations. They trolled through other magic wielders, but no one volunteered to serve as sperm donors."

She stopped to take a measured breath. "Whether it was the luck of the draw or simply desperation on both parts, we needed an infusion of power to avoid genocide. Working together, we discovered a way to strengthen our magic. Some of our men lay with them."

"The children?" Karin leaned forward. Genetic mixtures had always intrigued her.

"More Witch than Shifter." The woman rolled her eyes. "Thank the goddess for small favors."

"We never saw any of them in the sea," the male broke in, "so we assumed none of them had the ability to shapeshift."

"The next hundred or so years slipped by," the male continued in a low, musical voice. "But then they used the Witch magic that was a part of us to reel us in. They wanted more children." He swallowed hard. "That was when it sank in we were roped into the bargain from Hell. We'd stupidly assumed we'd provide a stopgap, and they'd figure something else out in the meantime."

Karin narrowed her eyes, not liking the sound of any of this. "They want Leif and the other male dolphins to serve as a stud service?"

"About the size of it." The female nodded sadly. "But it gets worse. Something about breeding with Witches sows the seeds of madness. The Shifters who were unlucky enough to be selected the first time turned into raving lunatics. They drowned themselves to avoid living with whatever demons tormented them."

"And subsequent batches?" Juan asked.

The whales exchanged glances. The male coughed, and an uncomfortable expression washed across his broad, flat features. "We developed a lottery. Whichever man lost became the sacrificial object. He serviced all the Witches, and then he had a choice."

"Some choice," the female muttered. "Either we killed him or let him wait until the madness grew so oppressive he took his own life. The problem only cropped up every hundred years or so. We did everything in our power to find a solution, but never did."

"We were hoping the Cataclysm wiped Witches off the globe," the male said.

"No such luck." The whale who'd been down on the platform marched onto the bridge with the other two trailing behind him, one male and another female.

Karin trotted to them, eyeing them closely. "How are you feeling?"

"We'll live," the female said. "Thank you." She bent her head to Karin's level. "You have no idea how close you came to me snapping your neck when your head was in my mouth."

Karin chuckled. "Then you wouldn't have gotten the medication. Beyond that"—she glanced from one whale to the next—"there must be some way to break the Witches' hold on everyone."

"If we could take on the Cataclysm—Tessa shuffled tarot cards —"surely we can manage a few Witches."

"No one knows how many *a few* translates to," Juan said. "We need a bombproof plan, folks." He stopped shy of reminding them his mate was one of the prisoners.

"Hang on," Karin held up a hand. "Let me raise Ketha. See what they've figured out. Presumably, our sea Shifter kin are stronger than the Witches."

"Yeah, we thought so too," the male who'd remained on the platform said.

"Never panned out that way," the female who'd made the crack about biting Karin's head off said, sounding bitter.

"Witches are sneaky," Becca said.

"Yeah. I bet if we scratch the surface, we can find the loose block," Tessa squared her shoulders.

"Loose block?" Juan looked her way as if she'd lost her mind.

"You know." She smiled coldly. "The one where when you drag it out from its spot, the whole edifice comes crashing down."

6

CUNNING BEATS TREACHERY—SOME OF THE TIME

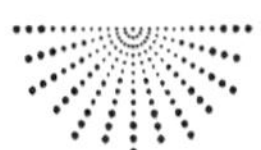

*D*aide unclenched his fists. At least an hour had passed since the Witches left them trapped in their spell. Worse, his few interactions with Karin had been terse. All business. Not that he wasn't more than willing to do everything he could to assist her in treating the whale Shifters, but the lack of anything personal cut deep. It shouldn't. Nothing had passed between them beyond professional courtesy.

He had to pull his head out of his ass and damned fast.

A blast of magic flashed. Ketha ducked, and an enchanted battering ram ran headlong into the invisible walls surrounding them. For a brief moment, the bones of their prison glowed, looking like vines twined together. Daide stared at them as an idea took shape.

"Goddammit," Ketha snarled. "What's that? Our tenth try?"

"I stopped counting a while back." Zoe patted her arm, but the corners of her brown eyes were pinched with concern.

"Brute force isn't going to defeat that thing." Viktor slapped a hand against the wall, drawing it back fast. They'd discovered touching the barrier long enough to activate it packed an unpleasant wallop.

"Focus your power at the bottom," Daide said. "The structure is weaker there."

"Sure and 'tis the only spot we haven't tried," Zoe chimed in.

"Isn't our power stronger together?" Viktor asked. "It worked that way when we fought the Cataclysm. You're leaving firepower on the table."

"Yeah, but you were Vampires then," Aura pointed out.

"I still think it's worth a shot," Recco argued. "It can't be too much longer before the Witches return. I'd just as soon not be sitting here like trussed boars."

"If we were boars, we'd be out of here," Daide muttered.

"Okay. You asked for this, so don't bitch if it backfires in some way I can't foresee." Ketha moved next to Viktor. "Zoe, you manage Recco's power."

"I'll pair with you," Aura told Daide. "Basically, open your magic to me so I can draw from it. It's similar to what we did when we stood against the Cataclysm."

"How do I open a channel for you to tap into?" Recco asked Zoe.

She exchanged a glance with Ketha, who nodded. "The animals. Turn things over to your wolf."

"Got it," Recco gritted.

Daide smothered a knowing look. He didn't like ceding control any better than Recco, but he also didn't want to muck up their best chance of escape.

"Aw crap. We have to hurry. I caught a whiff of Witch." Power shimmered around Ketha, turning the air incandescent. Magic formed, looking like loops of shiny silver rope. She threaded it through her hands, and the other women each grabbed hold.

"What do we do?" Boris asked.

"Don't take this wrong," Ketha said, "but you and Ted stay out of the way."

"Help is here," Moira crowed, sounding a lot like her vulture probably did. "Perfect timing if I say so myself."

Daide scanned the skies. An enormous flock of vultures blotted out the day's light. "Won't they die if they run into the barrier?"

"Some will." Moira set her mouth in a thin, tense line. "It's up to us to make certain they sustain as few casualties as possible. We have to hurry." Her nostrils flared. "That hint of Witch is turning into an absolute stench."

Daide reached for his coyote, activating his psychic parts for it to access easily. *Ready?*

"Yes."

The alteration didn't catch him by surprise this time, but allowing entrance to his inner landscape was harder than it appeared. It required a Zen state of mind, which he'd never been very good at. Recco had been the martial arts guy.

The reek of rotting vegetation and old, chewed bones surrounded them. If the Witches had a stink, he hadn't noticed it the first time. Maybe being sheathed in their spell amplified their magic, or muted his own.

Ketha chanted a few words in Gaelic. Aura, Zoe, and Moira repeated them. The rope glowed red and slithered from Ketha's hands to ground level where it butted against the barrier, making hissing sounds. From above, a cacophony from hundreds of pissed-off vultures rose in protest.

"Give me more magic," Ketha growled. "This isn't enough."

Daide felt power pour from him and feed into the rope. It grew to twice its girth and pulsated like a beating heart. Along with his power, he sent his will. Magic might not be his native environment, but concepting worked for everything else. Believing in the outcome often forced nature to come around. He'd had scores of patients who should have died, but hadn't.

Aura shrieked in Gaelic. The rope rammed the barrier, and black-tinged fire exploded around them. Smoke rose, thick and oxygen-stealing. He gagged and coughed. Had they succeeded? He peered through fire and darkness, totally disoriented.

Aura clamped a hand around his arm. "Goddammit! We did it."

She dragged him through burning debris and batted at places his clothing had caught fire. Blinking and gasping for air, he whacked the back of her smoldering jacket, singeing his fingertips in the process.

The vultures formed a protective arc around their new position, cawing furiously. Warm bird shit rained down on them, but Daide could have hugged every single bird.

"Are they all okay?" he asked around raw places where he'd inhaled smoke. The fire burned on, forming a twenty-foot column in the spot where they'd stood. What the hell was it using for fuel?

"Not sure," Aura croaked. "If anyone can find injured vultures, it's Moira. Look, there she goes now."

Moira pulled up her hood to protect her hair and dashed into the column of fire. She must have employed magic to find the birds, because only seconds passed before she ran back out cradling three vultures in her arms.

"Bring 'em here," Recco called.

Daide held out his hands and took two of the birds. One was dead, but the other might make it. He massaged its chest gently and puffed air through its beak.

"Magic is better," his coyote said. *"Let me."*

"Sure." Daide hadn't yet reclaimed his paranormal side. He watched carefully while the coyote worked fast, scrubbing the bird's lungs of smoke and stabilizing its erratic heartbeat.

"Excellent job," Daide told his bondmate. *"If I ever open another veterinary practice, you'll have to teach me some of your tricks."*

"Gladly." The coyote sounded pleased—and happy.

"I need your magic. Now," Ketha cried hoarsely.

Daide smoothed the bird's feathers and let his bondmate extract whatever magic he had left for Ketha and Aura to tap into. He turned and faced the direction the putrid smell was coming from. The vultures swung around as a group and flew hard for Witches running toward them. Dark lightning bolts surged from their extended fingertips.

"Yes!" Aura screeched. "Something we can target."

"Moira. Tell your birds to hold off until it's safer," Ketha said tersely.

"Will do," Moira said, followed by a spate of Gaelic. The birds rose another fifty feet into the air, remaining out of harm's way.

White shafts of pulsing magic crashed against dark. Where they collided, sparks flew. Off to one side, the column of fire kept right on burning. Was Witch magic a combustible substance?

Hands extended, Ketha marched toward the Witches, flanked by Aura, Zoe, and Moira.

"Come on, men." Viktor fell in behind his wife. Recco and Daide formed a line next to him, both still holding injured birds. Because he was adding his power to the mix through his bondmate, Daide focused on the vulture curved against his chest.

The closer the magics got to one another, the more violent the explosions when they collided. Understanding punched Daide in the gut. Ketha should have been a military tactician. She was herding the Witches toward the burning column. Surely, they wouldn't be stupid enough to get trapped in their own working.

He quieted his mind, in case Witches were adept at reading thoughts. Bright, blue-white light surged around the four Shifters, and their Gaelic chant picked up rhythm, cadence, and volume. Power flew through Daide as if someone had opened a spigot to its full-on position. He staggered but remained upright.

With a roar, a wall of magic bore down on the Witches.

"Now, vultures. Now," Moira shrieked.

The birds flew at the Witches from above, pecking out eyes and digging their sharp beaks into exposed flesh. Blood flowed, adding a metallic stench to the already overpowering Witch reek.

Ketha and the women had halted. Lines of strain carved deep into their faces, but their ploy was working. Inch by inch, the Witches stumbled backward. One screeched when fire licked at her backside, but her attention was diverted—along with her magic. It was exactly the opening they needed.

A mighty heave, and the magical wall Ketha had woven drove the Witches into the flames. Except for one.

"Move aside," Recco barked, followed by, "Daide?"

He scooped the vulture from his friend and feinted sideways. Recco raised the Remington to his shoulder in a single, fluid motion and fired. The Witch raised her hands, clearly intent on blocking the bullet with magic, but it ducked and wove like a homing pigeon, evading her power and burying itself between her eyes.

The vultures in Daide's arms squawked and squirmed. Daide understood, and he loosed his hold on them so they could wing skyward to join their kin. He hadn't counted how many Witches they faced, but none remained.

At least not here. Daide's ears rang from the rifle blast, and he shook his head to clear them.

"Listen up," Viktor shouted, his voice sounding garbled. "We can celebrate later. Come on. We're going back to *Arkady*, and then we'll figure out how to free Leif and the dolphins."

"Hang on," Daide said, scanning the ground. "We need to make certain there aren't any more wounded vultures."

"Sorry. Wasn't thinking. Bring them along," Viktor instructed. "They can fly free once you've fixed whatever ails them."

"Moira. Do you have some special way to locate hurt birds?" Recco retracted the rifle's bolt, and the expended casing bounced on the ground.

"My vulture is on it." Moira's dark hair was streaked with ash and blood, and she sank to her knees. Vultures perched on both shoulders and cawed at her. She cawed back, having presumably ceded her vocal chords to her bondmate. The vultures flew off in groups of twos and threes and returned carrying wounded birds suspended from their beaks. Altogether, half a dozen had sustained serious injuries.

Between Recco, Moira, and himself, they carted the birds back to the Zodiac. The vulture flock flew overhead, making a hell of a racket and clearly concerned about their fallen comrades.

"Here's a stroke of luck," Viktor muttered as he hastily untied the raft. "Surprised those fucking Witches didn't puncture the pontoons."

"They're arrogant," Ketha said.

"Aye. Never occurred to them we'd defeat their enchantment," Zoe cut in.

"We very nearly didn't," Aura muttered. "Damn but they're strong magically. If it hadn't been for Daide's suggestion about focusing our efforts at ground level, we'd probably still be trapped."

Daide felt quietly pleased by her compliment as he leapt nimbly into the Zodiac, checking on the birds he'd tucked beneath each arm. One had a broken wing. The other, a collapsed lung. *Want to help?* he asked the coyote?

Yes, but the broken bone will need time to mend.

Daide nudged Recco. "Let your wolf assist you, *amigo*. It will leverage magic to heal, which is way faster than how we were trained."

"Really?" Recco sounded intrigued.

Moira's birds cooed softly at her, not sounding like vultures at all. With a shake from heads to wingtips, both took off and joined the group still circling above. She smiled and climbed into the raft.

"Damn, you fixed them fast," Daide said.

"When it works, magic's the best potion there is," she replied.

Viktor fired the motor, and they edged toward where *Arkady* rode at anchor several hundred feet out in the bay. "Want to let Juan know we're on our way?" He aimed the question at Aura.

"Already did. I talked with him as soon as we were free. Wanted to make certain they didn't put themselves at risk sending the cavalry out for nothing."

Daide worked on the vultures with his bondmate as the raft skated across quiet surf. Quiet by Ushuaia and Antarctica standards. When he glanced at *Arkady*, he saw people lining the gangway's stairs and Juan at the bottom. Adrenaline still hummed through his body, leaving a sour taste in his mouth.

"Are Witches all that's left in Invercargill?" he asked.

"Good question," Moira answered him. "I know exactly who to ask." She tilted her chin skyward. "The birds will know."

The ones in his lap made small chirping noises as if to agree. They were stronger, but he hoped they'd remain aboard for at least a day or two.

"Can you talk with them?" Daide asked his coyote.

"Not exactly, but Moira's vulture bondmate can."

Moira drew her dark brows together until a vertical line formed between them. "Now that's damned interesting."

"What?" Ketha turned her penetrating gaze on the vulture shifter.

"My bondmate asked for information. Humans barricaded themselves into a fortress north of town. The birds aren't certain, but they believe there could be as many as a hundred left. Apparently, they formed a strange alliance with the town's two resident Vampires—"

"Aw shit," Ted groaned and looked from Viktor to Recco to Daide. "That's what you used to be, right?"

Moira made a chopping motion. "This gets stranger still. These Vamps protected the humans."

"Aye, like as not in exchange for blood," Zoe muttered. "Witches would have had sufficient magic—and knowledge—to kill off the Vamps, particularly if there were only two." She stopped to take a measured breath. "Do the birds know how many Witches there are?"

"They can't count," Moira replied.

"Then how did they know about the Vampires?" Zoe countered.

"They described two. When I asked if they'd ever seen others, they told me no. I'll take a crack at having them describe Witches and see if I can come up with a rough nose count."

The Zodiac chugged up to the gangway platform, and Viktor tossed a rope to Juan who tied it off and leapt into the raft. Falling to his knees, he wrapped his arms around Aura and held on tight.

"It's all right," she murmured. "I'm all right."

"But you nearly weren't," he said. "Last time ever you go anywhere without me."

"You couldn't have helped much," Viktor told him. "Move over so the rest of us can exit the raft."

Juan let go of Aura and scrambled back onto the platform and into position to stabilize things and help with the injured vultures. "I suppose this means you didn't locate any supplies for the boat."

Viktor grunted. "Christ, mate. How about, glad you're all alive? We tried to get inside that marine supply place we used to use, but it was booby-trapped. Probably how the Witches knew we'd arrived, now that I think about it."

Juan helped Boris, Ted, and the women onto the platform. They filed up the gangway, and he called after them. "Grab something to eat and meet on the bridge."

"See you soon," Zoe called from the rail spanning Deck Three, her words probably meant for Recco.

"Could you grab some chow for us both?" Recco yelled back.

"Aye." Her red hair flashed bright, illuminated by a ray of sunlight breaking through the cloud cover.

"Have you heard anything from Leif?" Daide asked. He still sat on a pontoon, holding his two vultures.

"No, and the whales are damned worried about him and the other dolphins," Juan replied.

Footsteps clattered down the gangway until Karin stood on the platform. Angling her head, she looked at the birds. "More patients for us?" Her white hair blew every which way in a moderately stiff breeze. "I'm actually warming to veterinary medicine. Not much difference when you cut to the meat of things."

"The whales," Daide said. "How are they?"

"The two I dosed are well enough to shift. The other three were in better shape to begin with, but they're still infested. If you'd been here, what would you have done?"

"We were hoping to use the whale tanks at the cetacean

institute," Recco answered. "And for their array of instruments. They'd have had robust enough equipment to introduce the medication intravenously."

"Does that mean I didn't give those two enough to totally treat their problem?" Karin asked.

"Probably," Daide said, "but you provided enough of a break, they'll grow stronger. See," he went on, "most animals have a resident parasite population. It doesn't bother them unduly and doesn't impact their lifespans."

"Maybe," Recco broke in. "We were never sure about it since even if you could find a specimen that wasn't infested, no one's done compare and contrast studies on longevity."

"Never mind the philosophy," Juan said. "Get moving so Vik and I can put the raft away and join you on the bridge."

Daide handed his birds to Karin to free his hands to exit the Zodiac. Once he'd taken his charges back, Karin did the same for Recco, and they trooped up the gangway steps.

"The birds want to be outside," Daide's coyote spoke up.

It made sense, plus the other vultures, which had been circling, were landing in groups of three and four on Deck Three's broad, flat open area. "We can leave them beneath this overhang," Daide suggested.

"Not inside where it's warm?" Karin asked, sounding concerned.

"They're wild creatures," Daide said. "*Warm* isn't important to them."

"Looks as if they'll be well cared for." Recco swept an arm to encompass the flock gathered on the deck.

Another vulture, larger and coal black, flew purposely from one of the upper decks. "Moira?" Daide asked.

She squawked at him before answering in telepathy. *"And who else? Leave them to me."*

Karin stuck out an arm, and Moira landed heavily on it. "Oomph," Karin made a face. "With all those feathers, I didn't expect you'd weigh so much."

"Never hassle a woman about her weight." Moira cawed laughter.

Daide laid his birds in a sheltered area against a bulkhead. Recco followed suit, and they moved into *Arkady* through the nearest door.

"I'm off to find Zoe and food," Recco announced, "right after I stop by my cabin and get rid of this jacket. It still stinks like cinders and Witches."

"See you upstairs," Karin said.

"Yup." Recco hurried down the corridor to his cabin.

Daide sniffed, surprised Recco had been right about Witch-stink. He hadn't quite acclimated to the stench, but he hadn't been paying attention to it, either.

"How rough was it?" Karin asked without preamble.

"Bad," Daide said. "We almost didn't make it."

"I'm not surprised. Witches are a nasty bunch. As unprincipled as Vamps, but in a totally different way. Their magic is far stronger, and they're smart, where Vampires are mostly arrogant." She eyed him. "Do you want to change your outerwear too?"

"Why? So I don't put everyone off their feed?"

"Something like that." She smiled.

Daide almost smiled back, but then remembered Leif and his arm around her. He stood straighter. "You must be worried about the dolphins."

"Oh my yes. We all are. I'll rustle up something for you to eat, so you can show up on the bridge once you've changed."

"Thanks. Appreciated." He didn't want to leave. Karin's energy drew him like a lodestone, but he'd be damned if he'd make a fool of himself fawning over a woman who cared about someone else.

"When the dust settles," she said, "I want to know more about the whales and their parasites. Plenty of dead worms shot through their blowholes."

"Sure. The medication you injected is a potent parasiticide. From the sound of things, it worked as fast as it did on the dolphins, which is how I titrated the dose."

"By guess and by golly?" She grinned.

"You nailed me dead to rights. Regardless, it appears to have been effective." He couldn't help himself. He grinned back right before he turned and hustled down the corridor to his cabin.

I cannot get sucked in, he lectured himself as he traded his clothes for something cleaner. By the time he headed for the bridge, he had his emotions under lock and key. And he hoped to hell they'd remain there.

7

THE ONLY GOOD VAMPIRE...

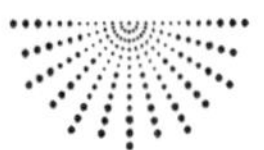

*K*arin detoured down one level intent on piling edibles onto a plate. At least she'd gotten Daide to smile, but it had been an uphill battle. The easy camaraderie marking their earlier interactions had all but fled. Should she apologize for not paying attention to her physical decline until she collapsed? Or was that even the problem?

Spreading biscuits with tinned preserves, she wished for freshly made strawberry jam to force her mind away from Daide's change of attitude.

"Yeah, for all the good wishing will do—about anything," she muttered and slopped a few spoonfuls from the previous night's casserole into a bowl. She wasn't all that hungry, but Daide might be.

As she worked, her thoughts returned to him, making her feel mildly guilty. She should focus all her energies on the Witch problem. Viktor and Juan hadn't said as much, but she suspected the supplies they'd hoped to find in town were more important than they let on. New Zealand had plenty of other cities along its eastern coastline, but all stopping would do was slow them down. At their current rate of progress, it would take years to reach Wrangel Island in the Siberian Arctic. Years when more wickedness poured through the gateway, infecting Earth until it reached a tipping point. For all she knew, they were already there, and all their efforts would be for naught.

She bit down on her lower lip, fighting frustration. Every place they made port, something went wrong. Maybe not exactly wrong, but they ran up against challenges. She'd overheard the conversation where Moira mentioned humans and Vampires. It seemed likely these Vamps wouldn't pose problems—not if there were only two—but she didn't trust any of them. She'd laid her antipathy aside when Ketha's seer skills revealed they had to work with Ushuaia's Vampires. Aura had clinched things with the fourth unfinished prophecy. Turned out, they'd both been correct.

Breath whistled through Karin's teeth. Her mind was really wandering. One moment it wanted to drool over Daide's dark good looks. The next it took a side trip backward in time to their fight against the Cataclysm.

She exhaled again, very slowly. If Daide's current attitude was to be trusted, he was a dead issue and thinking about him a waste of time. She'd been foolish to believe he might be interested in her, a woman at least four times his age. Never mind she wasn't old by Shifter standards. Still, she had white hair, lines in her face, and far from a girlish physique. He'd been kind. Professional. And she'd been so goddamned lonely, she'd misinterpreted his attention as romantic interest.

Christ! She was pathetic and needed to get over herself. Fast.

"Yeah. What I need to determine is why the hell Vamps survived here. They should be either human or Shifters."

She plopped two plates and a bowl on a small tray, along with silverware, and walked out of the kitchen. It was possible the vultures had gotten things wrong. Maybe there had been two Vampires, but the birds hadn't overflown the human compound lately. The more she thought about it, the more she believed it was a logical explanation. The Vamps had morphed into something else, but the birds didn't know about it.

Empty corridors and stairwells flashed past as she hurried up four decks and shouldered onto the bridge. The dishes made small clinking sounds as they knocked into each other when she set the tray on the floor near where Daide was seated next to Recco and Zoe.

"Sure and you'll join us." Zoe patted a chair next to hers. "I brought whiskey, but Juan vetoed it." Her mouth rounded into a disappointed moue. "Probably wise of him, though I'd dearly love a wee nip."

Karin settled into the indicated chair and eyed the fifth of spirits tucked between Zoe's knees.

"Thanks for getting the snack together," Daide said around a mouthful of biscuit and jam.

"No problem. The casserole is for you. I'm not particularly hungry." Her words earned her a quick, pointed glance from Zoe, but the coyote Shifter didn't say anything.

Boris, Ted, and the other three folk from Arctowski slipped through a side door. "Sorry we're late," Boris said. "Has anyone heard from the dolphins?"

The whale Shifters were lined up in front of the windows, staring at Invercargill's quays. They turned almost as a unit, and the man Karin had left on the gangway platform shook his head. He pinched the bridge of his nose between his thumb and forefinger and winced.

When he looked at everyone, he muttered, "I don't understand. I can't sense Leif or any of the other dolphins. It's like the Earth swallowed them. I've been trying to raise Poseidon, but that wily old bastard is never around when you need him."

Karin's eyes widened. Part of her expected the ether to part, revealing a very pissed-off sea god, but nothing of the kind happened. She put down the biscuit she'd begun nibbling and said, "It has to be one of two things."

"We figured as much out," the whale Shifter said before she could finish her thought. "Either Leif has cast a protective spell around himself and the others, or the Witches have. Either way, they're invisible, and it's damned disquieting."

"Is there a way to sort it out?" Viktor asked.

The whale rolled his broad shoulders amid cracking vertebrae unused to his human configuration. "If the question is whether I can tell the difference between Witch emanations and our own, the answer is yes. But when I send out seeking magic, what returns is nothing. Not Witch. Not ours. Just a void."

"Has to be Witches, then," Karin said.

"Why do you believe so, land Shifter?" the whale asked.

She considered her assessment, which had popped out before she sorted things through. "Shifters wear many faces," she began, "but we're not underhanded. I can see Leif shielding himself from Witches, but why bother to hide his presence from his own kind?"

"Fear," one of the female whales spoke up. "If he's terrified, he'd have built the strongest spell that came to mind."

"Aye," Zoe said, "but would he squander magic where 'twasn't needed?"

"I don't like any of this," Juan said. "We need to launch a raft and go hunt for him and the other dolphins. From what Recco told me, the Remington works against Witches."

"Bet the iron saber would too," Viktor broke in.

Karin hunted for Moira, but she wasn't on the bridge. She raised her mind voice and called the vulture shifter. "Could you open that door?" she pointed at the one leading outside near the glassed-in wall.

One of the whales moved faster than his bulk suggested was possible and propped a door open in time for Moira's dark, feathered form to breeze through. Cawing, she curved her talons around the back of a chair and fluffed her feathers.

"Shut that," Viktor called. "Some of us are cold."

The whale looked surprised but let go of the door.

"You want to know about the Vampires." Moira's lidless, avian gaze roamed around the bridge. *"In a nutshell, it's been years since the vultures flew anywhere near the human compound. Apparently, the group either still has ammunition, or some way to make more. They shoot at them."*

"Big surprise," Daide said. "Don't take this wrong, Moira, but vulture tastes a lot like turkey, and I'm certain food was in short supply during the worst of the Cataclysm."

She bobbed her head but stopped shy of squawking at him.

"What I'm wondering," Karin spoke slowly, "is if the Vamps replicated themselves."

"It would depend where they fell in their power cycle," Viktor replied. "At the front end of the Cataclysm, Raphael didn't have much trouble creating new Vamps, but that ability waned. And those of us he created lacked that skill."

"If the Vamps were satisfied with their arrangement with the humans," Recco said, raking hair away from his face, "there'd be no percentage to making more of them."

"You're right," Daide cut in. "More Vamps means more blood. Maybe they developed a détente of sorts with the humans."

"It's a whole lot of maybes," the whale Shifter Karin had come to view as their leader rumbled in his low, gravelly voice.

"I could take a few birds and fly close enough to see something," Moira suggested.

"Too risky," Viktor said.

"And too time consuming," the whale mumbled. Fisting one ham-sized hand, he brought it down on a chair, which broke apart like so much balsawood. "Damn it." Stooping, he gathered the pieces. "Sorry. I'll be more careful. Those of you who were ashore don't fully understand how critical it is we move quickly."

Ketha chewed her lower lip. "They'll kill them, won't they?"

"Not exactly," Karin said to spare the whale the humiliation of launching into his tale of misplaced bargains. "All those rumors about male Witches dying out centuries ago are true. Their solution to produce new Witches with credible power was to force the sea Shifters into serving as breeding stock. Only problem was whichever Shifter drew the short straw and serviced the Witches eventually went mad."

A long, hissing breath escaped Ketha. "Oberon's balls. Why weren't we ever informed?"

"By whom?" One of the whale shifters dragged the heels of his hands down the rough planes of his whiskered face. "We were ashamed. And the die was cast. Naught to be gained by whining about it."

"I hate to be indelicate," Karin said, "but it's damned hard to force a man to mate against his will."

"Witchy spells and love potions fill that void," the whale countered.

"I'm with Viktor," another whale spoke up. "Let's get our shore party into a raft and moving. We can stop by the human compound to solicit aid. I bet they'd give it willingly. Witches are the reason they're stuck hiding out."

"I'm returning to the vultures," Moira said. *"I'll handpick a group, and we'll meet you near where the humans are. It's two miles north of town and then off a side road that goes west. As I know more, I'll let you know via telepathy."*

The same whale Shifter who'd managed the door before held it open for her.

"I volunteer for the shore group," Karin said and finished the biscuit she'd been working on.

"I'll go too," Daide said.

"We need to think this through." Viktor glanced around the bridge. "Either Juan or myself must remain here."

"You went last time," Juan reminded him.

Viktor shot him a dirty look. "Your point?"

"Not sure I had one, but I'd like a shot at this. Seems our best bet would be resurrecting one of those jalopies you mentioned littering the roads. It's faster than travel on foot. Fuel separates, but we can strain off the water."

"You're not going without me." Aura trotted to Juan's side and trained her green eyes on him.

"Funny." He stared her down. "It's kind of the same thing I said when you got back with the raft."

"All five of us will be there," the lead whale Shifter said. "No arguments because we won't back down."

Karin got to her feet. "If the whales are coming, the best magical balance will be them, and six of us. If it's Daide and me, Juan and Aura, and Recco and Zoe, that would work."

"If something happens," Viktor countered, "you've wiped out our entire medical component."

"Nothing's going to happen to all of us." Karin stood straighter and hoped to hell her words were prophetic.

"I'd like to help." The zoologist from McMurdo stood. He looked determined—and frightened.

"You'd be a liability," Karin told him. "This isn't a fight for humans."

"Kind of what I figured," he mumbled and sat back down. "But I wanted to toss it out there."

"Appreciate you offering," Viktor said.

"Come on, Captain," the lead whale Shifter urged. "Time is everything. If we arrive after Leif or one of the others has been forced into being a sperm donor, we've lost them."

"Zoe and Recco, are you willing?" Viktor asked.

"More than willing." Recco shot upright.

"Me too." Zoe stood next to him.

"I'll drop the raft back in the water," Viktor said. "Those who are going get yourselves ready. You can't count on the weather, so put on your bibs and parkas."

"I'll help you with the raft," Ketha said.

Viktor headed out of the bridge with her next to him. "Thanks for not insisting on going—" he began, but his voice vanished once the door shut behind them.

"See you on the gangway." The whales filed out the door nearest them, muttering in their lyrical language.

"Don't worry about the debris from your snacks," Tessa said.

"Yeah, we'll take care of everything," Ted seconded. "I really wish I could be more than a third wheel."

"Someone has to hold down the fort," Karin told him.

He rolled his eyes. "Yeah, but I'd rather be out scouting for Apaches than making sure they don't burn down the stockade."

Karin hurried to her cabin and selected what she thought she'd need, including a medical bag. Clipping her life vest on, she bolted for the gangway, not wanting to hold anyone up. She was pleased Daide had volunteered to go right after she did, but she'd be a fool to read anything special into it. He was a doctor exactly like her. They put themselves in the line of danger so someone would be around to save lives.

Juan and the raft were already at the bottom of the gangway, so she trotted down the wobbly steps. The day had been mild by southern latitude standards, but it was shading toward night, and a nippy breeze had kicked up.

"Going to be a cold crossing," Juan noted.

Karin tucked her hair under her hood and cinched its draw cord beneath her chin. The whales were already in the raft, and everyone else joined them in the next few minutes.

"Feels odd not to swim," one of the whales mumbled.

No one else said anything as they crossed the stretch of choppy, dark blue water. Karin kept her magic deployed like antennae, scanning for Witch presence. What bounced back wasn't reassuring. While she didn't sense Witches, the absence felt empty, ominous, as if an unseen puppeteer manipulated strings just out of reach.

"Take the main highway out of town." Moira's mind voice blasted into Karin's head. *"Maybe three miles out, look for a battered sign pointing west. You can still make out 'Harrison Mineral Baths' on it."*

"How far from there?" Karin asked.

"Half to two-thirds of a mile, but Christ on a crutch they have that place warded nine ways from Tuesday. You'll smell Vampire long before you get there."

"I had no idea Vamps could construct bulletproof wards." Karin chewed her lower lip.

"Neither did I. The vultures told me you just landed. Hurry. I'm certain those fuckers know we're around, and I don't want any more of my birds hurt."

"What was that all about?" Juan asked and finished tying off the raft to a convenient concrete pier block with metal rings embedded in it.

Karin sketched out the gist of Moira's message. "Your vehicle idea is sound, but unless you find a truck, we won't all fit."

"Don't worry about us," the whale Shifters' leader said. "We have our own ways of traveling."

"We'll wait for you at the intersection where that spa sign is," one of the whales Karin had worked on added. "Would you mind if we brought the rifle?"

"Not at all." Juan offered it to him, along with a handful of spare bullets.

Before Karin could ask for details about their teleport plans, the area around the whales blazed so brightly, she shut her eyes. The air thrummed with Shifter magic. Compared with what she'd been sensing, it felt clean and welcome. When the glare receded enough for her to pry her eyes open, the whales were gone.

"Come on." Juan took off at a quick clip uphill toward where the town's streets began. "First car I can get started wins."

"We'll help," Daide said. "Recco and I weren't precisely delinquents, but we picked up a few illegal skills. Jumpstarting cars was a rite of passage where we grew up."

Karin tamped back a grin and exchanged glances with Aura and Zoe. "We'll keep watch while you're stealing us a car."

"It's not stealing," Daide protested. "Not when the owner's been dead for years."

"Hell, if he's not dead and living in that compound, he'll thank us for bringing his car close enough to actually use," Recco added with an engaging smile.

The men moved from one abandoned vehicle to the next. They worked fast, and in no time the ragged chug of a reciprocating engine filled the darkening sky with clouds of black smoke.

"Pile in," Recco yelled over the noise of the engine. "Probably won't go far, but it doesn't have to."

"Fuel?" Juan yelled back.

"Quarter tank."

Karin climbed into the backseat of a four-door Citroen, medical bag in hand. Daide and Recco got into the backseat with her, while Juan, Aura, and Zoe took the front, balancing the saber across their laps. The car lurched and stumbled down what had once been a broad boulevard. Potholes crisscrossed its surface, and Juan wove around obstacles.

"Your medical equipment?" Karin twisted to look at the men next to her.

"Popped it in the boot," Daide said. "We tried to fit the saber, but it was too long."

"I'm amazed the tires still hold air," Recco said.

"One was fairly flat," Aura informed him. "I used magic to inflate it."

"Neat trick," Daide said.

"Aye, but it willna work if we sustain a puncture," Zoe informed him.

Karin gazed at the ruined town. While the architecture was far different from Ushuaia's, the net effect was the same. Crumbling structures, rotting bodies, and bones. A horde of hundreds of rats scrambled out of their path from where they'd been perched atop something, no doubt feeding from it.

"None of this was here on our first trip," Aura said. "The streets and buildings looked pristine, as if the inhabitants had dashed off for a bite of lunch and simply not returned."

"All illusion created by the Witches?" Juan asked.

"Aye," Zoe said. "They're hella strong."

"Why haven't they intercepted us?" Karin mused out loud.

"I'm sure we'll find out," Juan said, a sour note beneath his words. "There are the whales. Must be our turnoff."

Karin craned her neck to look out one of the car's filthy windows. Vultures circled overhead. She swallowed around a dry, scratchy place in her throat, and her palms slicked with sweat despite the chill seeping into the car.

"It will be fine." Daide placed a hand briefly over hers. "We'll rescue Leif and his dolphins."

An image of Rowana dying in her arms rose to taunt Karin. She forced it aside. "Whatever happens"—she was surprised her voice didn't tremble—"some of us will make it out of here. Whoever is left has to continue to Siberia."

"Was there ever any question?" Zoe's soft brogue was soothing.

Karin wanted to scream at her. Of course there'd be questions. The pull of retreat to Ushuaia to wait out phase two of the apocalypse would be hard to resist in the wake of grief. Instead, she said, "No. No question at all."

Juan stopped the car in the middle of the road because it was the only place not riddled with fissures. He cranked his window down amid rusty squealing, and one of the whales moved next to the car, bending his head to window level.

"Not sure how close we'll get," the whale said. "The warding begins about a quarter mile down the road."

"Did you try to breach it?" Aura asked.

"No. Muscling our way through will take all of us."

"Even if we fight our way to the compound," Daide said, "they'll be loaded for bear by the time we show up. Is there some way to communicate with them?"

"Yes," Juan seconded. "We need to inform them we're playing on their team, although signing on for any team that includes Vampires sticks in my craw."

"We can try." Karin jimmied the latch until her door opened. Not much reason to drive any farther, so she stepped out of the car, reaching back inside to claim her kit.

What little daylight there'd been was gone. The darkness felt ominous, somehow. Nostrils flaring, she scented the air, certain she caught a whiff of Vampire. At least it wasn't Witch stench.

Not here, and not yet, she corrected herself.

She walked to where the whales stood in a line staring down the road to the compound.

"Look sharp," her wolf growled. *"You're about to have company."*

Zoe and Aura flanked her. "My coyote just told me—" Zoe began.

Aura cut her off. "Yeah, my mountain cat said the same."

Karin dropped her bag and extended her hands. Aura grabbed one, Zoe the other, and they wove their power together.

"Get behind us," the lead whale snarled.

"I don't think so," Karin countered.

A sound like a hundred bolts of cloth tearing at the same time made her ears ache. The slimy feel of Vampire magic cascaded around her, along with their characteristic rotten-egg reek. The fissure she expected formed about twenty feet away, and a Vampire complete with extended fangs and a black cloak stepped through.

Dark hair cascaded to knee level, and his eyes were a burnt-amber shade. Tall, beautiful, and with a body like a Greek god, his gaze traveled across their group. Shrewd and appraising, it suggested a sharp intelligence.

Karin constructed a protective spell with the other women and stood straight, waiting. The Vamp's primitive magic probed the edges of her ward, and then moved on. She began to relax, but only a little. One Vampire would never take on eleven Shifters. No. This fellow wanted something.

Surprise fluttered across the Vamp's striking features. "But you three"—he pointed at Juan, Recco, and Daide—"were Vampires until quite recently. What happened? I can fix whatever robbed you of—"

"Oh hell no." Daide took a step forward. "We were turned against our will."

Musical laughter trilled from the Vampire. "True for all of us, but the advantages are compelling."

Karin let go of Aura and Zoe. "Skip the sales pitch. You're here for a reason. Tell us what you have in mind."

"How about if I save the sales pitch for later?" he crooned. Karin forced her gaze away before he mesmerized her. "What I want is simple. I know what happened earlier. I also know you're Shifters. No love lost between you and the Witches. I propose an alliance."

"What kind of an alliance?" Juan's words dripped distrust.

"Simple enough. I lead you to your missing sea Shifters, and you help me kill the rest of the Witches." He dusted his palms together. "Rids me of an enormous problem, and then you can get back on that ship and leave. Unless my offer of eternal life and endless power begins to sound more attractive."

"How many more Witches are there?" Zoe asked.

"Ten. After the batch you dispatched today. Nice work, by the way." The Vamp retracted his fangs and smiled fetchingly.

"You have a bargain under one condition." Juan walked closer to the Vampire.

"What's that?" His alluring smile widened, and the air around him developed a shimmery quality.

"No coercion. Four of us spent a decade as Vampires. Plenty long enough to decide we'd rather die than be Vamps again."

"Tsk. Tsk. You weren't turned by the right Vampire. Why I could—"

"No deal. We'll find our companions on our own. Best of luck with the Witches." Juan turned on his heel.

"No need to be so hasty." The Vampire's tone was pure silk. "I agree."

The lead whale Shifter stomped to the Vampire. "Where are my kinfolk. Show me right now."

"Pushy. Pushy," the Vamp muttered.

Amid cawing and shrieking, the flock of vultures landed. The Vampire stared at them. "Fascinating. First time I've seen a herd of anything run by a Shifter."

Magic flared and flashed, and a buck-naked, furious Moira faced off against the Vampire. "They follow my bonded one of their free will, which is more than you can say about any of your blood-turned minions." Another flare, and her coal-black vulture returned, sharp beak opening and closing in anger.

"We need a plan," the Vampire said without preamble.

"Why?" the whale shifter asked. "We'll shoot the Witches—or behead them."

"First, we have to penetrate their wards," the Vampire's easy mien had vanished, and he bent to draw in the dirt with a long-nailed index finger.

"Is there more than one of you?" Karin asked.

"Yes, but my companion isn't well. Pay attention." He pointed to his rough sketch. "The Witches are about a mile from here in a cave system that butts against the sea. This area is weakest, but once we're within their lair, we..."

Karin listened with half an ear. How could a Vampire be *unwell*? And then it came to her in a rush. The other Vamp must have reverted to human—or bonded with an animal. For some reason, the Vamp a few feet away hadn't been able to turn him—or her— again, which was an intriguing piece of data. Apparently, the Vampire gate no longer swung both ways.

An uncomfortable sensation settled into her guts like a stone. Was the Vampire planning to use them to defeat the Witches and then imprison them for his own nefarious purposes? It would be very like a Vamp. Perhaps he didn't realize the full extent of what breaking the Cataclysm had done to his kind.

Why should he? None of us do, either.

She narrowed her mind voice to Zoe and Aura. *"Something about this stinks."*

"Ya think?" Aura mumbled.

Zoe's response was a collection of Gaelic words so old, Karin only caught one in half a dozen. Snatching up her bag, she followed the group.

Daide fell in next to her. *"A favor?"* His telepathy was garbled.

"Sure. What?"

"If that bastard turns me, take the saber and cut off my head."

"You don't have much to worry about it. I suspect it's what he meant by his companion being unwell. He's tried and can't manage turning the other one back."

"I feel stupid. Should have put two and two together myself," Daide murmured.

Karin held out her hand, and he gripped it hard. She didn't want to let go, and he didn't even try to extricate his fingers. Together, they ran after the Vampire.

8

ONLY WAY OUT IS THROUGH

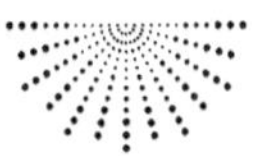

Daide battled horror as a Vampire stepped through the place where the air had split in two. The abomination looked a lot like Raphael, except for his eyes, which made this even creepier. His sense of unease had skyrocketed after listening to the Vampire. Raphael employed the same rapid-fire switches from flattery to coercion, mingled with Vampire compulsion. The combination was hard to resist.

Daide couldn't stand by and do nothing. Maybe all four of them who'd been Vamps would be susceptible to the siren tug of Vampirism. He remembered struggling to resist Raphael's streaming wrist—and the mixed sense of relief, gratitude, and revulsion when he'd glommed onto the Vampire, sucking down his blood as fast as he could.

No matter how strong he envisioned himself, he needed a fallback position. Telepathy was still a struggle, but he caught up with Karin and asked, *"A favor?"*

"Sure. What?" Her voice, warm and strong, steadied him.

"If that bastard turns me, take the saber and cut off my head."

"You don't have much to worry about. I suspect it's what he meant by

his companion being unwell. He's tried and can't manage turning the other one back."

"I feel stupid. Should have put two and two together."

Daide chided himself for being careless. He'd been so troubled when the Vampire appeared, he hadn't evaluated the thing's words. Vampires never got sick, so his comment about his companion being under the weather should have kicked up a host of red flags.

Karin held out her hand, and he gripped it hard. Grateful for her steady presence, he ran after the Vampire with her next to him. The vultures flew overhead, a darker place against the night sky.

Picking your allies was a luxury, he reminded himself. The Vamp knew where the Witches were. They didn't. Maybe they could behead him as soon as he'd uncovered their lair. It grated. He wasn't in the habit of killing something that hadn't threatened him.

In truth, he wasn't used to killing at all. Unless you counted for food, so he wouldn't starve. The corners of his mouth twitched. He'd been a sorry example of a Vampire. First time failing at something was a point of pride. "How come breaking the Cataclysm didn't affect this one?" he whispered.

"I have no idea." Karin kept her voice low. "He's very old, but then so was Raphael."

"Yeah, but he was dead before the Cataclysm imploded."

"True enough." Karin's medical bag banged between them.

"Let go," he said, not wanting to untangle his fingers from hers, but it wasn't as if she'd ever belonged to him. "I'll carry your bag. Good that we have supplies. Should have brought mine."

"It's not like anyone's going to steal your kit," she said and moved closer to him to avoid a lateral fracture cutting through the asphalt. She smelled of wild things, fresh and invigorating, and he inhaled hungrily.

"Depends if any of the humans leave their compound," he said to remind her they were far from alone here.

"Unless someone there isn't human, I don't see how they could penetrate the wards. Oh-oh. The Vamp slowed down. We must be close."

They left the road on a rutted side track. Daide borrowed from his coyote's night vision, which was far sharper than his own. The rotten vegetation stink of Witch grew stronger. At least the Vampire was upholding part of his promise. Not that they couldn't have located the Witches without him, but this was faster, and if the whales were to be believed, time was critical.

Daide dug deep and tried to be happy for Karin and Leif. He hoped they'd find the dolphins before one was turned into an unwilling stud service. The whales' story about madness had been chilling.

Recco closed on his other side, not saying anything, but tension rolled off him. "I'll be happy once we get to the other side of this," he muttered.

"Makes two of us, *amigo*," Daide grunted.

"No matter what happens," Juan chimed in from behind them, "we are never, never going back to being Vamps. Agreed?"

"Not a question you even had to ask," Daide replied without bothering to elaborate he'd already chosen death over Vampirism.

The Vampire drew to a halt. "As you know, I have exceptional hearing. You needn't continue your tirade."

Daide's head snapped up. If he didn't know better, the old bastard had actually sounded hurt. Except Vamps didn't have feelings. Certainly not the old breed like this specimen.

"The rear entrance to the Witches' lair is about fifty feet that way." He pointed his long-nailed index finger.

"Aren't you coming with us?" the whales' leader asked.

"No. I did my part."

"Well then, we don't need you anymore." Juan raced forward, iron blade in hand.

"No!" the Vampire shouted. "You can't. Don't you understand? I was the first. I'm who forged an alliance between the devil and Sekhmet to create a master magical race. And now I'm the only one left." He'd been edging off to one side as he spoke. Power rose around him, thick and glistening.

"All the more reason to end you," Daide shouted.

He and Recco ran to Juan, who'd followed the Vampire's retreat. Juan swung the blade, but it bounced off an invisible barrier threaded with the Vampire's power. Fury boiled from Daide's guts. "Oh hell, no," he cried. "You're not getting off that easy."

Juan swung the blade again and again, grunting with strain as it ran up against the impenetrable blockade. Sparks flashed where it connected, but the barrier didn't give. The Vamp had begun to chant, low and guttural; the air surrounding him took on an insubstantial aspect.

"We can't let him leave," Karin yelled. Magic flashed from her hands.

Daide snatched the Remington from the whale shifter and hurtled forward with it in firing position. When he got so close heat from the Vampire's magic seared him, he pulled the trigger. It was a risk. The bullet might not have any better luck than the saber and could ricochet, but if they didn't act fast, the source of Vampirism would elude them. Daide wasn't under any illusions they'd ever find him again.

Vamps might not indulge in emotion, but this one's mask had slipped enough, fear shone through. The rifle blast deafened Daide, but he yanked the bolt back to eject the spent cartridge and seat the next one. Smoke holding the stink of magic rose around him, obscuring his vision. No one yelled at him to stop, so he fired again, blind this time. The bullet Recco fired earlier in the day had evaded the Witch's efforts to escape its trajectory. Maybe these bullets would be just as dogged.

"Can anyone see?" he screeched before firing a third time.

"No," Karin yelled back, her voice distorted because his ears were still ringing from the gunshots.

"He's dead," one of the whales bellowed. "Good work."

Daide lowered the rifle, gasping like a landed fish. The carrion stench of Vampire twisted his guts into a painful, burning knot.

"Here." The whale thrust fresh shells into his hand, and Daide chambered them. The rifle held four rounds.

"Quick thinking with the rifle. He had to go," Karin said from where she'd moved next to him.

"Indeed, he did, dearie," an unfamiliar voice cackled from the darkness. "My thanks to you will be allowing you to leave."

"Not without our kin," the whale nearest Daide growled, his tone low and menacing.

"You weren't listening, Shifter." The Witch's voice oozed venom. "Leave now before my good nature deserts me. Personally, I don't care if you live or die. I was being kind, but kindness isn't part of the natural order of things for Witches."

Daide stiffened and raised the rifle to his shoulder. Could he shoot blind again? Would it matter to the silver-and-iron-infused shells?

"Do it," his coyote urged. *"Let me switch our vision to your third eye."*

The blackness and smoke ceded to a gray-green, and the Witch became fully visible. Shrouded in a dark shawl that covered her from head to toe, her arms were extended. Mini lightning bolts arced back and forth between her fingertips as she held power in abeyance.

The knowledge she stood ready to mow them down made his decision for him.

The rifle was already in position. He tightened his finger around the trigger and aimed the sights right between her eyes. Slow, steady, he pulled the trigger. The rifle's report blasted, making his ears hurt worse, but the eerie part was the bullet. He watched it travel as if someone had taken a time-lapse video.

The Witch knew she'd been targeted, and she slid to one side, certain she'd escape, but the bullet doubled around behind her and buried itself in the base of her skull, which exploded. Blood and bits of bone and tissue geysered, and the stench of decaying Witch joined the reek of Vampire.

Now that Daide could see, the Vampire had degenerated into a pile of bones sticking out of the cloak he'd jauntily wrapped around himself. Made sense. They decomposed fast when they were old like that, reverting to their true age immediately.

"Focus, people," the whale leader bellowed loud enough for Daide to hear despite his ringing ears. The Shifter hurried toward where the Witch had collapsed into a reeking pile of blood and bones and kicked her aside. Light shone around him as he searched for an opening into her lair.

Daide did a double take. The light was the same phosphorescence common to marine life, shining a pale blue-green. Impressive the whale could summon up elements of his marine self while in human form. Daide drew the bolt back, replaced the spent bullet, and then trotted to an uneven pile of boulders and brush. The whales scented the air as they moved from spot to spot.

"Here," one of them cried. "Found it."

Daide wanted to tell him to be quiet, but that was stupid. The Witches knew they were here. And they probably had some way of knowing their messenger was dead. If the Vampire's count had been correct, it left nine, all of whom would fight to their last spell.

"Won't open," another whale grunted.

"Big surprise," Juan muttered. "I'd bar the gates if I were them too."

Karin, Aura, and Zoe ran toward the gateway. "It's enchantment," Karin said. "I believe we can break through it."

Daide wanted to argue it was simpler to shoot through the lock, but maybe it wasn't such a straightforward proposition if magic powered it.

"Are you sure?" one of the female whales asked.

"Because we can go around and find other entrances," another whale chimed in. "There must be more than one."

"Hold tight for a minute," Karin said.

Daide both saw and felt magic boil from her, Aura, and Zoe. A sheet of gleaming green-white coated an old-fashioned wooden door studded with metal crosspieces. The door shuddered and groaned. When it began to vibrate, Daide positioned himself off to one side, rifle raised to address whoever burst through the door when it opened.

A squealing, splintering crack battered his already damaged hearing. Rather than swinging open, the door shattered, falling into clumps of dust and debris. A gush of stale air whooshed through the opening, suggesting it wasn't one the Witches used often.

He waited, but no one materialized.

"Damn it." Zoe added Gaelic to her curse. "Means there's an inner door also firmly locked."

Karin shrugged. "We figured out the secret of this one. Another will yield faster. It's a rare magic-wielder who bothers with more than one type of lock."

"Particularly not here," Aura agreed. "Why would they? They run the place."

"Not anymore," Daide muttered.

The bioluminescence around the whales intensified, and they moved through the shattered doorway, standing in a line to light the way. Karin and the other two women walked briskly through, chanting softly in Gaelic. As Daide passed the whale sentinels, the one nearest him whooped. "Yes. Finally. I sense the dolphins."

"Must mean the Witches have redirected their power and are mobilizing to launch an all-out attack on us," Karin said. "Ward yourselves."

Juan threaded through them until he stood in front of the women, holding the saber. "Safer than bullets in here," he said.

"Noooooo!" the whale leader thundered. "It's not us in their gunsights. They're killing the dolphins." A blast of magic knocked Daide to his knees, and the whales vanished.

"They teleported!" Karin yelled. "Hurry."

Daide raced down a winding corridor, alternating between his coyote's vision and his psychic view. Adrenaline pumped through him. Sure enough, a stout door, this one far more modern, blocked the tunnel.

A blast of white light flew from the women's joined hands, but the door didn't so much as quiver. They tried again. Still nothing.

Breath rasped through Daide's teeth. "Move over. I'll try the gun."

"Bad idea," Karin said.

"Open your magic to us," Aura twisted to face him and Recco and Juan. "All of you. Have your bondmates help."

Daide turned his focus inward. *"Do your stuff."*

The coyote yipped and yowled. The same sensation he'd had before when the women siphoned power from him prickled up and down his spine. The women shouted in Gaelic. Magic buzzed, pressing inward until the corridor came alive with it. Behind them, an enormous crash told him the ceiling had caved in.

The only way out was through. He breathed as deep as he could and willed the coyote to mine deeper and find scraps of magic he hadn't tapped before.

Power swirled in a vortex that threatened to draw him off his feet. Deep booming began in his belly until he felt he'd burst if it didn't release. A huge rush of sharply defined magic wound through the vortex and headed straight for the door, splitting it cleanly in two.

The women bolted through before the dust settled, with him and the other two men right behind them. Firelight or maybe candlelight flickered, illuminating stone walls. This was an old corridor, clearly built by humans. Two twists and they emerged into a high-ceilinged cavern with a firepit dead in the middle. Whale shifters grappled with some Witches, while others stood with their arms extended, black-tinged power shooting from their fingertips.

"Move over," Daide yelled. "Whales stay down." Shouldering the rifle, he waited a split second until a clear path opened before him.

Finally, his obsession with target practice was paying off,

although this rifle—or maybe it was the bullets that were magic—would have excused a whole lot of slop. He squeezed off three shots, and three Witches dropped like stones. One bullet remained. He trained it on a Witch with red hair spilling to her knees.

She raised her hands above her head, magic no longer flowing from her. "I surrender," she said in a clear, ringing voice.

"Well I don't," a dark-haired woman who'd been standing in shadows said. "Nona. Stand up for your kind, or I'll strip you of your power."

"No." The redhead squared her shoulders. "They're going to kill me. I'd rather live without magic than be a dead Witch."

Juan had circled around behind the raven-haired Witch while her attention was on her companion. In one easy motion, he swung the saber, cleanly decapitating her. Blood spewed, flowing across the cavern's dirt floor.

The whales grunted, snarled, and snorted as they literally ripped Witch bodies apart. Three Witches lay dismembered and bleeding. The fourth was well on her way out with two Whales grabbing handfuls of her body and shredding her flesh to grisly bits amid shrieks and howls.

Daide stared at Nona. "Where are the dolphins?"

"Where else?" She eyed him defiantly. "We herded them into the sea once you killed Catriona."

"The one who met us outside?" Karin asked.

"Yup. What are you going to do with me?" Nona tilted her chin.

"Depends on how you behave," Aura said.

"I'm the last one left," Nona muttered sullenly. "How the hell do you think I'll behave."

"Leif!" Karin shouted. "Lewis. Lynda."

Dolphin song trilled faintly from the far side of the cavern. Daide sprinted around limestone formations, avoiding rocks and holes. Another corridor wound away from the cavern. Heavy steps thumped behind him. He didn't have to look back to know several whale Shifters were close.

Intent on following the most obvious path, he was surprised when one of the whales called, "Back up. You missed the turn."

Daide retraced his steps. The path was empty, but he sensed where the whales had turned right. The track took a definite downward cant, and the smell of the sea slapped him hard. He hoped to hell Karin had her bag. God only knew what they'd find down here.

The ceiling lowered until he had to stoop to keep moving. The whales must have had a hell of a time since all of them were at least half a foot taller than him.

Whoops and hollers reached him. He rounded a bend and came out in another rounded cavern, this one with very little headroom. The whales had dragged the dolphins out of the water onto a sandy spit. Shifter magic glistened and flashed as they worked over them.

"What's wrong?" Daide asked. "How can I help?"

"Drugged," one of the whales gritted out.

"That's good news. I can take blood samples and figure out an antidote."

"By the time you did all that, they'd be dead," the whales' leader said. "Quiet. Let us work."

Recco pelted into the cavern, followed by Juan and the women. Karin shouldered her way to one of the comatose dolphins and laid her hands atop its head. "It's a wonder they didn't drown," she growled.

"They were well on their way when we arrived," one of the whales twisted to look at her. "You're the one who leverages magic to heal."

"I am. Let me test something." Karin settled into a low chant. A visible thread of power—green woven with white—left her fingers and wound around the dolphin she was crouched next to. The pitch of her chant lowered until it almost disappeared from Daide's hearing, but he was certain the sea creatures could hear the low notes. The ribbon pulsed and brightened.

The dolphin shook itself; a cascade of hoots and bleats

tumbled from it right before it shimmered into Lewis's human form. "Thank you." He threaded his arms around Karin, hugging her.

She looked at the whales' leader. "Summon the Gaelic spell for healing and wholeness. Once it reaches its zenith, mix water with your casting. The resulting cord will circle your patient. Keep feeding water, but mix in air until the cord turns color. When that happens, wait."

"Did you all get that?" the whale asked his companions. Amid a chorus of yesses, each of the whales settled next to a dolphin.

"I'll take another," Karin said and moved to the next closest dolphin.

Recco elbowed Daide. "We need to learn that spell."

"For now, let's do what we can to keep their lungs working while they're waiting for magic to heal them." Daide settled next to a dolphin, massaging its chest cage.

Recco did the same.

"Those look like chest compressions," Juan noted.

"They are, but you can press harder. No hyoid bone to break off," Daide said.

"We'll work on the last two," Aura said, motioning to Zoe.

Daide focused on the animal beneath his hands. The feel of its skin. Its warm breath. Running on instinct, he used his mind voice. *"Can you hear me?"*

"Yes."

"Who are you?"

A rumbling chuckle preceded. *"We all look alike, eh? Leif. I'm Leif. Although you might be better off leaving me here."*

A deeply sinking feeling rocked Daide, and his hands stilled. *"You had sex with one of them?"*

"At least one. They ensorcelled me, so I have no memory."

"They're all dead. Will it matter?"

The dolphin rocked beneath his touch, struggling against the effects of whatever he'd been dosed with.

"Karin," Daide called. "This one is Leif." He didn't tell her anything further. That tale was Leif's to impart.

"Hang on. Just finishing up here."

She crawled to where they were and repeated her incantation. Maybe because Leif wasn't under too deep, the dolphin shifted into his human body quickly. He shook his blue-gray hair until water sheeted from him, and then he struggled to sit.

"You say all the Witches are dead?" He looked right at Daide.

"All but one," Daide said.

"There might be hope for me yet, so long as she isn't pregnant." A grimace twisted his features into something harsh and foreboding.

Understanding carved worry lines into Karin's forehead. "Crap. We didn't get here in time."

"So long as no child of mine is born, all should be fine," Leif answered.

"That's right." A whale stood over them. "We left two of us riding herd on the Witch who surrendered."

"Surrendered?" Leif barked a bitter laugh. "What a joke. She said what she had to to save her own skin."

"Regardless." Karin pushed to her feet, standing bent over because of the ceiling. "I'll check her over right now. Even if she's pregnant, we can make sure she doesn't stay that way."

"Wrong," Leif said. "We do not kill the unborn."

"To save your life?" Daide looked askance at him.

"For any reason." He struggled partially upright. "Let's go see what my fate is."

"Be right there." Daide scanned the cavern. Between them and the whales, all the dolphins were in various stages of recovery. Most had shifted to human, so it seemed safe to follow Leif. He'd been surprised by the dolphin Shifter's reaction to abortion. Karin had suggested that path, so clearly land Shifters didn't share their sea kin's philosophies.

He turned his attention inward. *"Can you shed some light on this?"* he asked his coyote.

"No, but we should hurry. I don't trust that Witch."

"Good point. Neither do I." Daide hurried after Leif, hoping against hope the redhaired Witch wasn't carrying his child. If she was, he'd have to figure out a way to make sure the baby was never born—even if it meant killing the Witch. The more he thought about it, the better he liked that solution. It sidestepped the sea Shifters' aversion to abortion nicely.

9

LIES AND ILLUSIONS

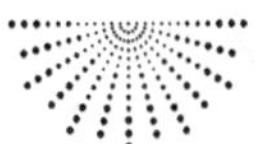

Karin trailed after Leif, Daide, and a couple of whale Shifters, mulling over the sequence of events. Her medical bag dangled from one hand. Maybe Nona had acquiesced so quickly because she was protecting her unborn child. Surely there was a way to extract the child's magic. She shuffled through possibilities, grateful when the tunnel expanded vertically, and she could walk upright.

One spell popped up several times. It would strip the child of all its magic, Witch and Shifter alike, but leave it viable. If they needed to take action, it would be the one they'd employ.

Maybe. The casting was intricate, and Karin wasn't certain how well it would work on an unwilling participant. The Witch certainly wouldn't view relieving her unborn baby of magic as a plus, and her fighting the spell would complicate things.

We'll cross that bridge when we have to.

Ready for damn near any development, Karin trudged onward. Still weary from her near brush with death, she marshaled her resources and sent warm thoughts inward to her bondmate. It whined softly.

Nona sat next to the fire with a whale on either side of her. She looked up as everyone filed into the cavern. "See?" She furled both brows into an insolent expression. "The dolphins were right where I said they'd be, weren't they?"

"Were you always this unlikeable?" Karin asked.

"Probably. Were you always an overbearing bitch?"

Karin laughed. "I've been called worse, young woman."

"Bet I'm not much younger than you."

Karin wasn't going to go there, so she didn't take the bait. Instead, she shouldered to the front of the line and stood a foot in front of Nona with her magic engaged as she hunted for a developing embryo.

A harsh laugh interrupted her search. "I'm not pregnant. Not for lack of effort, mind you, but the spawn didn't take."

"You'll excuse me if I don't take your word for it." Karin moved closer. Since the Witch knew what she was up to, she employed an obvious spell. "Fascinating," she muttered. "You told the truth. You were pregnant, but you aren't anymore."

Nona shrugged. "Maybe the sea Shifter would care for a rematch?" She batted aquamarine eyes Leif's way.

He didn't dignify her suggestion with a reply.

"We should get out of here," Juan said.

"I'm coming with you," Nona announced.

"The hell you are," Aura countered. "We hate Witches, and you're none too fond of us."

"Aye," Zoe chimed in. "Aura is correct. You'll remain here."

"But I'll die if I'm by myself." The defiant tilt to her chin lowered a notch, and she sounded worried.

"Throw yourself on the humans' mercy," Karin suggested.

"Pah. They've been Vampire fodder for ten years. Assuming any remain, which is doubtful, they're unlikely to have warm fuzzies for me."

"The Vampire is dead." Juan leveled his gaze at her.

"One of them," she shot back.

"How long since you've laid eyes on either one?" Aura arched one blonde eyebrow.

"Why do you suppose there are only two since they can easily replenish their ranks?" Nona blew out a noisy breath. "It's not as if any of us went looking for them. Vampires never make good bedfellows. They only want one thing: blood. Now. About taking me with you…"

The air in the cavern altered, but so subtly Karin might not have noticed if she weren't paying close attention. She took a measured breath, assessing her impression before she reacted and spooked everyone unnecessarily. Maybe she was imagining the difference. It wasn't as if she weren't on edge. Moving quickly, and she hoped accurately, she latched onto the place where the warp and weft of the ether felt off.

A vibration, one that shouldn't be present, pinged sourly, twisting her gut into an unpleasant knot. A second pulse—stealthy and faint—throbbed beneath the first before winding around it.

"Enough!" Karin dropped her bag and lobbed magic at Nona from both hands. The whales on either side of the Witch didn't ask questions. They threaded their brand of power into Karin's spell until Nona was encased in silvery interlocking metal rings.

"Ought to hold her," one of the whales observed.

"What was she doing that we missed?" the other guardian asked.

The vibration ceased abruptly, and Karin unclenched her jaw. She narrowed her eyes. "Plotting to unhinge the integrity of this cave. Bet there's a magical lynchpin somewhere. Give it a good, hard tug, and the whole shebang would have crashed on our heads, burying us."

"You can hardly blame a Witch for trying," Nona muttered. "If you'd been willing to take me with you, I'd never have considered such a thing. In fact, you can still change your minds."

"Why?" Zoe sneered. "So you can move on to more creative ways to kill us?"

"We do need to leave." Juan ignored Nona and repeated his earlier words.

"What about the humans?" Aura asked.

"What about them?" Juan sent a pointed look her way.

"We should blast through the warding, so they're not prisoners in that compound any longer."

He grinned crookedly. "One of many reasons I love you, my softhearted darling. Come on. The corridor we didn't take when we were hunting the dolphins should lead us out of here."

"What about me?" Nona strained against the metal rings, making them rattle discordantly.

Karin shrugged. "We'd have let you walk free. Once we're gone, the enchantment powering my spell will fade gradually. Give it a month."

"But I'll starve."

"Eh. Not my problem. Never was." Karin retrieved her bag and turned to follow Juan and Aura, shooing the others ahead of her. As she trotted briskly down the well-trodden dirt, mage light suspended off to one side, Nona's screams, screeches, and curses followed her.

She snorted. Being cursed by Sirens worried her a whole lot more than being cursed by one lone Witch. And a Witch who'd brought fate crashing down on herself for being stupid.

Daide caught up with her but didn't say anything. Just loped by her side. The tunnel ended abruptly at a gate fashioned similarly to the first one they'd used magic to annihilate. Everyone was arranged in a semicircle, waiting for them. The night was clear, black, and cold. The sky shot with thousands of stars. The Cataclysm might be hatching evil, but the beauty of the moment stole her breath.

"We're going to split forces," Aura said and looked at Karin. "You, Zoe, and I will stop by the human compound, along with Moira and the vultures." As if in response, the whir of wingbeats sounded overhead.

"Aye, and in case the Vamp's not as defanged as we'd like to believe, we're taking these with us." Zoe pointed at the rifle and saber lying on the ground in front of her.

"Good idea. I didn't like it much when Nona suggested there might be more than one other Vamp behind that ward. What's everyone else doing?" Karin glanced around the group and said a hasty prayer to the goddess for keeping them all safe.

"We're returning to the sea to speed our healing." Leif bowed slightly. "Once we've fully recovered from the witchery and the chemical incursion, we shall join you aboard *Arkady*."

"We're going with the dolphins," the nearest whale rumbled. The salt smell of the sea thickened around them. Light flared, blue-white and green. When it cleared, the sea Shifters were gone.

"They must be in decent shape if they can teleport," Karin murmured.

"Aye, 'tis quite a relief," Zoe seconded the sentiment.

"We need supplies," Juan said. "Now that the Witches aren't around to boobytrap everything, I'm going to do a quick reconnaissance. Feel like helping?" He looked from Recco to Daide and back again.

"Sure." Daide smiled. "Do you have your radio?"

"I do. Assuming we get lucky, we'll begin collecting items and piling them on the piers. A few Zodiac trips, and we'll be set for another ten thousand miles."

"Maybe you'll come up with food." Aura sounded hopeful.

"I'll do my best, but don't set the bar too high. At most, we'll find canned and powdered items."

"If we can get it started, we'll bring the Citroen back to the pier," Aura said.

"Excellent." Daide nodded in her direction. "We have supplies in the trunk."

"We'll make certain not to leave them," Karin assured him.

Juan kissed Aura and took off with the men pacing him on either side.

Moira fluttered to the ground, wings extended. *"Damn that Witch. I can still hear her."*

Karin knelt next to her. "Do you want to come with us?"

"Will you have need of us?" She glanced at the vultures circling overhead.

"Probably not," Karin replied. "Why?"

"I would very much like to spend time with my friends, and then I'll return to the ship."

Karin held out an arm, and Moira hopped onto it, long shiny talons curving around her forearm. "You'll have to tell us all about it, sister. In all my years as a wolf Shifter, no wild pack has ever welcomed me. Tolerated me, maybe, but it began and ended there." A wistful note ran beneath her words, and Karin understood how much she would have loved to commune with her wolfy kinfolk.

The vulture spread her wings, flapped them a time or two, and rose effortlessly.

Karin pushed upright. "Let's get this over with." She snapped up the saber, surprised by how heavy it was.

"Yes, let's," Zoe said. "Here's hoping Vampire number two doesn't offer us cause to use the weapons."

"No shit. And that Nona was wrong, and we don't end up facing off against Vampires three, four, and five." Aura swung the rifle over one shoulder and pocketed the small pile of shells.

"Too bad we can't teleport like the sea Shifters," Karin muttered and plodded away from the Witches' lair, cutting cross country in the general direction of the crossroads where they'd met the Vampire. His death had been quite a coup. If he was telling the truth about being the father of his race—and she was pretty certain he had been—any sovereignty they retained had just ended.

"Tonight is almost enough to make me not want to stop anywhere ever again," Zoe said in a low, tired voice.

"Not much has gone according to any type of plan," Karin agreed. "But we've done some good. First in Grytviken where we saved that priest from an eternity of damnation. And wiped out those Vamps in stasis.

"And then at Arctowski, where we rescued those poor sods hiding in an ice cave," Aura murmured.

"Don't forget McMurdo and the sea dragon," Karin said.

"See?" Zoe stepped up her pace. "'Tis exactly what I mean. Everywhere we turn, there's bad shit."

"Is that a scientific term?" Aura chuckled.

"No one loves a smartass." Karin dialed up the lumens in her mage light. The road appeared ahead. She could see it, and they'd move faster once they reached the pitted stretch of asphalt. Bad as it was, it beat the collection of ankle-grabbing brush and holes they were slogging through.

"What if some of the humans want to come with us?" Zoe asked.

"Why would they?" Aura countered.

"Sure and we've collected humans elsewhere. This batch like as not won't be much different, particularly if they've been Vampire food for ten years." Zoe stumbled, caught herself before she fell, and cursed in Gaelic. "I hate shortcuts. We should have retraced our steps."

"We couldn't," Karin reminded her. "The ceiling collapsed behind us."

"Details."

Aura sprinted lightly ahead. "Stop it you two. Here's the road. Let's play the human equation where it lies. If some want to join us, we'll see who they are and what skills they offer. We're still short on crew."

Karin hurried, surprised how quickly they came across the car they'd left. It felt like part of a lifetime had elapsed since they'd all piled out of the Citroen. She opened the driver's door, dropped her medical bag inside, and tugged the keys from the ignition. "Lucky for us, the men didn't hotwire this one. We can drive back."

Aura charged down the side road leading to the mineral baths. Karin ran after her with Zoe right behind. They came to a crashing halt in front of a swirling darkness, blacker than the night around them.

"Moira told us this compound was well-protected"—Aura craned her neck, looking upward—"but she didn't say it rivaled Fort Knox."

"Fort where?" Zoe asked.

"Never mind." Karin switched to her psychic view to make the ward's elements visible. "Holy fucking godhead. I don't get it." She turned to the other two women. "The Vampire is dead. How could his working transcend his demise?"

"It does add fuel to the argument other Vampires are still viable," Aura mumbled. "Shit. This thing is endless."

Zoe walked a few inches closer, peering at the barrier while power jetted from her fingertips. Wherever the bright motes contacted the ward, they sizzled and sparked.

"Help us." A disembodied voice that sounded as if it belonged to a child, echoed around them. "Please. Help us."

"What in the goddess's name is that?" Karin shook herself to clear her thoughts.

"A trap," Aura replied, her tone sharp.

"Has to be," Zoe seconded.

Karin ground her teeth together. "Playing devil's advocate, why is it a trap? Humans produce children."

"Aye, but not youngsters who can project messages through a magic-imbued barrier. Our hearts were in the right place, but we should leave while we still can." Zoe dropped her hands to her sides.

"I'm good with that." Aura nodded tersely. "The humans got themselves into this mess. One of the Vamps is dead. Maybe they can overpower the remaining ones."

Karin hefted the saber. "Human versus Vampire? We know the outcome to that contest, but we can kill Vamps. Once and for all."

Aura draped an arm around her shoulders. "I admire your courage, but it will take hours to slice our way through that ward."

"I'm not so certain even hours will do it," Zoe muttered. "Not unless we put out a call for reinforcements."

"That's it!" Karin snapped her fingers, and the ghostly voice began to wail in the background. No words this time, only a pathetic keening that tore at her heart.

"You said the magic word." Karin stared at Zoe. "Reinforcements." Without putting it up for a vote, she raised her mind voice and hoped the whales wouldn't ignore her.

One corner of Aura's mouth twisted downward. "Calling the whales, eh? They can teleport, but I bet this ward will stymie even them." She let go of Karin after a quick, hard hug. "You never did like to lose."

"You've got that right, sister." Karin sucked in a breath, waiting. If the whales didn't show up, they pretty much had to leave. The crying child kept right on wailing.

The air off to one side developed an incandescent aspect right before it split into a gateway depositing two whale Shifters. The leader and another male. "Yes?" The lead whale inclined his head.

Meanwhile the other whale strode to the edge of the barrier. "Holy kelp. I understand why they asked for help, but this isn't straightforward."

The leader joined him. Power pulsed around him, forming bioluminescent streaks. "Not straightforward at all. Not if we look for a way through it. That ward has more twists and turns than the Minotaur's labyrinth."

The ghost child had fallen silent when the whales showed up, but it commenced howling again.

Both whales snapped their heads up. "Poseidon's balls. What is that?" one asked.

The lead whale shut his eyes and tilted his head to one side, listening. "I'll be damned," he muttered and opened his eyes. "It's a Vampire. If it can be believed, which is unlikely, it's just as trapped as the humans, and it wants out."

"Damn. Zoe called it when she said the wailing had to be

something magical." Karin bit hard on her lower lip. "It said help *us*. I assumed it was a human requesting aid for his kind. If it's a Vamp, who the hell does *us* refer to?"

"Not certain I want to find out," Aura said, "but the Witch did suggest there were several of those fuckers."

Karin sucked in a tight breath, aware she'd tuned out that part of Nona's message because she didn't want it to be true.

"If Vampires are concerned, do we have the luxury of walking away?" a whale countered.

"We can teleport in there," the other whale said.

"Tell me something I don't know." The lead whale rounded on him. "The question is if we'll be able to teleport back out."

"Can you bring us with you?" Karin thrust her shoulders back. Last place she wanted to enter was a Vampire den, but they'd be stronger together.

"Yes, as long as it's not too far," the whale replied.

"How about the weapons?" Aura asked and waggled the rifle.

The whales exchanged glances. "I'll handle the saber and rifle," the lead whale informed them and held his hands out for the weapons. "My compatriot will watch over you."

"Come close enough to touch me," the other whale instructed. "This will happen fast, so be ready to launch a defense once we're on the other side."

Karin handed over the saber and ran to the whale's side. He wrapped his beefy arms around all three of them, and magic built around them. Familiar, yet not. She did the best she could to prepare herself. Smoky darkness pushed in from all sides, vanishing almost as soon as it formed. The report of the rifle blasted her ears, and she blinked, willing images to form out of the haze swirling around them.

When it didn't happen fast enough, she switched to her third eye, but it didn't help. The rifle blasted again, and she heard the clang of iron against rock. The saber. Who'd snatched it up? She felt for the whale who'd escorted them across the barrier, but he'd moved on. Apparently, his senses were more finely honed than hers.

The barricade obscuring her vision fell away. One whale held the sword. He stood over a rapidly decomposing corpse oozing black ichor. The other swung the rifle, clearly hunting for more Vampires. The two he'd shot lay in crumpled heaps of mottled flesh sloughing off bones. The rotten-egg stench of Vampire was thick and putrid.

Karin switched to shallow breaths and turned in a full circle, taking in a ramshackle, turn-of-the-century structure with a broad veranda. Peeling white paint had flaked off leaving patches of black mold beneath. Smaller buildings lay scattered about, no doubt cabins from when the hot springs was in full operation.

She sent her magic, what was left of it, winging wide and cursed. No humans. Not a single life form beyond theirs met her seeking spell.

"How the hell did they fool the vultures?" Zoe gritted out.

"Simple enough," Karin replied. "The birds aren't magical. They'd overfly this place—and even they admitted they hadn't been near it for a long while—and see humanlike figures moving about."

"Because they assumed only two were Vampires, the others had to be human by a process of elimination," Aura growled.

"Precisely." the lead whale said. "Since we're here, we should give the place a quick once-over."

Karin swallowed back a bitter taste, certain whatever they found would turn into fodder for nightmares. Instead of arguing, she said, "I'll start on this side," and ran for the cabins to her right.

After the third one proved empty, her ragged heartbeat settled into a plodding rhythm. A shout from one of the whales brought her to the main house at as quick a pace as she could manage. He stood at the top of the steps and shook his head.

"Better you don't go inside," he said.

Karin tried to push past him, but he grabbed her arm. "You don't listen well, land Shifter. I found abominations inside. The basement is sealed to contain the smell. It's full of cages so small a man couldn't stand or barely even turn over. Most of them have bodies in them, and the stench is atrocious. The Vamps kept them alive as long as they could. Once they died, they didn't bother to bury them. The place reeks of pain and fear and death."

"That bastard outside the cave lied to us." Zoe drew her lips into a snarl. "He wasn't the last one after all."

"Vampires lie. What a surprise," the lead whale growled.

"But I netted him with a truth spell," Karin protested, feeling stupid and used and like she should have known better.

"Seems he was able to circumvent it," the other whale said. "Apparently, he was also the only one who could come and go through the wards, probably to protect the weaker Vamps from the Witches."

"Can you transport us back to where we left the car?" Zoe asked the whales.

"No need," Karin said. "All the Vampires are really dead this time, so the barrier should have fallen."

"Shall we find out?" The lead whale angled his head, a grim smile in place.

They made their way out of the yard. No one said much. Karin had no idea if they were just tired or blaming themselves like she was. Night was fading, and the precise, prickly magic she associated with the ward didn't rise up to halt their progress.

When they got to the car, she stopped and turned to the whales. "Thank you for heeding my call."

"Our pleasure." The lead whale bowed and laid the saber on the ground.

"Indeed." The other whale handed the rifle to Aura. "We shall see you back on the ship." A shimmer and a flash, and they were gone.

"Here." Karin dug the keys out of a pocket and handed them to Zoe. "It's all yours."

"Why me?" Zoe settled into the driver's seat.

"Right hand drive, and I'm exhausted." Karin climbed into the passenger side and dragged her bag atop her lap.

"I'll take the back," Aura said. "I'm still wrapping my mind around how sneaky Vampires are, and why the hell they survived here."

"It was the ward." Karin slumped against the broken-down seat feeling springs poke into her back.

"Huh?" Zoe fired the engine and turned the car around.

"I want to know too," Aura said.

"The Vampire who led us to the Witches probably was the original one." Karin bit back a groan as puzzle pieces clicked into place. "It's why he was powerful enough to construct a ward to hold back the changes when we defeated the Cataclysm. Also why his tale about being the first Vampire didn't set off my truth spell. Even with his ward, I bet the group here felt the effects and were weakened by them."

"They were obviously out of blood, at least the human variety." Aura sounded thoughtful. "I'm trying to splice two and two together and figure out what was in it for that Vamp to lead us to the Witches."

"We're not known for killing indiscriminately," Karin said. "I bet he assumed we'd leave enough of the Witches alive, but weakened, to provide blood for a while."

"We'll never know." Zoe pulled up near the docks and shut off the wheezing engine. The sky had developed the pearlescent gray of dawn, and a wind had kicked up.

"Probably not." Karin pushed her door open. "Pop the trunk, why don't you? The men's medical supplies are inside."

"Sure thing." Zoe got out and walked around to the back.

The distant thrum of a Zodiac's motor filled Karin's ears and made her glad she had a home to go to. Never mind she'd never envisioned herself as the seafaring type. She grabbed Daide's bag, and Zoe snatched Recco's. Aura carried the saber and the Remington.

The three of them walked downhill to the pier where the raft had let them off. "I learned something today," she said.

Aura snorted. "I learned a whole bunch of somethings. Which particular thing caught your attention?"

"You can't ever take anyone else's word for anything. And I still loathe Witches."

Zoe snorted back laughter. "Aye. If we hadn't strapped on our Crusade outfits and gone off to save the humans, we'd have been in our bunks hours ago."

Karin dropped Daide's medical bag at her feet next to her own and held out her arms. The other women let go of their items and crowded close, hugging each other. "We're damned lucky," she said.

"You bet we are," Aura seconded.

"Aye, because we have each other." Zoe detached herself. "Zodiac's here. I'm going to grab the rope, and then we can go home."

Karin tossed medical bags and weapons into the raft. She huddled on a pontoon, and must have fallen asleep because Juan's hand on her arm shaking her awake was the next thing she remembered. The trip up the gangway and along the corridor to her cabin passed in a haze. Using the boot jack, she pried off her Wellingtons and pitched head first into her bunk.

10

TIME FOR TRUTH

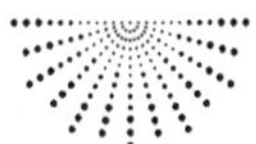

*D*aide strode onto the bridge. Two days had elapsed since their confrontation with the Witches. Two busy days where he'd made at least a dozen trips with one of the Zodiacs, ferrying supplies back to *Arkady*.

Viktor was bent over a list, checking items off it. He nodded Daide's way. "You've gotten good handling the rafts."

"Thanks. It's not the first time I've operated one. How are we doing with your punch list?" Daide pulled the door shut behind him.

Viktor shrugged. "Better than I'd hoped. We're still missing a few items, and I'd dearly love to pull up to one of the piers and top off our fuel."

"Are we low?"

"Nah. Not at all, but I never pass up opportunities. At least I never used to." He straightened. "Have we heard from the sea Shifters recently?"

"What do you mean *heard from them*? They've been on and off the boat."

"Mmph. They haven't checked in with me. Or Juan."

Daide thought about it. "I'm pretty sure they don't realize they're supposed to. Recco ran into Leif earlier today."

"And?" Viktor raised tawny brows.

"He had some kind of blow up with Poseidon. This is secondhand, but apparently he showed up and told Leif he'd been waiting forever for the sea Shifters to shake off the Witches' yoke."

"Bet that didn't go over very well."

"You'd be correct. Leif was furious. He confronted Poseidon, asked why he hadn't intervened on their behalf."

"And he didn't care for the sea god's answer." Viktor made a sour face. "Obviously, I know less than nothing about magic and gods and suchlike, but Ketha's told me they almost never intercede in mortals' affairs."

"We're scarcely 'mortal' anymore," Daide pointed out.

"Doesn't matter. They still won't go out of their way for us."

"Not how it looked when Poseidon and Amphitrite first showed up down on Deck One, but Leif's made it clear he harbors bitterness because his lieges sat back and did nothing while so many of his kin died."

"Beyond the sea folks' political maneuverings, how are you and Leif doing?" Viktor's question came out of left field, and Daide sputtered for a reply.

"Fine. Why wouldn't we be?"

"Not sure." Viktor glanced at Daide with his green-eyed gaze. "For a while there, something seemed off. Not on his side, but on yours." Without giving Daide opportunity to respond, Viktor kept on talking. "I watch the folks on my crews carefully. It's one way to nip trouble in the bud, before it turns into something unmanageable. These ships aren't big enough to accommodate a bunch of prima donna personality issues."

Daide took a step back. "Prima donna? Is that how you view me?"

"No. Sorry. Poor choice of words. I was only sharing an example. And I'm glad I was wrong about you and Leif."

Daide stood straighter, not wanting to rip the lid off that particular can of dead fish. The stench of jealousy was never pleasant. "I originally stopped in here to see what else needed doing. And when you're planning to pull anchor."

"Are you done treating the whales?"

"Recco is finishing up with the last one right now. Since they spend most of their time in the sea, it's not reasonable to knock out every single parasite. But we reduced the population enough, their strengthened immune systems should kick in and function normally."

"Good. It was one of the things I was waiting on."

"Where are we headed next?"

Viktor smiled crookedly. "Aye, mate. That's the question of the hour. We should have a meeting and kick it around. Tonight over dinner would work. Could you make certain the sea Shifters are there?"

"I'll do my best. I can probably catch up with Recco. If he's still working on that whale, I'll have my messenger."

"Thanks." Viktor went back to scanning his list and making notations on it.

Daide recognized he'd been dismissed and retraced his steps out of the bridge. He wasn't looking forward to dinner with everyone. Not if it meant seeing Leif and Karin cozied up next to one another, but he was being petty. Karin hadn't made an appearance yesterday. According to Ketha and Aura, she was exhausted and catching up on rest.

He'd seen her at breakfast a few hours ago, and she'd nodded his way, looking more or less like her usual brusque self. He unclenched his jaw. Why the fuck was this so hard? He'd had women tell him, "thanks, but no thanks" lots of times before. Why did this feel so different?

Because it is different. Before I had my work to fall back on. And Recco and our good old boys niche we'd carved out for ourselves.

When I was a Vampire, women were the last thing on my mind.

Maybe that was part of it. This was a new life for him. Everyone was pairing up, and he wanted what they had. A special someone to cherish. Their survival was far from certain. The specter of destruction added urgency and a fine edge to his yearning. He didn't just want to be in love, though. He wanted Karin. She was everything he admired in a woman. Strong. Gutsy. Principled. Intelligent.

He squared his shoulders, determined to make the best of however things shook out. It had been a plus having back-to-back tasks moving goods from various shuttered shops in Invercargill to *Arkady*. When he was busy, he didn't perseverate about Karin.

To redirect himself, he catalogued the supplies they'd collected. The ones he recognized, anyway. He'd need manuals to figure out the proliferation of cables, shaft splicers and sleeves, pulleys, lubricants, and other engine parts that had thrilled Juan and Viktor. In addition to the ship's needs, they'd unearthed cases of canned goods, and a store specializing in freeze-dried camping foods had provided some exotic-sounding blends. Curries and Asian-spiced dishes that might or might not prove palatable. They'd also located sealed tins of rice and wheat and corn and oats. And cases of liquor. Arkady's storerooms were stuffed to overflowing, which might come in handy if they added to their slender crew.

He pushed through a door, welcoming the rush of damp, marine air. Whenever he licked his lips, he tasted salt, but at least it wasn't as cold here as it had been in Ushuaia. Cold came in gradations, and this wasn't the type where his hands began to ache immediately. It also wasn't the type that lent itself to living outdoors. A hardy soul would probably survive, but it wouldn't be a pleasant experience.

He trotted down the extended gangway because he expected to find Recco at the bottom. The whale floated alongside the platform, but Recco wasn't there.

"Where'd he go?" Daide hunkered next to the whale.

"Inside for something." The whale's voice rumbled through Daide's head.

"It's all right. You're the one I need. We're having a meeting at dinner, and Viktor wants all of you there."

The whale repositioned itself, directing a laterally placed eye Daide's way. *"Why?"*

"We'll be deciding where we sail next. It's a group decision, and you should have a say."

Air spewed out the whale's blowhole. *"North. We're headed north. I fail to see why I should bother with my human form for that."*

Footsteps clattered down the risers, and Recco joined him on the platform. *"Amigo.* What's up?"

"Meeting at dinner. Vik sent me to make sure the sea Shifters were part of it."

"Hear that?" Recco squatted next to the whale.

"Of course I heard it," the whale trumpeted, not bothering with telepathy.

"Will you at least tell everyone else about it?" Daide persisted. "Let them make their own decisions."

This time briny spume spurted from the whale, catching Daide square in the face. He didn't think it could possibly be accidental. Wiping himself with the crook of one arm, he regarded the whale. "You don't have to remain with us."

Magic pulsed so hard, Daide grabbed hold of one of the many metal rings dotting the platform at water level. Light flared, bright white, and he shut his eyes against the glare. When he opened them, he wasn't surprised to see the whale, wet and streaming, in human form.

Female, she skewered him with her pale-blue eyes. Hair the coppery green of kelp shrouded her to her feet. "You have no idea what it's like to lose everyone you love. To long for death yourself because you have no more reason to live. My mate is gone. My child withered and died in my womb. Once the seas were alive with whale song. Not anymore. Sorry, but I can't get excited because the Shifter who considers himself king of this ship says jump. You may need him. I don't."

"You scarcely have a corner on pain and loss," Recco murmured. "Daide and I were veterinarians. We had a cozy little practice, a spot we'd carved out for ourselves in Ushuaia. Friends. Family a few hours north in Buenos Aires. Within weeks of the Cataclysm, we'd not only lost all of it, we'd been turned."

"Try being a Vampire for a decade," Daide cut in. "I hated blood so much, it made me puke for the first several months."

"It's all about you, little man." The whale who towered over him by at least half a foot poked him in the chest with an index finger. "Have you ever heard our song? The one whales sing when they're dying? It's how we say farewell to everyone we've ever loved. Try listening to variations of it over and over until you want to puncture your own eardrums. So you'll never have to hear it ever again."

"I'm sorry about your people. Truly I am," Daide said.

"We were amazed anything that lived in the ocean remained," Recco added. "The way the water looked around Ushuaia, nothing could have survived in it."

"You know what's left of us," the whale countered. "Not many. No thanks to Poseidon and his consort." She lowered her voice, but fury boiled around her, giving the air a reddish tinge.

"Why would you expect help from them?" Daide asked.

"I'd like to know as well," Recco said. "According to the land Shifters, none of the Celtic deities ever aided them. Nor the Norse ones or any others."

The whale shrugged, and more water sluiced down from her tangled hair. "Decency, for starters? Never mind. I'm not looking for an answer. No answer will bring my mate or child back to life."

"Will you make sure your sea kin know about dinner tonight?" Daide prodded, sensing the whale's anger and discontent had run its course.

"Yes, coyote Shifter. I will do that much."

Recco laid a hand on her arm. "We've all lost a lot. It's as if the Cataclysm took pride in stripping us of what we held most dear."

"It might still beat us," Daide said. "But wouldn't you rather go down fighting than sunk in feeling sorry for yourself and your situation?"

"I am not—" Her voice broke off, and she looked away. "Maybe I am. Thanks for speaking plainly." Breaking away from Recco's grip, she dove sideways off the platform. The water bubbled and tumbled as she shifted form. With a splash of her tail that got both of them good and wet, she plunged for the ocean's depths.

Daide wiped water off his face for a second time and glanced at a bag hanging from Recco's hand. "What didn't you finish?"

"I was going to take a blood sample. It can wait. I'm fairly certain she won't need to be dosed again." He tugged on his jacket's zipper, bringing it to chin level. "Brrr. That wind has a bite to it now that I'm wet to my skin. I can't wait until we hit Micronesia."

Daide headed back up the gangway with Recco behind him. Not sure what was driving him, he glanced over his shoulder long enough to make eye contact. "Got a minute or two?"

"Sure. How about if you follow me back to the lab. For once, it's me who left it in less than pristine shape."

Daide moved aside at the top of the stairs and let Recco walk in front of him. He took advantage of the few minutes to organize his thoughts. Part of him was reluctant to say anything about Karin. Not much he could relay that wouldn't make him look like a weak, stupid, lovesick fool who didn't know when to back off. But Recco'd had some rough moments before he was certain of Zoe's affections. Moments when he'd considered leaving *Arkady*.

More important, Recco would never judge him. Hell, Recco didn't judge anyone. He was one of the most tolerant men Daide had ever come across.

"I recognize that look." Recco set his bag on a table and regarded Daide intently. "What's going on?"

"It's more about what's not going on." Daide angled a foot and kicked the door shut.

Recco drew his dark brows into a frown. "Humph. Should we move this discussion to the bar?"

"Nope. I'd rather keep it private."

"I can run up there and bring a bottle back. One of the things we've replenished is our liquor stocks."

Daide thought about it. Alcohol had a certain appeal, but he might decide not to reveal anything in the time it took Recco to leave and return. Reticent by nature, spilling personal problems wasn't exactly his style. He shook his head. "Nah. We might end up there afterward, though."

"All right. Man up, and tell me what's bothering you." Recco crooked two fingers his way. Twisting a chair around backward, he fell into it and folded his arms across the backrest.

Daide clasped his hands together behind him. Standing still was hard, so he paced from one end of the good-sized room to the other. "It's Karin," he said at last.

"What about her? She'll be fine if you're worried about any residual ill effects."

"How can you know?" Daide was hedging, avoiding diving right into his problem, and he kicked himself.

"Because she was in here late yesterday running tests on her blood and asked me to corroborate her findings. They were quite normal."

Daide sucked in a breath, blew it out, and did it again. Recco's attention never wavered, but he wasn't pushing, either, and Daide blessed him for his patience. It had made him an exceptional vet and an even better friend.

The words wouldn't get any easier, so he went for it. "I'm glad she'll recover completely, but that's not what I wanted to run by you."

"I figured as much." Recco didn't make any move to straighten the lab. He probably sensed Daide's discomfort and offered his full attention.

"I care about Karin. More than friend-type caring." His words were jerky, disjointed, but Daide kept talking. "Not sure when I became aware of it. Maybe when she hung in there with me after those atrocities used my essence to garner a free ride from Hell. She was so accepting and matter-of-fact. She didn't treat me like I should have known better."

"I'm not seeing a problem, *amigo*." Recco angled his head to one side. "She'd make a stellar mate for you."

"Sure she would. If she weren't involved with Leif."

The shock etched into Recco's face was deep and genuine. "Really? And you know this, how? Because I haven't seen any evidence of it."

"He was there when the sea Shifters called her back from death. Not just there. He was the one who orchestrated the healing. I saw them together afterward. He had his arm around her."

Recco spun both hands in small circles.

"What's that supposed to mean." Daide pushed his shoulders back to the accompaniment of cracking joints.

"It means go on. There must be more for you to give up on a woman you claim to care about."

"I do care about her." Daide bristled. "A lot. So much it scares the crap out of me."

"Aha!" Recco nodded knowingly. "Maybe that's it."

"Maybe what's it?"

Recco rested his chin in his crossed arms. "Easier to accept she's already taken than fight for her."

Daide rolled his eyes and plopped into a chair of his own after angling it to face Recco. "This isn't the Middle Ages, *amigo*. Where I challenge Leif to a jousting match and whoever unseats the other one wins the damsel."

"It's not so different, either. Does she know how you feel?"

"Of course not. I don't want to make her uncomfortable."

Breath hissed from between Recco's teeth. "Bullshit. You hate to lose. You'll go to any lengths to avoid looking like a fool. Easier to assume something than do what's hard."

Hot words crowded in the back of Daide's throat. He swallowed them down. Recco knew him better than anyone. It was why they were closeted in this room and he was baring his soul.

"You have to talk with her," Recco went on. "At least let her know you care about her. You might be mistaken about Leif. I'm fairly certain the sea Shifters never mate outside their own kind."

"Yeah. I knew that, but the prohibition originated long before the Cataclysm. When they had lots of potential mates to choose from. They're going to have to change the rules since this batch are all interrelated in one way or another. If they're too stiff-necked about it, they'll die out."

"That's a sideline philosophical diversion. You're very good at them, particularly when you don't want to deal with something."

"What if I'm right, though? About Karin and Leif. Not about the sea Shifters needing to broaden their horizons."

Recco shrugged. "If you're right, you'll know for sure. And you'll wish them the best."

"Bitter medicine." Daide swallowed around a dry place in his throat.

"Better the devil you know than whatever you've conjured up with your imagination."

After a brief tap on the door, it swung open and Karin strode in. She stopped and looked from him to Recco. "Is this a private conversation, or can anyone join in?"

Recco smiled and got to his feet. "We were pretty much done. I'll be back later to straighten up my mess. Told Zoe I'd meet her about now."

Before Daide could craft an excuse to ask Recco to stay, he sauntered out of the lab whistling an old Argentinian love song.

Karin focused her intense copper gaze Daide's way. Her white hair had been braided, and she was dressed in black from head to toe in a stretchy top, sweat pants, and a vest. "I apologize if my appearance was ill-timed."

"No. It really wasn't."

"I don't know. Looked pretty serious to me. Is everything all right with the whales and dolphins?"

"Recco finished with the last whale a little bit ago." Daide got to his feet. He needed to master his churning emotions, but words didn't come easily.

"Something's bothering you. What is it?" Before he had a chance to answer, she forged ahead. "Did you have a recurrence of the demon problem? If that happened, you should have come to me, not Recco. He's a gifted healer, but his grasp of magic is still developing."

"No recurrence." He tried to smile reassuringly.

"If not that, then what?" She tilted her head in the way she did when she was assessing a thorny problem.

Daide realized he'd balled one hand into a fist, and he flexed his fingers. "This is about me. And you as well." He walked closer to her and placed a hand on her shoulder. "I care about you. More than I probably should. I know you're involved with Leif—"

"Leif? Where did you ever get that idea?" She leaned into his touch.

Daide's chest tightened. How could he have read the signs all wrong? "So you and he aren't a couple?"

"No." She pursed her mouth into an unreadable expression. "Before you get any ideas, young man, I'm old enough to be your great-great-great grandmother."

"If it's the only problem we have, we'll be golden." Never a spontaneous man, Daide took a chance, wrapped his arms around her, and brought his mouth down on hers.

11

CUPID'S ARROWS

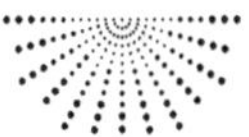

Karin stood in the storage room tucked behind the galley. Organizing food stocks they'd collected in Invercargill was a big job, but easier to do it now than once they were underway. She looked longingly at a series of raised beds and grow lights. She'd tried her hand at making use of them, but none of the seeds aboard *Arkady* had been viable after ten years. They'd helped the humans grow crops in Ushuaia, so maybe she'd be able to grow at least a few items here as well—if she could get hold of more seeds.

She made a mental note to make one more trip into town and hunt down a garden supply store. Those seeds might not have fared any better than the ones aboard the ship, but she wouldn't know until she attempted to sprout them. Lettuce and spinach grew fast, and fresh vegetables would be a welcome addition to their canned and powdered diet. Not that she was complaining. Compared with what she'd survived on in Ushuaia, she'd eaten like a queen since coming aboard the ship.

"Interesting discussion across the hall," her wolf said in a sly, enigmatic tone she recognized.

"Were you always a gossip?" Her words might be sharp, but she

133

grinned indulgently. Not much got past her bondmate, and she was grateful for its vigilance.

"I watch out for us," it countered. *"Gossip is such a common word."*

Karin went back to lining up cans, tins, and pouches in cupboards.

"If you tarry, you'll miss it."

"I figured you'd give me the lowdown."

"I could, but this is one time you'd be better served to be there yourself."

Something about the wolf's tone caught her attention. It rarely pushed her toward any action unless it was truly important. She straightened from where she'd been crouched in front of storage cabinets and shut them. Her hands were gritty, and she dusted the palms together as she made her way through the galley and then into the main dining room. It was empty, but her wolf had said *across the hall,* which must mean the other dining room.

When she got there, the four scientists from McMurdo were bent over steaming cups of coffee, chatting intently. They nodded at her and then returned to their conversation. The only other possibility on this deck was the lab, so she trotted toward it.

"Are you going to offer up any more clues?" she asked her wolf. It didn't answer.

The door to the lab was shut, but it was often closed. She knocked briefly and walked inside. Recco and Daide sat across from one another, and the air fairly crackled with emotional residue. "Is this a private conversation," she asked, "or can anyone join in?"

Recco smiled and stood. "We were pretty much done. I'll be back later to straighten up my mess. Told Zoe I'd meet her about now." He sauntered out of the lab whistling a catchy tune.

Karin stared at Daide. He exuded his usual heartbreakingly handsome charm in formfitting clothes that made his lanky, well-muscled body even more appealing. She shut down that line of thought fast. "I apologize if my appearance was ill-timed." She stopped there, choosing not to mention her wolf's prodding.

"No. It really wasn't."

"I don't know. Your discussion looked pretty serious to me. Is everything all right with the whales and dolphins?"

"Recco finished with the last whale a little bit ago." Daide got to his feet, but he seemed edgy. Not like himself at all.

She considered employing magic to read his thoughts, but decided to try to get to the bottom of whatever had alerted her wolf the old-fashioned way. With words. "Something's bothering you. What is it?" Before he answered, she forged ahead. "Did you have a recurrence of the demon problem? If that happened, you should have come to me, not Recco. He's a gifted healer, but his grasp of magic is still developing."

"No recurrence." He glanced her way and smiled, but it looked forced.

"If not that, then what?" She angled her head to one side, shuffling through possibilities.

Daide's nostrils flared. For a moment, she would have bet money he was about to run out of the room, but he held his ground. "This is about me. And you as well." He walked close enough to place a hand on her shoulder. "I care about you. More than I probably should. I know you're involved with Leif—"

Shock waves hit her like a runaway train; she sent truckloads of thanks to her bondmate for making sure she was right where she needed to be. "Leif? Where did you ever get that idea?" Daide's touch felt exquisite—warm and solid—and she leaned into it.

Passion laced with hope flared in the depths of his dark eyes. "So you and he aren't a couple?"

"No." Karin reeled in an inane desire to throw herself into Daide's arms. His thinking she was involved with Leif was one hurdle, but they faced many more. She'd lived without a man in her life for more than a century. If that was going to change, she had to be damn sure it was the best thing—for both of them.

"Before you get any ideas, young man"—she stressed the *young man* part on purpose—"I'm old enough to be your great-great-great grandmother."

"If it's the only problem we have, we'll be golden." Daide wrapped his arms around her and brought his mouth down on hers.

She wanted to sputter they needed to work things out, carve out a path before they dove blindly down a black hole. Instead, she kissed him back. His lips were firm and demanding. Whiskers scratched the sides of her face, heightening her awareness of how male he was.

Strong hands kneaded her shoulders as he teased her mouth with tongue and teeth. He licked along the seam of her lips, and she opened to a quick tongue dart inside. Because it was so fast, she followed his tongue with her own, sparring with him, hoping he'd swipe back in again, and again. The comparison with intercourse was obvious and heat spiraled outward from her belly.

Sex had been a clinical experience for so long—release coming from her fingers when she was so desperate, she had to come so she could think—she wasn't sure how to behave with a partner. His cock swelled. Long and thick, it pressed into her belly. She longed to touch him, wrap her fingers around that hardness and savor it, but she didn't want to appear too forward. It was one of the downsides of being born two centuries before when social conventions were very different.

Breath clotted in her throat, and the world hazed over with desire. Her hips writhed against him, and she threaded her arms around his torso, splaying her hands across his muscled back.

He raised his mouth from hers, a soft smile playing about the edges of his chiseled lips as he moved a hand to cup the side of her face. "I can't tell you how long I've wanted to do that."

Karin wasn't sure what to say. Should she admit she'd lusted after him? Would it make her look like a slut? Heat rose from her neck to the top of her head. "Sorry," she mumbled. "'Fraid I'm terribly out of practice at this sort of thing."

"We all are." He caressed her cheek with a calloused thumb.

"Some of us way more than others." She looked up and lost herself in his enticing dark eyes. "I wasn't referring to the lost decade in Ushuaia. I've pretty much kept to myself for a long time." She inhaled briskly to encourage her heart to beat a little more slowly. This was an opportunity for the serious conversation she'd sought before their kiss. Maybe not exactly the same thing since remnants of the kiss eddied between them, but close enough.

"That surprises me." His voice was deep and sensual.

"It shouldn't. Shifters only marry other Shifters. There weren't any men who appealed to me, and after a while, casual affairs lost their zing. Easier to concentrate on medicine and keeping my skillset up to date. And on supporting the younger women. Rowana and I were kind of like den mothers."

"You must miss her."

"Oh, I do. Even more than everyone else. She and I were peers. We understood one another in ways the others don't."

He continued to stroke the side of her face and her neck, and he snugged the arm behind her back. "You know a lot about me. Tell me about you."

Creeping unease pushed her to disentangle herself from his embrace. Intimacy meant sharing life histories, and she'd concealed anything personal for a long time.

He angled his head until his gaze caught hers. "Did I say something wrong?"

"No. Of course not." She twisted a chair around until it faced him, dragged another opposite it, and said, "Sit." Shaking her head, she added, "Sorry. Didn't mean to sound like a drill sergeant."

"You didn't. You sounded like yourself. No worries. I'm partial to self-assured women."

She settled into one of the chairs and waited until he'd taken the other. "It's hard to know where to begin, but I'm probably not the best choice for mate material. I've hidden behind being a doctor for a very long time. This probably doesn't apply to vets, but doctoring people means I find out everything about them while disclosing nothing about myself. It will be a hard habit to break."

"Do you want to?" His words thrummed with emotion.

"To be totally honest, I'm not certain. How I've operated has insulated me from being hurt. It's also cut me off from joy, but I've considered it a quid pro quo." She smiled crookedly. "It's not that I'm not attracted to you. I am, but when you asked me to tell you about myself—and trading histories is something prospective lovers engage in—I didn't exactly panic, but neither did I warm to opening the vault around my private self."

"I'm a patient man. I can wait."

A warm place bloomed deep within her, but she reached for rationality. It was where she lived. "I appreciate the thought—and the kiss. It's been a long time since a man held me in his arms."

"But?" He arched a dark brow.

"You're quite perceptive because there is, indeed, a *but.*"

"The perceptive part comes from working with non-verbal patients. Come on. What roadblock were you about to toss between us?"

She blew out a breath. Was she being a fool? Or worse, a coward? Ignoring her indecisiveness, she soldiered on with what was in her mind. "You'd be so much better off with one of the younger women. They'd welcome you without reservations, be the partner you deserve—"

Reaching forward, he placed a hand over her mouth. "I don't want them. It's you I want. You that I long for. If I were attracted to them, we wouldn't be sitting here. Want to know what I think?"

She angled a pointed glance his way. "I have a feeling you'll tell me whether I say yes or not."

"You'd be correct." He moved his hand from her mouth to her knee and scooted his chair closer. Warmth from his touch ratcheted through her. "You're a strong woman, Karin. Strong and used to being in control—of everything. Not that I'm much of an expert on relationships, but I'm pretty sure they're about sharing power, or ceding power." He shook his head. "I'm making a botch of this, maybe power has nothing to do with putting the other person's needs first."

"Each person giving a hundred ten percent has always been my assumption too, and it's a tall order," she murmured, never wanting him to stop touching her and conflicted as hell over her need.

"Don't take this wrong, but I suspect you're afraid. I convinced myself you and Leif were an item. It was easier for me to pine for a lost love interest than to put myself out there and risk being shot down. It's what Recco and I were talking about when you walked into the lab."

"What'd he think?"

"He convinced me I had to talk with you, that I'd never know for sure about you and Leif unless I asked."

Karin placed a hand atop his. "You didn't exactly ask. You told me you knew."

Daide smiled softly. "I was having a hell of a time getting any words out. What I did worked. It's all that matters."

Karin turned over what he'd said. "It's not that I'm afraid, or maybe I am in a backhanded way. I've carved out a niche for myself. It's a comfort zone, and it's filled with watching over my patients." She swallowed hard. Now was a time for truth. "Sometimes, there's not much left. Certainly not enough for a mate."

"Even if that mate can share patient care—and worry—with you? I always practiced with Recco, and it was a relief to have a second brain and second set of eyes on the difficult cases. It also lessened the guilt when we lost patients."

"I can see where it might work that way."

"Were you always a healer? I'm guessing you were born in the 1800s. Women weren't doctors then, at least not many."

"Early part of the 1800s," she confirmed.

"Where were you born?"

"Cumbria in northern England in a large, sprawling Shifter community. Magic wasn't such an oddity back then, even though the Church called us abominations and occasionally went on a rampage when they hung a few magic-wielders to make a point."

"Keep talking," he urged. "It's intriguing."

She smothered a snort. "You're smooth. I hadn't planned to give up anything personal."

"You haven't said much. When did you become a doctor?"

"Officially? Because I've always manipulated magic to heal."

"Yes. Officially."

"I enrolled in medical school in the 1940s. They didn't want to allow me in, but a wee bit of compulsion magic solved that problem." She tilted her chin at a defiant angle. "The residency system wasn't as entrenched as it is today, but I completed a fellowship in internal medicine."

"I assume you practiced in Wyoming since it's where your group was living before you headed for Ushuaia and the eclipse."

"Yes. I'd been there for maybe twenty years."

"Before that?"

She started to laugh. "You're one determined man. A few more hours here—and about a hundred more questions—and you'll have my entire history laid bare."

"I want to know because I care about you."

Karin wasn't sure if that made it better or worse. Caring was dangerous ground. She'd loved Rowana, but no magic in the world would have been enough to save her. Her Shifter companion and friend had died in her arms, and it still haunted her.

Part of her—a small part—wanted to tell Daide he was a sweetheart, but they had no future together. A much bigger part balked at such a Draconian approach.

"What are you thinking?"

"How do you know I'm thinking anything?" she countered.

"Because you get this little line"—he traced a fingertip vertically between her brows—"when you're considering something."

He'd apparently spent a lot of time watching her, and it both pleased and scared her. "I propose a compromise."

"I'm listening."

"Let's work on getting to know one another, not as professionals

—that part is already nailed down—but as people. I'll do my best to not hide behind my carefully crafted persona."

"You're going to give us a chance." He broke into a broad smile. "I'm elated."

She didn't know how to respond, so she nodded and muttered, "I hope to hell I don't disappoint you."

"How could you? You're going to try, which is all anyone could ask." His smile faded, and his tone grew serious. "I'll never hurt you."

Karin rolled her eyes. "All men say that."

"Yes, but I'm not them. We won't always agree because it's not possible, but so long as we keep talking with one another, we'll find common ground."

"How can you be so sure?"

"Because I've never wanted anything as much as I want you."

Sincerity shone through his words. He meant them with every fiber of his being. Anxiety shot through her, tightening her gut into a knot. "I can't be responsible for your happiness."

"I'm not asking you to be."

She tried to draw her hand away, but he laid his other one atop it, sandwiching hers between. "You're like a skittish colt, ready to break and run the second something's not right."

"Figures you'd use an animal analogy."

He nodded. "Sure. They're what I know." Bending forward, he brushed his lips across her forehead. "Maybe this is enough for now. Will you have dinner with me tonight?"

"Yes. I will. Speaking of which, I should get something started. It's my turn to cook." Feeling like an awkward teenager who'd just accepted her first date, Karin got to her feet.

Daide stood too and bowed slightly. It was a courtly, old world gesture that tugged at her heart. "Until then. Is there anything I can help with?"

She gazed into his bottomless eyes, encouraged and frightened by turns. "Maybe straighten up in here." She swung an arm to encompass the lab where things sat out on tables and ledges. "I could use a spot of time by myself to process our conversation—and my feelings."

"So long as you don't process me out of your life, all will be well. See you at dinner. Say six thirty?" He turned and began sorting lab accoutrements.

Karin walked out of the room, feeling like she was floating and trying her damnedest to rein in her happiness.

"*At least you didn't tell him to get lost,*" her wolf spoke up.

"I came close."

"*I know. I live here too.*"

"How come you didn't say anything?" She avoided the smaller dining room and angled for the one off the galley.

"*Because it was important for you to listen to him.*" The wolf whined softly. "*In a lot of ways, I've filled the role a mate would. You and I are close, closer than many Shifters and bond animals. Before the Ushuaia years, when you still had choices, I wasn't displeased when you chose to remain aloof. It meant more of your attention flowed my way.*"

Karin trod through the dining room and shouldered into the galley, relieved it was empty. Rather than begin dinner, she leaned on a counter and focused inward. "Why tell me these things now? If it hadn't been for your nudging, I'd never have known Daide and Recco were discussing me."

"*Because Shifters and bond animals were never meant to totally fill each other's needs. I have the other animals. You've mainly had me—and Rowana. You asked why. Maybe my decision is rooted in Ro's death. You need an emotional link to someone besides me.*"

Tears pricked behind her lids. "I love you."

"*I know you do, and I love you just as much. We were a good choice for each other, but I want you to give Daide a chance. He's a good man, and his coyote is coming along.*"

Karin snorted and began dragging supper items out of the pantry. "Coming along, eh? You're ancient. The coyote is very young. You might cut it some slack."

"*I am. If I wasn't, I'd have punished it for misreading the sea dragon.*"

"How would something like that work?" Karin kept her words casual as she covered dehydrated vegetables with water. She wanted to know more about the bond animals and their society. Long ago, mages had breached the borders of the animals' special world. If they'd garnered knowledge of such things, it was long since lost.

Her wolf snarled and left; the place it dwelt within her echoed with its rapid egress.

"Fine. Be that way," she told the air. Maybe the wolf could still hear her. Maybe not. Her eyes widened as an analogy smacked her in the gut. In many ways, her relationship with her patients had elements in common with Shifters and bondmates. The wolf knew everything about her, whereas her knowledge of it was patchy. She saw what it wanted to show her and not a jot more.

"Jesus. It took me two-and-a-half centuries to figure that one out," she muttered. Covering parboiled rice with water, her thoughts turned to Daide. Why he wanted her was one of the mysteries, but truth had rung cleanly off his words and feelings. He was sure of himself. The question was if she could lay her ambivalence and uncertainties aside long enough to let herself care for him.

It was one thing to yearn for him while she lay alone in her bunk. Quite another to move from dreaming about the impossible to something real. A smile wanted out, and she understood she not only liked the idea, but she'd rise to meet the challenge.

She'd have to ask him why he'd assumed she and Leif were involved. It had to have something to do with when the sea Shifters had healed her, but how Daide had gotten from her nearly drowning to being spoken for would make for an interesting story.

Maybe she'd bring it up over dinner...

Yeah. Dinner.

She bent to her ingredients. If she didn't get moving, no one would have anything to eat.

WEDDINGS

rkady chugged northeast along New Zealand's coastline. Daide stood at the railing watching seabirds dive for fish. The proximity of land offered better hunting opportunities for blue-eyed shags, the only type of cormorant found in Antarctic regions. The fast-disappearing coastline also yielded some level of protection from storms, but for the moment the sea was cooperating. As much as it ever did at these latitudes. The roaring forties and fifties were notorious for sinking ships. He recalled maps with Xs marking wrecks throughout the Southern Ocean. Even though those losses had occurred over a hundred-year timeframe, the statistics were still sobering. While he'd enjoyed kayaking and kicking around Ushuaia's harbor, he'd never entertained a hidden desire to run away to sea.

They were passing Bay of Islands, which meant nothing but open ocean lay ahead. At least everyone had been of one mind about not stopping at any of New Zealand's other cities, like Christchurch, for example. They didn't need supplies after Invercargill. Additional crew would be welcome, but it wasn't as if they could steam into port and hang out a sign.

God only knew what would materialize. His brief brush with the

Witches still chilled him. He'd always envisioned them like Samantha on old episodes of *Bewitched*. The reality was far darker and deeply disturbing. He didn't have to try too hard to recreate the Witch's shrieks after they'd left her swathed in spells in her lair, surrounded by her dead kinswomen. He'd talked with Karin about Witches in the days since then, and a hundred other topics too.

The thought of her made him smile, and a warm spot bloomed in his chest. She really was trying. At times, he sensed her struggle with their growing intimacy. He backed off then, offering her space to move toward him at her leisure. In many ways, it reminded him of working with animals whose distrust of humans ran deep. They did better when you provided opportunities for them to approach you. Sometimes it wasn't possible. If they were too badly hurt, the only option was a tranquilizer to knock them out while you did your damnedest to save their lives.

In the handful of days since their conversation in the lab, he and Karin had shared every meal together. He'd accompanied her into Invercargill, and they'd tracked down the seeds she wanted. Working with Recco, they'd also assessed blood samples from all the sea Shifters. One whale required more medication, but everyone was doing far better than Daide had expected they would.

It made his heart glad. Now that he wasn't eaten up with jealousy, he'd discovered he liked and respected Leif, the sea Shifters' alpha. It was a relief to move beyond the small, petty part of himself that had cropped up out of nowhere. He'd never been one to be jealous, but then he'd never been interested enough in a woman to give a good goddamn if some other man wanted her too.

One of the birds dove in a graceful arc and emerged with a decent-sized fish clamped in its sharp beak. Wings pumping, it headed toward one of many islands dotting the channel. Shags nested year-round, so the bird was probably gathering food for nestlings. Daide silently wished it well. Parts of the world were recovering from the Cataclysm's ravages, and it gave him hope they wouldn't arrive on Wrangel Island too late to do some good.

He'd truly enjoyed the interval between the Witches' cave and now. For the first time since they left Ushuaia, he didn't feel stretched thin, balanced between a precarious present and an uncertain future. The uncertain future hadn't gone away. It still extended before him, but at least he didn't have the eerie sensation death was waiting in the wings for an opportunity to strike.

Recco emerged from a side door and strode to his side. "Watching the cormorants, eh?"

"And the sea." He turned to face his friend. "Rumors abound, *amigo*."

Recco furled his dark brows. "About?"

"Karin tells me plans are afoot for a double wedding."

Recco's coppery skin developed a warm hue. "I knew the women were cooking up something. Wonder when they were going to get around to telling me and Juan?"

"From what I understand, Shifter matings are planned and driven by the women. All we have to do is show up and say yes a few times."

Recco laughed. "Does your use of *we* imply a triple wedding?"

"Oh hell no. It's far too soon." Daide walked himself back from the longing that beat a path through him. If he had his way, Karin would be his wife, but they needed more time under their belts. More cozy meals and warm embraces. They had yet to move beyond heated kisses, but they would—and sooner rather than later.

"How are things going between you and Karin?" Recco's words broke into Daide's mental meanderings. "You're looking pretty happy together, but I haven't wanted to pry."

"So, how come you're prying now?" Daide smothered a snort. He knew damn good and well why, but Recco needed to come clean.

Recco slapped him on the back. "Zoe put me up to asking. Apparently, Karin is very closemouthed, and the women haven't had any success dredging information out of her." He narrowed his eyes. "You knew what I was going to say, didn't you?"

"Yup. Karin and I are getting to know one another. I'm enjoying the hell out of how we are together. And she hasn't slammed the door in my face—not yet, anyway."

"Has your bond animal weighed in?"

Daide nodded. "It wants me to be happy, but Karin's wolf scares it to death."

"How do you know?" Recco followed the question by pointing at whales and dolphins swimming alongside *Arkady*. The sea Shifters romped and hooted and bleated, clearly delighted to be strong and healthy again.

"I don't. Not for sure," Daide replied. "It's only a guess on my part. Karin's bondmate is ancient. Mine is young. It's kind of like Padawan and a Jedi master."

"You always loved *Star Wars*."

"I did." Daide blew out a breath. "I dreamed of travel to other galaxies."

"Well, see? You got the travel part right."

Daide slugged him in the arm. "You're funny."

"Yeah, the original comedian. When's the event? You never did say."

"What event?"

"The double wedding. Be a real shame if I missed it."

The snorts he'd ridden herd on emerged in a burst of laughter. Daide spread his arms wide. "Where are you planning to go?"

"You never know. I could launch a Zodiac at any moment, but I wouldn't do that. I love Zoe, and I'll be proud to be her mate."

"The gals are casting tarot spreads. It's why they vanished after breakfast. Once they come up with an auspicious day-time combo, I'm sure you'll be one of the first to know. You and Juan, that is."

"Sure you don't want to make it a threesome?" Recco angled a pointed glance his way.

"Why does that sound smutty when you say it?"

"Maybe because I'm a smutty kind of guy. You didn't answer me, though."

Daide dropped the banter that had always been a staple between him and Recco. "I would love to marry Karin, but it's not going to happen in the next couple of days."

"Women like a man with a take-charge attitude." Recco's words were deadpan, but he couldn't pull it off and started to laugh.

Daide joined him. When he caught his breath, he muttered, "Take charge could get my balls handed to me on a platter."

Recco was still chortling. "No kidding, *amigo*. Mine too. Never did see the appeal in that type of approach myself. If a woman needed that kind of heavy-handed direction, I didn't need her. Way too high maintenance for my taste."

"You stole my thoughts."

"What are friends for?"

Footsteps clattering down metal risers drew Daide's attention to the stairs winding down from bridge level. Juan joined them, grinning from ear to ear. "Aura just stopped by the bridge. We're getting married at seven tonight."

"Grand news." Recco held up a palm and high-fived Juan. "Same time for Zoe and me, right?"

"Same time. Vik will do the honors. I'm not sure who's more excited, him or me."

Zoe hurried through a side door and glanced around the group. "You told him." She aimed her words at Juan.

"I did. No one said not to."

Zoe's expression softened, and her brown eyes brimmed with tenderness as she regarded Recco. "It's fine. I wanted to be the news bearer, but it doesn't matter." Tendrils of her curly red hair blew across her face, and she brushed them aside as she bent over the railing.

Two dolphins slapped their tails in greeting.

"Plan to be inside around six," she told the dolphins. "Recco and I are getting married."

"Aura and me as well," Juan called out.

The air grew heavy with Shifter magic, and the salt tang of the sea increased, tickling Daide's nostrils. One by one, a bevy of naked sea Shifters popped out of the shimmery, salty air shouting congratulations. Dripping wet, they threw their arms around Recco and Juan and Zoe, leaving puddles on the deck.

Leif took a step away from where he'd been hugging Recco. "I'm not sure if they're anywhere close, but of course you'll want to invite Poseidon and Amphitrite."

Something about his tone—formal and strained—probably meant he hadn't let go of his bitterness toward the king and queen of the sea. Yet he understood the wisdom of including them. Many nautical miles lay between New Zealand and eastern Siberia, miles during which they'd no doubt run into bad weather and magical beings out for blood. Poseidon and Amphitrite were both ancient and powerful. Having them as allies was far better than inadvertently alienating them.

"Certainly," Zoe agreed. "What's the best way to contact them?"

"What you did last time worked," Leif said.

Zoe nodded. "Lower level of the ship and going through our bond animals?"

"Yes. I'd offer to help, but I've had no communication with them since they chided me—again—for our ill-conceived bargain with the Witches."

Daide kept his mouth shut. Chided was a mild term for what had happened, and his respect for Leif expanded another few notches.

"I'm headed back upstairs," Juan said.

"I'll gather the women and see what we can do about the sea gods." Zoe gave Recco a quick kiss before trotting across the deck.

Daide draped an arm around Recco's shoulders. "*Andale, amigo.*"

"Why? Where are we going?"

"To make you presentable for your wedding."

Recco made a face. "That's for women."

"Not in the tribe I came from. There, the men painted themselves and spent days preparing for their nuptials. We only have a handful of hours, but we'll do the best we can."

"You're serious, aren't you?"

"You bet I am. Now let's get moving."

GETTING Recco dressed had been an uphill battle, but he'd finally cooperated. As Daide had suspected, Zoe was nowhere to be seen. Nor would she appear until the ceremony. Some customs crossed cultures and species, and the one where bride and groom remained separate was damn near universal. Although he'd had little time to spare, Daide had jumped in the shower and changed clothes. Peering at himself in his cabin's small mirror, he slicked his hair back, not bothering to gather it into a single rubber band or braid it. Satisfied he was dressed adequately for the occasion, he turned to leave.

A knock on the door was followed by Karin poking her head inside. "Oh good. You're decent. Ready to go?"

"What if I were indecent?"

"We might miss the ceremony. Not a good idea." She sucked in a breath. "The sea gods are here. I swear, Poseidon and Viktor almost got into a knock-down, drag-out fight."

"Let me guess. The sea god wants to do the honors."

Karin nodded. "Exactly. Viktor drew a line. Said it was his ship, and if anyone was going to do the marrying for his oldest friend, it would be him."

Daide leaned forward. "Did Poseidon back down?"

"They compromised. Viktor will marry Aura and Juan. Poseidon will marry Zoe and Recco."

"Good thing we had two couples, huh?" Daide's gaze swept over Karin. Dressed in her black robe with runic markings on it, she'd left her hair unbound. Swinging in curls, it hung past her waist.

"Do I pass muster?" Her mouth twitched into a smile, and her scent rose, enveloping him in forests and greenery and something unique to her.

"More than pass muster. You're gorgeous."

He closed the distance between them and wrapped his arms around her. When she turned her mouth upward, he kissed her. She threaded her arms beneath his and spread her hands across his back as she returned his kiss. Her nipples hardened against his chest, and desire surged. Familiar heat filled his nether regions, and his cock thickened. Never one to indulge in masturbation—not since he'd passed twenty or so—he'd brought himself off more in the past couple of days than he had in the last fifteen years.

She butted her hips against his and broke their kiss. "Soon, but not right now. We need to get moving. There's work to be done before the ceremony, and precious little time."

He held her close for one more long, delicious moment before letting go. "No matter how much time we spend together, I never get enough of you."

She laughed and tugged the cabin door open. "The litmus test will be if you're still saying that a few months from now."

"Sounds like you think we might have a future." He kept his tone light, but her answer meant everything to him.

She raised a white brow. "Oh. Did I say that?"

"Not in so many words, but yes."

"Well then, it must be true. Or maybe I'm being swept away by all the wedding energy."

"Enough to want to join them?" Daide couldn't believe he'd said that, but he couldn't take the words back.

Karin stopped at the bottom of the stairs and turned to face him. Laying a hand on his shoulder, she focused her shrewd copper gaze on him. "I appreciate you being willing to throw caution to the winds and take a chance on me, but this isn't our time. I'd know if it were."

She moved her hand from his shoulder to thread her fingers with his. Daide squeezed her hand. Elation ran through him like high-voltage electricity. She hadn't told him he was a fool. Hadn't laughed. Hadn't run the other way. "Not their time" didn't mean no.

"You're all right with that? I didn't hurt your feelings?" She spoke low, the words aimed only for him.

"More than all right. I'd wait for you forever, but I have a feeling I won't have to."

"No. You won't."

"There you are!" Ketha emerged from the larger dining room.

"Sorry, sorry. Point me where you need me." Karin smiled. Color bloomed on her cheeks, lending her an almost girlish appearance mingling with her timeless allure.

"I'm an extra set of hands too," Daide said.

Ketha made shooing motions, and then followed them into the dining room.

Daide glanced around, amazed at its transformation into a festive bower. Tiny shimmery lights, no doubt powered by magic, surrounded every table in a bevy of colors. Tablecloths and silverware had been laid out, and wonderful smells wafted from the galley.

"Guess we got those extra supplies from Invercargill just in time," he joked.

"Tinned butter we didn't have to ration made a cake possible," Ketha said. "And it will be lovely to have something beyond our limited menu."

"Speaking of cake, I promised to help decorate it. See you soon." Karin strode toward the galley and shouldered through the door.

People drifted into the dining room in small groups and settled at the tables. Daide picked his way across the room. Viktor was resplendent in a white uniform trimmed in gold braid. Juan wore something similar, but with a red sash tied around his waist. Recco sported the dark suit and art deco tie they'd borrowed from Juan. He nodded Daide's way.

"I hear we're expecting royalty," Daide said.

Viktor made a sour face. "If they don't show up, it's fine by me."

"Hush." Juan sliced a hand downward. "Just because we can't see them doesn't mean they can't hear us."

"Right you are," Viktor agreed. "It's not that I don't appreciate the help they've given us, but—"

"We came up with a workable agreement," Juan inserted smoothly. "It's all that matters."

"We're here," rang from the doorway, and the sea Shifters filed in, dressed in a variety of clothing they'd filched from the ship's stores. Tiny pearls had been woven into their hair, and a few had sea horses draped around their shoulders. Daide wondered how they were managing to breathe, but they looked very much alive.

Viktor beamed at them. "Grab seats wherever you'd like."

Leif crossed the expanse of the room and looked from Juan to Recco. "Need a best man?" Reaching into a pocket, he extracted two tastefully carved gold rings. One was set with a large fire opal, the other with a clear, deep-blue stone that might have been a sapphire.

"Those are beautiful," Juan said.

"Wherever did you come by them?" Viktor asked.

A small smile played about Leif's mouth, and he shrugged. "A wreck here. A wreck there. You'd be surprised how littered the seabed is, and the dead have no use for baubles they've left behind."

"Thank you," Recco said. "We'd love to have you be our best man and ring-bearer combined."

"Ringbearers are generally children, aren't they?" Leif asked.

"Only in really large weddings," Daide replied.

Music blared from the ship's PA system. Tinny and scratchy, it took a moment before Daide recognized Wagner's *Wedding March*. Recco and Juan straightened, staring at the door.

"Are you men ready?" Viktor asked. "Not getting last minute cold feet or anything?"

"Never been readier for anything in my life," Juan replied.

"Me, either." A catch in Recco's voice betrayed his emotion.

Magic swirled behind them, heady and redolent with smells of the sea. Daide didn't have to turn around to know Poseidon and Amphitrite would soon be among them.

Karin walked through the kitchen door bearing a lavishly

decorated cake. She placed it on a side table and made her way to where Daide stood. The other Shifter women emerged from the kitchen and formed an aisle from the dining room door to the front of the room.

"We are here. You may begin," Poseidon's deep voice boomed.

Daide twisted to look at the king of the sea and Amphitrite his consort. Poseidon wore a robe made of glistening silver fish scales and belted in gemstones woven with hammered silver. Blue-gray hair fell to his feet, and his eyes reflected the sea, shifting from gray to blue to silver as he regarded them. Amphitrite's gown sparkled in mother-of-pearl shades. Pearls draped around her neck and dripped from her ears. Snow-white hair was braided with glittering multihued gems and lay close to her head.

"Such a joyous occasion. We appreciate being included." She regarded them through silver eyes.

"I hope you'll stay and eat with us afterward," Viktor said.

"Thank you, Shifter. We may do that."

The music, which had quieted, started again. Aura and Zoe walked through the dining room door hand in hand and moved to the front of the room. Aura's blonde hair drifted around her in a cloud. Zoe's red locks had been braided in an intricate pattern. Both women wore their dark robes, garments woven with magic they'd brought from Wyoming. Aura's was sashed in red, Zoe's in blue.

Karin inserted a hand under Daide's arm. They moved aside as Zoe and Recco stood before Poseidon, while Aura and Juan positioned themselves in front of Viktor.

"You first." Viktor smiled encouragingly at Poseidon.

"Thank you, raven Shifter." The king of the sea draped strands of glistening blue-white magic around Recco and Zoe, chanting all the while in Gaelic. He touched their foreheads, leaving marks that looked like runes, but that faded almost instantly. Leif handed Recco the ring with the opal, and Poseidon waited while he slid it onto Zoe's finger.

Poseidon switched to English. "You two are bound through this life and all others to come for I have marked you as partners, and such can never be sundered by man or mage or demon."

The glittery light surrounding Recco and Zoe faded, and she turned her face up for a kiss. Happiness streamed from them, and Daide was deeply glad for his closest friend and doubly grateful their decade as Vampires hadn't destroyed their capacity to love.

"Married by a god. Imagine that." Karin's voice whispered across his mind. She tightened her hand around his arm.

Viktor waited until Poseidon took a step back, signaling his part was done. Drawing a small book from his pocket, he opened it and began to read. This wedding ceremony was far more familiar. Daide felt his chest tighten as the familiar words about richer, poorer, in sickness and in health, and until death do us part rolled from first Vik and then Juan and Aura. Leif produced the sapphire ring, and Juan placed it on Aura's finger.

All too soon, Viktor was saying, "You may kiss the bride."

The room erupted in cheers and wishes for a long and healthy life together. Daide steered Karin to a nearby table and pulled out a chair for her to sit. "I can't. Not yet," she said. "I have to ferry food from the galley."

"I'll help you." He followed her across the room. They'd just reached the galley door when the ship lurched hard to port.

"What the hell? The one time I trust the autopilot, and it's not good enough," Viktor bellowed and took off at a dead run out of the dining room with Juan on his heels.

Aura stared after them, looking stunned, but her expression changed rapidly. "I married a seagoing man," she announced to the crowd. "Please. Stay and eat. I'm sure this is nothing, but if it's all the same to you, I'll join my brand-new husband on the bridge."

Karin hustled into the galley, the vertical line between her brows growing deeper by the minute.

"Do you know what's out there?" Daide asked.

"Not exactly, but magic is behind it. I'd bet my last spell on that."

"Shouldn't we do something? Beyond serving dinner and pretending everything is normal?"

Karin squared her shoulders. "Yeah. We should. Convenient we have Poseidon here. I hope to hell he'll help."

"No time like the present to find out." Daide reversed course. Fighting the ship's motion, he lurched across the dining room to where they'd left Poseidon and Amphitrite. Their pleasant expressions had fled, and Poseidon set his mouth in a harsh line as he gestured at them to hurry.

13

STORMS AND KELPIES

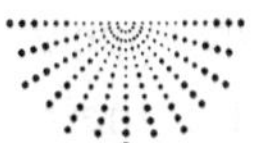

Karin hurried after Daide, scattering seeking magic in a broad swath. What came back to her was so unbelievable she started over. And ended up with the same impression.

Before she could ask Poseidon anything, he sputtered, "They have no right here. None at all. I shall simply order them home."

"Who?" Daide asked, managing to appear ready for anything and puzzled at the same time.

Karin sucked in a tight breath, hoping to hell she was wrong. "It's Kelpies, isn't it?"

"What are they?" Daide cut in before Poseidon could ruin her day with his reply.

The king of the sea nodded, his expression grim and bitten off. "Yes. Kelpies. Hybrid Satan spawn. They have no right here," he repeated as if that explained everything.

"Other's rights never stopped them before." Amphitrite's words were lined with fury—and fear.

Daide stomped a few feet closer to Poseidon and tried again. "What. Are. They?" He left a space between each word, as if that might encourage a response. "Surely, you all wouldn't be so spun out about an Australian sheep dog."

"Not dogs," Karin said, recalling there was indeed a breed some idiot had named after the Scottish water sprites. She took a measured breath. "They're shape-shifting water spirits that live in the lochs and pools of Scotland."

"Shifters? Like us?" Daide broke in.

"No. Nothing like us. They appear as horses, but they're able to adopt human form, except for their hooves, which don't change. Almost every sizeable body of water in Scotland has a Kelpie myth attached to it. They lure humans and eat them."

"You missed a few key points," Poseidon muttered. "Like how they can be snared and their power harnessed."

"Eh. I never believed those parts." Karin looked the sea god dead in the eyes. "I'm surprised you do since they involve Christian symbols like crosses."

Sadness flickered behind Poseidon's eyes "Crosses predate the imposter god, and you know it."

"So they do, but the tales of harnessing a Kelpie in horse form with bridles adorned with the cross don't."

"Do you know how many are out there or what they want?" Daide cut into what was turning into a philosophical argument that was doing nothing but wasting time.

"They never want anything good," Karin said flatly.

"A lot of them, but it gets worse." Amphitrite answered Daide's initial question and set her mouth in a thin line. "Kelpies can't move the sea, so they must have teamed up with something even darker and more malevolent than they are."

Karin had never retracted her magic, so she urged it to greater sharpness, searching ley lines for clues and coming up empty-handed. "Maybe the Cataclysm added to their power?" She bit her lower lip, thinking.

Leif and the lead whale Shifter loped close. "We're returning to the sea," they said in unison. "All of us."

"It's where we belong as well," Amphitrite said. "Perhaps we can reason with them."

"At the very least, we'll figure out what we face." Leif dragged his blue-gray hair back from where it hugged his tall form.

Magic with a dull, dark bite blasted Karin. A quick peek through her third eye showed glowing ley lines drawing closer to one another as if girding for battle. The metallic taste of blood alerted her she'd bitten through her lip. Still relying on her psychic view, she spun, hands raised to concentrate her magic.

"Don't leave yet." She aimed her words at Leif and the whale. "Whatever was out there is headed our way."

Glass first cracked and then shattered as two of the dining room windows blew inward, littering the floor with shards. Karin's nostrils rebelled as the reek of death and rot mingled with musk in a scent too horrible to inhale, yet enticing at the same time.

Daide moved next to her. Determination to launch whatever countermeasures were necessary streamed from him, and she blessed his steadfastness. Not many men would have the courage to stand fast in the face of Kelpies.

He snorted wryly. "For once, I was inside your head. It's not courage, darling, but ignorance. Hard to fear something you only heard about a few minutes ago."

Poseidon pushed in front of all of them and stood tall. "Show yourselves," he cried, following the English with the same command in Gaelic.

A shadowed place slid between two ley lines, and Karin switched to her normal vision in time to see a tall, swarthy figure emerge. Straight black hair fell to the man's knees, covering his nakedness. Beautiful as any Vampire, his skin glowed with a warm, inner light. Dark eyes with obscenely long lashes glittered from beneath perfectly formed brows. A square chin, full lips, and chiseled cheekbones drew her, but Karin recognized enchantment in the thing's pull.

"Don't waste your magic on me," she snarled, showing her incisors much as her wolf might have.

"Where are the rest of you?" Poseidon sounded as friendly as a feral cat standing guard over a kill.

The Kelpie gestured vaguely toward the ship's wall and moved toward them, its feet making clomping noises. When Karin glanced down, she wasn't surprised to see hooves. She'd had one run-in with a Kelpie in horse form when she wasn't much more than thirteen. The animal had been stunning, the most perfect horse she'd ever seen. Its mane and tail flowed behind it, coal black but reflecting all the colors of the rainbow. When she'd darted forward, intent on running her fingers through that glorious mane, it turned to hissing, writhing serpents, and she'd sensed foul magic.

Magic it had shielded when it was luring her. Karin knew the myths and stories. She'd summoned power of her own to protect herself and run the other way.

"Begone!" Poseidon thundered. A glowing driftwood staff circled with hammered bronze materialized out of the ether, and he banged it on the deck beneath them for emphasis.

The Kelpie laughed, a musical trill that sent shivers of longing down Karin's spine. No wonder the creatures had such success luring women to their doom. Always male in human form, Kelpies were notorious for sniffing out virgins and deflowering them—prior to the carnage that came next.

"Ye doona command me nor my kind." The Kelpie's brogue was so thick as to be almost unintelligible.

Karin resisted the urge to roll her eyes. Last thing they needed was a pissing contest between two power-mad males. "What are you doing here?" she demanded.

"Aye, and what do you want with us?" Amphitrite added.

The Kelpie's gaze bounced between them. "Who knows why we ended up here. We've been trying to get home for ages, which answers your second question."

Karin's eyes widened as understanding struck home. "But we're not going to the U.K."

"Details. Ye could. And now, ye are. Keep in mind, Shifter, 'tis your ship we've need of, not ye nor your companions."

He angled his head, and Karin felt his power envelop her, thick, slimy, and compelling. Cursing herself for a fool for not warding herself at the front end, she blasted him with power. When her magic ran up against a perimeter he'd been smart enough to erect, sparks flew.

The Kelpie winced but clearly wasn't hurt. The momentary distraction gave her the opportunity she needed to build her own ward. It might not be enough to quell the longing burning through her, but at least it was something.

"You will leave now." Poseidon directed his words at the Kelpie and stood tall. His staff clattered against the deck a second time.

"I think not." The Kelpie sashayed forward, its hooves yielding a swaying motion that emphasized the roll of its hips.

The tip of an erection poked through the curtain of hair surrounding him, and Karin fought a wave of lust so intense all she could think about was wanting to see more of that cock. Deep within, her wolf growled, and its presence strengthened her, held her back from something she'd regret forever. Once you touched Kelpies, they had power over you. She wasn't certain how deep their hold would extend, but nor did she want to find out.

Clearly intuiting the Kelpie's intent, Daide raised his chin and his hands. Magic, primitive and unfocused, shot from his fingertips and collided with the Kelpie's ward. "She's mine."

The Kelpie shrugged. "Women come cheap. They always have. Someone aboard this vessel will appreciate my attentions." He brushed a hand over his crotch, and the slice of cock disappeared, proving he'd displayed himself on purpose.

Karin felt disgusted with herself. She was far from a blushing, virginal maid to be sucked in by tawdry tricks.

The dining room door slapped against its stops. Viktor and

Ketha burst into the room. "Who the fuck are you?" Viktor shouted, skidding to a halt in front of the Kelpie.

"Damn my eyes," Ketha hissed. "Get back, Vik. It's a Kelpie. Bastard. Fucker. What in the goddess's name is he doing here?" Light flared from her hands as she shot magic its way.

"Let's do this right," Karin yelled. "Women. To me."

Ketha ran lightly to her side, followed by Moira, Tessa, Zoe, and the others. Magic slammed into her as they joined their power, weaving it together.

"We want you off this ship," Karin announced.

"Immediately," Viktor added in a tone that could have etched glass. He'd put a bit more space between himself and the Kelpie at Ketha's command, but not much.

The Kelpie bared squared-off teeth, reminiscent of his horse form. Any semblance of his unnatural beauty fell away, and he appeared fell and threatening. "We'll sink your puny excuse for a ship. All we require is passage to the nearest port in the British Isles. Hell, it could even be Ireland, though 'twouldn't be our first choice."

"And why not?" Zoe inquired caustically. "Sure and ye'll not be finding fault with my native soil."

"Damned stiff-necked Shifters," he growled. "We're practically kissing cousins, and—"

Rage boiled over at being compared with Kelpies in any version of reality. Karin checked the integrity of their shared magic and heaved an enormous ball dead center at the demon spawn. Shifter enchantment sputtered and crackled as it raced up and down the Kelpie's ward. Visible cracks extended around the creature, but his ward held. Barely.

Ketha began to chant, low and urgent, in Gaelic, to potentiate their power. The Kelpie's stench changed as he understood they were playing hardball with him. He turned, attempting to leave, but he was mired by their magic. Trapped where he stood.

"We must kill him," Poseidon urged.

"Canna we bargain with him? His life in exchange for—?" Zoe never took her eyes off the Kelpie.

"Nay," Amphitrite broke in. "His kind never keep to their end of barters. If we kill him, maybe the others will leave."

A crafty gleam formed in the Kelpie's dark eyes. "They won't. They'll retaliate if ye take my life."

The light around him began to change, developing rainbow-hued coloration. Karin understood he was trying to shift. His power was far more potent in horse form since it was his native manifestation. The edges of his body took on a blurry, insubstantial aspect.

She ground her teeth. They didn't have the luxury of time to discuss the fine points of killing versus bargaining. She didn't want to make a mistake, but once the Kelpie's transformation was complete, who knew what damage he'd do to *Arkady?* Even absent magic, a 1500-pound horse was a far more dangerous adversary than a 200-pound man.

Ketha's chant turned low, feral. Karin joined in with her, as did the other nine women. What few humans were still in the dining room had clumped together in a tight knot next to the back wall. She wanted to tell them to flee to their cabins but couldn't divert an iota of energy away from the power surging around her, turning the air electric with its potential.

The Kelpie's warding developed a high-pitched, oscillating hum, pulsing right before it shattered and fell to the dining room floor in uneven bits of gray and black. The reek of frantic Kelpie twisted Karin's stomach into a disgusted knot, and she swallowed bile. Death, rot, and decay trumped the musky seduction smells from earlier.

She took a deep breath and stared at the creature. At least they'd stymied his efforts to shift. He spread his hands, palms upward. "Let me leave."

"Give me one good reason to offer you clemency?" Viktor stomped closer.

"You'll soon outrun our ability to swim." The Kelpie tossed his head defiantly. The only thing missing was a whinny. "We reside in Bay of Islands."

"How did you end up there?" Poseidon pushed between Viktor and the Kelpie.

A pained expression flickered across his high cheekboned face. "None of us ever figured that out. One fine day we were at home in Britain. The next, we floundered in unfamiliar waters. It took days to swim to land. Ye must take us with you. If ye have another few ports of call afore ye see us home, we'd not get in the way of that."

"No." Viktor crossed his arms over his chest. "If you'd done things differently, requested to come aboard, and stated your problem, I might have made a different decision."

"I don't trust Kelpies," Karin said.

"Aye, nor do any of the rest of us," Zoe tossed in. "You've done a damn fine job of ruining my wedding day."

Black flashed around the Kelpie, and he dove for Viktor, who was closest to him. Winding strong arms around him, he drove him to the floor. The men grunted and heaved, each trying to get the upper hand, while Karin hunted frantically for a way to leverage the magic still pointed at the Kelpie without harming Viktor.

Daide and Recco shouted their fury and jumped on the squabbling men, punching and grabbing handfuls of the Kelpie's long hair. Karin would have shouted a warning about not touching the creature, but it was far too late for that.

"What's that myth about touching them?" Ketha hissed.

"Gives them power over you," Zoe replied.

"Once he's dead, the geas no longer holds sway. Here's a project for me." Poseidon leapt into the fray, staff swinging.

Grunts, shouts, and curses filled the air. Maybe because he had magic on his side, Poseidon landed blow after blow. The solid crunch of a bone breaking was followed by the Kelpie shrieking in pain.

Poseidon herded Viktor, Recco, and Daide off to one side to give Karin a clear shot at the Kelpie and yelled, "Now," in Gaelic.

Karin didn't hesitate. She gathered every whit of magic from the women and drove it straight into the creature's heart. Its cries turned to the tortured sounds of a dying horse. Indeed, its human form turned wet and glistening, and a shaggy, black stallion took shape, hooves churning and eyes rolling back with the whites showing all around them as it thrashed in death throes.

"Jesus Christ and all the blessed saints." Boris detached himself from the group of humans.

"If I hadn't seen it with my own eyes, I'd never have believed it." Ted joined his partner.

"How the hell will we get him out of here without cutting him up?" Viktor was breathing hard, and blood tricked from a gash running down one side of his face.

"Won't be a problem," Poseidon said. "Magic returns to itself."

After one last pathetic scream, the horse quieted. Poseidon barked a few words in a form of Gaelic so old Karin couldn't interpret it. The Kelpie shimmered, shuddered, and broke into ribbons of iridescent brilliance. Rising as a unit, they streamed through one of the broken windows.

"Is he still alive?" Daide asked.

Karin shook her head. "According to legend, he'll turn into seafoam."

"The important thing," Poseidon said, "is the others felt his death like a sharp blade in their chests. Still, I must meet with them. Tell them this ship is forbidden."

"Would you like reinforcements?" Leif leveled his gaze at the king of the sea.

"Thank you, son. I'd very much appreciate your support."

"We're all coming, then." The lead whale joined Leif. He bowed in Zoe's direction. "Best wishes on your nuptials, lady."

"Thank you. Please return when you're done and eat with us."

"We shall." Poseidon nodded, and the air grew heavy and slick with magic as he, his consort, and the fourteen sea Shifters teleported out of *Arkady*.

Karin exhaled sharply. "Of all the creatures we might have run into, Kelpies were last on my list."

"Mine too," Ketha muttered. "Below last, actually."

Viktor turned to leave, but Ketha caught his arm. "Where are you going?"

"Out on deck to offer what support I can with a high-powered rifle."

"Nice thought," Ketha said, "but you can't shoot them."

"Not with the iron and silver-laced shells?" He raised a tawny brow. "They were pretty damned effective with the Witches."

"You might have a point there, but I'd just as soon have you out of harm's way," Ketha retorted. "You can't touch Kelpies. Once you do, it gives them power over you."

"Mmph. He wasn't doing much mesmerizing when I punched him."

"It's because three of you were bashing him," Karin said. "Four if you count Poseidon. Given enough time, he'd have cleaned your clocks. Maybe not the sea god, but the rest of you."

"What should we do about dinner?" One of the McMurdo scientists spoke up.

"What else?" Karin retorted. "We can't let all this food go to waste."

"Will those things come back?" Boris asked.

"I don't know," Ketha replied, "but Karin's right about our supper."

"The cake survived." Recco angled his gaze at it.

"We'll take it as an omen," Viktor said. "I'll run up and let Juan know where we're at. I'll take him and Aura a plate while I'm at it." He angled toward the kitchen with Ketha by his side, murmuring softly.

Karin looked at Daide. Aside from a darkening bruise across one cheek, he'd emerged unscathed. "You were brave, but foolhardy," she chided.

He shrugged. "That description fits ninety percent of men. Feel like dinner?"

"Let's take a short walk, first."

"Lead out, Madam Doctor. Where are we going?"

"The main deck. I want to make certain our sea kin don't require assistance." She also had something to say, and she didn't particularly want an audience.

They trotted up one flight of stairs holding hands. When they got to the closest door leading to the broad open expanse of the anchor deck, she stopped. "I owe you an apology."

"For what?" He drew his dark brows together.

"My attraction to the Kelpie. Seduction is how they've survived all these years, but it's no excuse."

Daide dropped an arm around her shoulders and turned her to face him. "I'd have killed that thing before I'd have let him anywhere near you. My coyote and I were ready."

Warmth flooded her heart until it wanted to crack wide open. "I don't deserve you."

"Deserving has nothing to do with anything." He wound his arms around her and kissed her forehead. "One of these days, I want a list of every single supernatural being with rules for how they pose a danger."

She leaned into his embrace, loving the feel of his body plastered against hers. "I'll get right on that, but it won't do you much good without me to tell you which things are which."

"So, see?" His lips tracked across her forehead and down one cheek, leaving a trail of heat behind. "You have to stick around. Save me from myself."

It took all her willpower to break away from their hug. "Come on. I'll start the tutorial while we're outside. If things turn to shit, it will happen fast, and I need to be there."

He pulled one of many storage lockers open and handed her a

thick parka, helping her into it before he selected a larger one for himself. "I'll pay closer attention if I'm not shivering."

The only thing she wanted to pay attention to was him, but the Kelpie had kinfolk out there in the sea, lots of them judging from Amphitrite's comment. If the legends about them were true, they'd be out for blood.

14

YOU MUST SAIL SOUTH

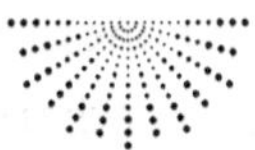

Daide held the door for Karin and followed her outside. Wind blasted him in the face. Narrowing his eyes to slits against its onslaught, he zipped his parka all the way up and stuffed his hands into his pockets wishing he'd grabbed a pair of gloves.

Karin ran ahead. He hustled to catch up and followed the tense line of her extended arm. Water boiled around Arkady's hull, churned to a froth by a circle of Kelpies. In horse form, they'd established a rough circle around the dolphin Shifters and were screaming as only outraged horses could. Daide remembered that sound. He'd heard it often enough when he'd been called to Ushuaia's ranches to deal with injured equines.

The whales' fins were visible where they'd erected a barrier beyond the Kelpies to make it difficult for the horses to swim back to shore.

"Are they always black?" he asked Karin. It was an inane question, but the scene spread before him was so surreal, he needed to anchor himself in something simple and non-magical.

"According to the myths," she replied without turning her attention away from the group. "I've only seen one before today."

Daide counted twenty-two Kelpies. Their long necks adorned

with lush manes were visible above the waterline. Foam eddied around them. Was it the remains of the one they'd slain?

A luminance pulsed within the circle. The water smoothed over, and Poseidon shimmered into view with his consort by his side. They stood atop the water as if it were a solid surface. Wonder battled awe and horror as myths collided. Maybe the Christ story was based on something real after all. Daide's mind was wandering, and he cleared it of everything nonessential.

"Should we call Ketha and the others?" he asked.

"Maybe. I'm in communication with her," Karin replied. "If things escalate, then yes. Right now, more of us would fall over one another."

Two of the horses surged toward Poseidon. Lightning flashed from his outstretched fingertips. When it hit home, the horses squealed their outrage but didn't fall back.

"Enough!" Poseidon thundered. "While you remain in the sea, you are my subjects to command."

Black light tinged with violet flared around one of the Kelpies. With a grinding, tearing sound, a man formed in its place. Dark hair eddied around his torso, but he wasn't expending obvious effort to tread water. He tossed his head back and focused pale violet eyes on Poseidon.

"We have never answered to ye." The man's English was garbled, his brogue so thick, it took Daide a moment to unscramble it.

Poseidon swept an arm downward; a wave gathered momentum in front of him and crashed over the Kelpie, who laughed. The oddly entrancing musical trill sent chills tripping down Daide's spine, and understanding crept in.

"It's how they lure their victims, isn't it?" he asked Karin.

"Exactly," she said, still focused intently on the drama unfolding in the water.

One of the horses swam close, and the Kelpie in human form threw a leg across its broad back. Facing Poseidon and Amphitrite, he tilted his chin at a defiant angle. "We require passage on your ship. 'Tis the first we've seen since the unfortunate accident that landed us halfway around the world."

Leif pushed his head above water level. "Why not summon the demon who made you?"

The Kelpie's laugh developed bitter edges. "Do ye not think we've tried? 'Tis always been every god—or, in this case, fiend—for himself, but some things never change. If 'tis a wee bit on the inconvenient side, they forget they ever knew ye."

Leif snapped his jaws shut. Daide knew what he was thinking since he'd said as much about Poseidon's conduct during the years of the Cataclysm. One of the other dolphins jumped into the breach. "Doesn't matter that your god has forsaken you. We will not allow you aboard."

"Listen and listen well. Your companion is dead," Amphitrite pointed out in a harsh voice. "If you persist in fighting us, the rest of you will join him."

The foam that had eddied about the Kelpies clumped together and headed straight toward her. Amphitrite stood tall and barked a command in a language Daide had never heard. The foam did an about-face and made a beeline for one of the horses. It whinnied outrage and pounded the waves with its front hooves. The foam kept coming, surrounding the Kelpie and covering it from its front legs to its neck. When it got to its head, it formed a white shield over its nose and mouth.

The whinnies died to nothing, and the creature thrashed, clearly struggling for breath.

Daide leaned close to Karin. "What the hell did Amphitrite do?"

"Reversal spell. There's not enough left of the one we killed for it to alter its course once it targeted her. She merely redirected the energy."

"I will release your companion if you agree to leave," Amphitrite shouted over the Kelpies' outraged bellows as they regarded their kinsman.

The herd surrounded the dying Kelpie. The one in human form

grasped the mask, attempting to pull it away or break its hold before the creature suffocated.

"Decide now." Amphitrite glowed like the otherworldly goddess she was. "Or it will be too late."

The human Kelpie twisted his mouth into a rictus and cursed in Gaelic. "We canna attack this shielding with magic, or 'twill immolate his brain. 'Tis made of the same stuff we are, so there is no way to sort Twraca's essence from Gwendacal's. Release Gwendacal, and we shall trouble ye no more."

Karin nodded once sharply. "They've offered up names. It's a good sign."

"Why is that?" Daide stared as a blast of green-white magic turned the air sparkling, and the mask covering the Kelpie's face vanished as if it had never existed. The sharp tang of the sea mingled with a chemical overlay he associated with expended magic.

Gwendacal gasped and choked. Daide leaned forward, willing the horse to breathe. They had elongated airways to accommodate their anatomy, and it didn't take much to damage them.

Karin grasped his arm. "Not your patient," she ground out.

"Maybe not," he countered, "but old habits die hard. I never could stand to see an animal suffer."

"It's not an animal." Karin's words were deadly quiet. "It only looks like one."

"Good point."

Rearing back, Gwendacal pounded the water with his hooves and shook his head from side to side. At least his eyes weren't rolling back in his head anymore. Baring his squared-off teeth, he lunged toward Amphitrite.

"None of that," Poseidon snapped. "We made a bargain. Keep your end or be forever shunned by dark and light magic wielders. Make no mistake, word of your perfidy will spread through all worlds until none of them welcome you."

"Wouldna be far different than 'tis always been," the human

Kelpie snarled. Switching to yet one more language Daide didn't recognize, it spouted a mix of syllables and horse noises.

The herd turned as a unit and swam toward the nearest shore on the boat's port side with Poseidon and Amphitrite behind them, skimming over the water's surface. The whales parted to allow them passage. Leif whistled, followed by a series of bleats and honks. He glanced up at where Daide hung over the railing and said, "We shall be back inside presently."

"Excellent," Karin called back. "Way too much food for us to polish off without your help."

The dolphins slapped the water with their tails and dove, presumably headed for the whales to discuss what had just happened. Daide watched the Kelpie herd swimming. They'd covered perhaps a third of the distance to shore. Poseidon and Amphitrite seemed satisfied because they shimmered into nothingness.

"Do you think we should wait until they've made land?" Daide asked, concerned Poseidon had abandoned his post too soon. Perhaps he and Amphitrite knew something they didn't, but it didn't pay to take chances.

Karin creased her forehead in thought. "Maybe not all the way, but until they're a hell of a lot closer than they are right now. We need to make certain they don't double back."

Her words mirrored his thoughts. "Back inside, Amphitrite said Kelpies can't make the sea rough. How do you suppose they accomplished it?"

"I'm not sure. The Cataclysm altered everyone's magic to some extent, and they've had ten years to plan for what they'd do if a ship ever materialized." Breath steamed from between her teeth. "I'm grateful they left. The Kelpies from myth would have fought to the last horse."

"Because we killed one of them?"

"Exactly."

He threaded an arm around her. "Do you suppose we'll ever escape from evil?"

A corner of her mouth twisted downward. "What a big question, Dr. Vegas. The short answer is no. A far longer one would involve a discussion of evil always being part and parcel of our lives. You can't have light without dark, so you don't want to wipe wickedness off the map. If you do, we won't be long for this world, either."

Something about her words resonated in his memory. "Ketha told Vik something like that when we were in Ushuaia, before we took on the Cataclysm, didn't she?"

"She may have. It would make sense since we figured we'd be annihilating Vampirism. They were always the balance point for Shifters." Karin rolled her eyes. "Never in my most vivid imaginings did I suspect we'd do nothing but face off against enemies after we left Ushuaia."

"What did you expect?" Daide was genuinely curious.

"Not sure." She rolled her shoulders back and leaned into the arm he had looped around her. "After we ran into those Vamps in stasis on South Georgia Island, though, I altered my mindset."

The Kelpies had almost reached land. Daide didn't think they'd turn around now, so he said, "We can probably go inside. It's not cold by Antarctica standards, but it's pretty damned chilly."

"Yeah. This particular crisis is behind us. Let's enjoy Aura and Zoe's wedding day." She offered him a wry grin. "Wonder if those four from McMurdo are sorry they signed on with the Good Ship Calamity."

Daide laughed and steered her toward the nearest door. "Haven't heard that word in years. And I always associated it with Calamity Jane."

"Aha!" She shook a finger beneath his nose. "Your weakness for Western television shines through once again."

"What did you used to watch?" He dragged the door open and shepherded them through. The warmth inside was like a balm, as was the absence of wind.

"Mostly old movies. Discontinued television series like *Fringe* and *Warehouse 13*. Stuff like that."

They stopped at the same locker he'd taken the parkas from and left the gear where they'd found it. Viktor had stressed how important that was onboard a ship. Otherwise, gear got misplaced and someone else had to waste a pisspot of time hunting it down.

"Why the paranormal shows?" he asked as he latched the locker.

She smiled, and it lit her copper eyes to their depths. "Always pays to keep an eye on the mortal population. See what they believe, and what they don't." She turned to face him. "I've always been a paranormal creature. You never even suspected anything magical was more than a child's pipe dream."

"If I admit you're right, will my coyote rise up in rebellion?"

"Why ask her when you could ask me?" his bondmate piped up.

Karin laughed. "I heard that."

She looked so beautiful and carefree, he cradled her face between his hands and kissed her. Karin wrapped her arms around him, returning his kiss with such enthusiasm warmth spilled through him. Along with lust and heat and need. When her nipples pebbled against his chest, he dragged his mouth from hers.

"If we don't join the others now, I won't be responsible for what happens next." His voice had a low, husky catch in it.

Her eyes sparkled mischievously. "So, now I'm a bad influence, eh? You are right, though. Aura and Zoe would never forgive me if I missed drinking toasts to marital bliss."

"Never is a long time." He ran his hands along the firm, lean muscles in her back.

"Shifters have long lives and even longer memories. Let's join the others." She thrust her hips against his erection. "A short walk will return all that excess blood to your brain."

"I swore I'd never get hooked up with another medical person."

Karin arched a brow. "Did the bimbos work out better for you?"

He snorted. "Not really, but they kept me single. You should be pleased you don't have any fond memories to displace."

"There wouldn't have been much in the way of *fond memories* left once you were turned. Either you'd have had Raphael turn her too, or you'd have fed from her."

Daide winced at the truth in her words. "There's not a day that goes by I'm not thankful I'm not a Vampire anymore. I have no idea how I got through those years. Mostly by turning my brain off and living from day to day."

"Yeah. You can deal with most anything so long as you don't examine it too minutely. Problem with being a scientist is we're trained to approach everything in an up close and personal manner."

He stopped in the corridor outside the dining room. Sounds of merriment drifted from within. "Are you ever sorry we left Ushuaia?"

"Sure. Sometimes. We were rebuilding something, and it was a comfort zone, but we didn't have any choice."

"We didn't know it at the time," he reminded her.

"True enough. But if we'd stayed, by the time we realized Armageddon had us in its gunsights, it would have been too late to launch effective countermeasures."

His smile faded, replaced by a solemnity to match hers. "I've heard you refer to the goddess. Do you see her hand in our journey?"

"If the question is do I think something bigger than us guides our actions, the answer is yes. None of us questioned the decision to sail away in *Arkady* to see what was left of Earth after the Cataclysm."

"Backtracking a few steps," he cut in. "We weren't certain we'd defeated the Cataclysm in its entirety, and it appears we didn't."

The dining room door flew open, framing Zoe and Aura. "We thought we heard you out here," Aura said.

"Come on in." Zoe motioned. "The toasts are about to begin."

"Are the sea Shifters back?" Karin asked.

"Aye." Zoe smiled. "Poseidon and his consort too."

"Only ones missing were you." Aura looked askance at them.

Recco joined Zoe and Aura. "There you are." He elbowed Daide. "How long does a man have to wait for his best friend on his wedding day?"

"If we hadn't been interrupted by Kelpies"—Daide defended his absence—"I'd never have left at all. There's cake, remember?"

"Indeed I do." Recco laughed. "Never could keep anything sweet around with you in the house."

Daide followed the others into the dining room. As he gazed about the room, he was struck by a sense of coming home. These people were his family. The tribe he'd been cheated out of as a child. For long years, it had been him and Recco, but they weren't alone any longer.

"Where would you like to sit?" he asked Karin.

She gestured at a table with Tessa, Moira, Becca, and two of the McMurdo scientists. He pulled out a chair for her and said, "Back in a moment with libations."

Some thoughtful soul had dragged two crates of the liquor they'd appropriated in Invercargill over by the table that held the cake. Squatting, he looked through the boxes. One held champagne, the other whiskey. The first was more appropriate for a wedding, but after what they'd just experienced, he grabbed a whiskey bottle, noting with pleasure it was thirty-year-old single malt scotch. He grinned to himself. If they were going to steal liquor, no reason not to take the best they could find. He hadn't been part of that particular shore party, but they'd done a most excellent job.

He cracked the seal and went in search of something to drink it out of besides the bottle. Boris met him in the galley doorway carrying a tray of tumblers. He glanced at the bottle and nodded approval. "Appears I'm timely with the glassware, eh?"

"More than timely. How about if you set that tray down over by the cake?" He scooped a glass off the tray and poured it half-full, inhaling the rich scents of oak and burnt cork.

Daide turned to face the room and raised his glass and his voice so everyone could hear him. "I propose a toast to Recco and Zoe, and to Juan and Aura. May their marriages bring them much joy."

After a chorus of "to the newlyweds" and "to Recco and Zoe and Juan and Aura," Daide banged on his glass with a knife. "I'm not quite done," he announced. "The toast was a start, but no one knows Recco better than I, and I'm going to tell you a story about him."

Recco groaned. "Aw crap, *amigo*. On my wedding day? You're going to roast me?"

"What better time? I'm hoping Vik will have a tale about Juan, and the women can tattle on Aura and Zoe."

The room erupted into laughter.

Poseidon got to his feet from where he'd been sitting near the front of the room. Turning to face them, he raised his hands. "Before you begin, I have a few things to say. First off, congratulations to the couples who've chosen to join their lives. It's always auspicious when magic marries magic. Keeps the strain strong."

Amphitrite walked to his side and looped a hand around his arm. Bending close, it looked like she whispered something into his ear. Poseidon didn't even look her way before he went on. "Once you've finished the festivities, you must return to points south. It could be Invercargill or Ushuaia or Christchurch. Or it doesn't have to be the ruins of an urban area at all—"

"Hold on a minute, mate." Viktor loped in front of Poseidon. "Last I checked, I determine where *Arkady* sails, and I do that with input from all aboard. Your opinion is noted, but it's only one opinion. If the majority do not agree—"

The staff from earlier materialized in the sea king's hand, and he thumped it on the deck. "Stop before I turn you into a fish—or kill you on the spot. It's rude to interrupt, but inexcusable when the one speaking is a god."

Viktor rolled his eyes. "Fine. Say what you will, and then leave my ship."

"Sail where you choose, but my sea Shifters and I will not be part of your ill-conceived plan to take on evil in the northlands. It's a fool's errand, and—"

"You lost your right to speak for me when you abandoned us," Leif thundered from the far side of the room. He crossed it in a few long strides and stood shoulder to shoulder with Viktor.

"We will follow Leif," the lead whale announced.

"You don't have that choice." Poseidon stood straight and brought his staff down again. "You are my subjects."

"Once we followed you out of loyalty," Leif pointed out. "That loyalty died when you forsook us."

An indecipherable expression, part sorrow, part resignation, and perhaps part disgust, flickered across Amphitrite's patrician features. Her figure took on an indistinct aspect, the air glistening in myriad colors before she faded from sight.

Poseidon did glance her way then, or at the space where she'd stood. Surprise etched into his high forehead, but he tilted his chin and said, "You've barely scratched the surface of the evil set loose by the Cataclysm." He looked straight at Leif. "You blame us for not helping you. We weren't strong enough. We came as soon as we could once your land kin aimed a blow at evil."

Leif shook his head. "I have a hard time believing that. Maybe your ability to travel around the globe was truncated, but you didn't even assist the sea Shifters in your immediate vicinity." He fisted a hand and brought it down on a nearby table. "None of that matters. If you won't help, leave."

"Leave" echoed around the dining room as all the sea Shifters chanted the single word over and over again.

"There will be a time you regret your decision." Poseidon's words held a pointed edge right before he left in a flash of light so bright Daide squeezed his eyes shut.

Leif turned to face the room. "I apologize for the sea god. Please, let's get on with the roasts and toasts. In truth, we severed our ties with Poseidon long ago, he just didn't realize it."

The din of conversation rose once more, and Daide elevated his glass. He wanted to talk with Karin. The small vertical line between her brows was back, which meant she didn't interpret the sea god's exit as anything good, but that conversation would have to wait.

"Attention, everyone!" he shouted, and eyes turned his way. "Let me tell you about Recco and the whale. None of our current company," he amended quickly. "This was Recco's first whale patient, and he damn near drowned."

"Ha!" one of the whale Shifters cut in. "Bet the whale did it on purpose."

"I always thought so, but the whale was damned closemouthed about its intentions." Recco grinned and motioned for Daide to keep talking.

"We were fresh out of vet school," Daide said. "Had just hung out our shingle, and we got a call from the Cetacean Institute in Buenos Aires…"

15

LOVE IS A SNEAKY BASTARD

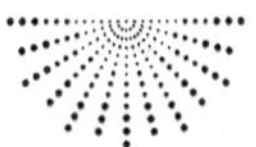

Karin fought a sinking feeling when Poseidon threw down the gauntlet, urging the sea Shifters to obey him. Whose side was the sea god really on? And what had Amphitrite been thinking? Judging from her face, she wanted to pound her consort into a million bits of seal meat.

She tried to pay attention while Daide told an amusing story about Recco and how he pissed off a whale who then made it his personal mission in life to crush him. The whale Shifters were practically rolling around on the floor, but she couldn't stop thinking about Poseidon.

Him showing up when he had couldn't possibly be coincidence. No. He'd materialized not because they'd called him but because he had ulterior motives. For all she knew, he'd been hovering in the ether hunting for precisely the opportunity they'd handed him on a platter...

Easy access to their group.

"So long as 'tis roasts we're after, Karin has the goods on Aura." Zoe ran lightly to her table, jarring her out of the bleak pit her thoughts had become. Karin looked up, and Zoe's smile vanished.

"Och, and whatever is the matter with you? Perk up, darling. 'Tis my wedding day."

Karin smothered her thoughts fast before Zoe could mine for details. "Not so very much wrong. I haven't laid eyes on a Kelpie in close to two hundred years is all." Karin made light of things and glanced around the room until her gaze fell on Aura. "Are you certain you want me spilling your secrets?" Karin arched a brow.

"It wasn't me who suggested it," Aura retorted. Color spread across the bridge of her nose turning her fair skin a lovely shade of pink.

Daide walked to Karin and offered his arm. "Would milady care for an escort?"

Karin swallowed a snort. "To the front of the room? I'm fairly certain I can make it there on my own, but if I run into problems, you'll be the first to know."

"So long as I'm not the last." Daide dropped a hand on her shoulder for one lengthy, delicious moment.

Damn him. He was attractive as sin, and he knew what effect his touch had on her. She shelved her worries about Poseidon, burying them deep as she made her way across the room. Aura and Zoe and their men deserved at least a few unfettered hours where they weren't worried sick about some monster lying in wait around the bend. Grabbing a glass off the tray next to the cake, she tipped the nearest bottle into it, noting it was whiskey.

Good enough. I could stand a bit of a break from being stone-cold sober.

She took a deep swallow, enjoying the burn as the alcohol made its way down her throat. "Aura, sweetheart." She sashayed close.

Aura cringed. "Crappity, crap. Not that one."

"But I haven't even opened my mouth yet," Karin protested.

"You don't have to. I know that look. And that tone."

The crowd took up a chant of, "Karin. Karin." At least it drove her worries away from center stage. Even if Poseidon out and out betrayed them, there wasn't much she could do about it.

Karin set the glass down and clasped her hands in front of her. She'd always loved telling tales, maybe because when she was born it was the primary means people had of entertaining themselves. "There's a good reason Aura majored in history," she began.

Aura groaned and dropped her face into her hands. Juan placed a protective arm around her and murmured. "It can't be that bad."

"Just wait." Her voice was muffled, but Karin heard her clearly.

"Once upon a time, Aura planned to be a doctor," Karin went on. "Only problem was she needed chemistry and zoology and physics to get into medical school. Math never was her strong suit, so she leveraged magic to bypass the normal channels. She took the classes and bluffed her way through exams. Almost made it too, until the day she blew up the chemistry lab. Hell, she nearly burned down Weber Hall, the building the lab was in. Luckily, it was a Saturday, and she was the only one there."

Karin took a measured breath and another sip of her drink before continuing. "Her bondmate was so freaked out by the fire, it forced a shift, and the campus cops ended up chasing a mountain lion down the college's main street until it headed for the woods. Shot at it with tranquilizer darts. Some even hit it, and no one could figure out why the creature didn't drop in its tracks."

A snicker emerged, followed by another. Karin bit her lower lip to keep herself from bursting out laughing. "The Shifter community found the whole thing hysterical, a sore point for Aura when she finally surfaced, which was a couple days later."

"I was almost killed." Aura tried for dignity, but missed the mark by a mile. "No one cared. You still think it's hilarious."

"Yeah, I do." Karin nodded. "There are a whole lot of disciplines where you can take shortcuts and get away with them. Medicine isn't one of them. If you'd been doing something other than daydreaming in chemistry class, you'd have understood you couldn't mix whatever reagents got away from you."

"I didn't listen in class. It's why I was in the lab that day. Trying to make sense out of the gibberish in my textbook." Aura shrugged. "I was young. It's no excuse, but that fire was a real wakeup call."

"You never would admit that out loud before. You have no idea how many nights' sleep I lost worrying about you misdiagnosing someone or blundering through a procedure and—"

"Enough!" Aura sputtered. "No one realized that better than I. My cat gave me nine kinds of hell about that incident. For years." She shook her head. "Are you done? Or were you planning to share more pithy anecdotes?"

"I vote for more." Juan smirked. "Only way I'll find out everything about my blushing bride."

"You'll have to pry them out of her on your own," Karin said and moved to where Daide stood.

He poured more liquor into her glass. "Cheers!"

"Back at you," she said and drained the tumbler.

"Would you like more?" he asked.

Viktor had begun spinning a story about Juan, one that turned the Argentinian's face a shiny red.

"No thanks," Karin said. "I need food before I drink any more anything."

"That can be arranged. I can make us plates."

Karin smiled fondly at him. "How about if we both sneak into the kitchen."

"Don't you want to hear the end of Vik's tale? Who would have guessed Juan was such a hellion as a Vampire?"

"You, for one." She leveled her gaze at him. "You were there."

"So were you, but not in quite the same capacity." He gazed intently at her. When he looked at her that way, she felt stripped naked, like he was seeing through the layers she hid behind.

Viktor finished talking amid applause, hoots, and hollers from the crowd. While everyone was occupied, Karin slid around the back of the room and through the galley's swinging door. All the food had long since grown cold, but it still smelled delicious, and she piled items on plates for both of them.

"Let's carry the platters into the dining room before we eat," she suggested. "That way, everyone won't have to detour through the galley."

"And we'll have it to ourselves."

"Exactly."

Daide picked up two serving dishes and shouldered back through the doors. Karin followed him. It didn't take many trips before all the food was arranged on the long table near the cake. Karin ferried plates and silverware next. Once they were done, she retreated to the kitchen and stood over the one of the plates she'd prepared.

"If it's privacy you're after, we could go to one of our cabins," Daide suggested.

"I'd love to, but I don't want the gals to think I abandoned them." Karin dragged two three-legged stools over and hoisted herself onto one of them.

Daide positioned the other one closer to her before sitting. He chewed and swallowed thoughtfully. Just when she was convinced he hadn't picked up on her worries about Poseidon, wasn't planning to pin her to the wall with questions she had no answers for, he angled a pointed look her way. "Well?"

"Well, what?" she hedged.

"If you didn't want privacy to talk, we'd be out there"—he waved an arm toward the swinging door—"with everyone else. Besides, I know your worried look. What got your goat?"

She finished swallowing and set her fork down. "You missed the precise usage for that expression."

"Not what I asked." He twisted to face her. "If you don't want to tell me what's bothering you, say so. I won't pry."

Karin pushed strands of hair out of her eyes. "I don't have anything like hard evidence," she began.

"Maybe not, but something beyond our run-in with the Kelpies upset you. I figure it's bound up in Poseidon's unexpected announcement."

Karin offered him points for shrewdness. "Doesn't the timing seem awfully coincidental to you?"

"What do you mean?"

She took another small bite of the dried beef casserole before answering. "We know a few things." She counted on her fingers. "One, Poseidon vanished during the Cataclysm. Two, he allowed virtually all his subjects to die, apparently without lifting a finger to intervene. I don't buy for a moment he was trapped. He's a god. They can teleport and go where they wish." She stopped to suck in a ragged breath.

"Go on," Daide urged, his tone somber.

"Three, he's Johnny on the spot when the women and I called the sea Shifters. When he showed up, both he and Amphitrite were the embodiment of attentive lieges, and Leif was far too ill to contradict them."

Daide narrowed his eyes. "You believe he was close and searching for an opportunity to come aboard."

"That's exactly what I think. The question is why, except he answered that today, albeit in an oblique manner. For whatever reason, he doesn't want us running around loose on Earth's oceans."

"I don't know. He helped with the Kelpies."

"Maybe it only appeared he was helping. For all we know, he was plotting strategy when he followed them part of the way to that island." She jumped off her stool and walked to the sink where she flipped the taps to fill a glass with water. "Want one?"

"Sure. This beef dish is salty, but you don't have to wait on me." He joined her at the sink and drank from his cupped hands, not bothering with the glass she held out. He wiped his mouth with the back of one hand. "Poseidon stood by while you murdered one of the Kelpies."

Karin shrugged. "Collateral damage, plus it makes it appear he's on our side. So, when he pitches what he's really after, which is for us to turn around, we're more likely to acquiesce."

"Makes sense. Do you think they'll come back?"

"Who? The Kelpies?" At his nod, she said, "No. Even they understand they wouldn't fare well fighting all of us. And they figured out we're not about to roll over and give up *Arkady*. For all we know"—she shrugged again—"Poseidon put them up to the attack."

"He was pretty convincing when he was whaling with his staff on that one we killed."

"Yes, but he wasn't the one who meted out the death blow. Not that I've ever run into gods before, but legends are quite clear they can kill with a look. They don't have to get down and dirty with weapons."

"Have other gods fallen from grace? Beyond Satan, that is."

"Satan was an angel, but oh my, yes. Anubis, for one. He was the first known wolf shifter, leader of those like me. I suspect it's why we no longer have a structure ruled by alphas."

"What happened?" Daide steered her back to their places at the counter and lifted her onto her stool, letting his hands linger on her waist.

His touch ignited longing, but Karin's attention was focused on his question. She ground her teeth in helpless rage. The Anubis tale always made her wish she'd been the one to kill him. "He sold out to a Vampire but continued to masquerade as our leader for a thousand years."

"Who took him down?" Daide had returned to his plate and was eating quickly.

"A group of Shifters and gypsies, of all things. In Germany, during the Nazi regime in the 1940s."

"Fascinating and not that long ago. For some reason, I assumed it occurred back in the Dark Ages."

"Why?"

"Because it seems like the sort of thing you'd share sitting around a fire."

"Sharpening stone tools?" Karin asked wryly.

"Something like that."

They ate in silence until their plates were empty. "You're quiet," Karin observed.

"So are you. Any ideas how to proceed?"

"Not really, since we don't know anything beyond my suspicions." Her shoulders sagged, and she longed for a simpler time. She'd give anything to move backward to before a Shifter spell gone bad had spawned the Cataclysm that damn near destroyed their lives.

"What's the worst part of this for you?" His question was soft, almost not there.

"You'd think I'd have gotten used to there being no safe haven," she replied. "Those years in Ushuaia should have hammered that expectation out of me, but they didn't." She turned to face him. "I never expected Ketha's plan to defeat the Cataclysm would work, but we didn't have any other options. When we beat it back, and the ocean started to return to normal, I let myself hope."

"Like the Pandora myth." He smiled softly. "Wasn't Hope at the bottom of the box?"

"Not sure about that, but she emerged last, at the tail end of all the world's evils." Karin inhaled briskly. "Mythology aside, it felt good to hope. Right in a way not much had since we ended up trapped in Ushuaia. I'd been hanging on by my fingernails for so long, wondering what grisly death would befall us, I wasn't careful. Didn't apply my usual, inductive approach. Or deductive, either. Nope. I figured we had good shit coming our way. After everything we'd lived through, we deserved the cards to yield aces."

She shook her head. "I should have known better. I was a fool."

"You're being too hard on yourself." He placed a hand over where she'd folded hers in her lap.

"No. I'm not. If I hadn't been lost in a fantasy world, I wouldn't have been so shocked when we ran into one form of evil after another within days of leaving Argentina."

He stood and moved behind her, wrapping his arms around her shoulders. "No matter what happens, we'll get through it."

Karin yearned to say something optimistic, but she didn't want to lie. "Maybe we will. If we get as far as Siberia, our odds of coming out on top against whatever's determined to keep that gateway open aren't good."

"Maybe not, but we still have to try."

Karin got to her feet and turned so his arms crisscrossed her back. She leaned into him, breathing him in. "Of course we have to try. I never said we didn't."

He tilted her chin with a finger. "Are you willing to take a chance on me? We've been dancing around our attraction, and I've done my damnedest to give you space, but I want you in a way I've never wanted a woman before. Maybe you don't feel quite the same way. Not yet, anyway, but—"

"Hush. I…" What could she say? That she didn't think she could survive if she opened her heart all the way and he was killed? Life didn't work like that. When you stopped taking chances, you obliterated parts of yourself and ended up a shell of a person.

"Good insight," her wolf inserted dryly. *"What are you going to do about it?"*

"Was that your wolf?" Daide asked. He looked away. "I know my coyote might not quite measure up, but I love you both."

Karin's eyes widened. "Love? You can't know you feel that way about me. Not this soon. Of course you'd love your coyote; it's how the Shifter bond works, except—" She shut her mouth abruptly, aware she was babbling.

"It's an emotion, Karin. Not a null hypothesis that requires A and B split testing to confirm."

Slowly, taking his time, he closed his mouth over hers. His lips were warm and firm, and he kissed her with a singlemindedness that stole her breath. She traded kisses, bites, and suckles as they moved from mouth to ear to neck and back again. He caressed the length of her spine, and she hooked her arms beneath his, loving the feel of his firmly muscled back beneath her fingertips.

Breath caught in her throat, and desire surged. The same need she'd been riding herd on since the first time he kissed her raced through her in a scorching tide. She moaned, a low, urgent sound that shocked her because it meant her control was crumbling.

"Karin." The way he said her name was part entreaty, part prayer. His voice was filled with hunger, need. A raspy catch in it made her crotch flood with lust and turned her nipples to exquisite points of delight.

She stopped thinking, choreographing every movement, every nuance, and dragged magic into a sloppy shield around them. "Hurry," she said. "No one will notice us when we cross the dining room."

"Even if they're looking through their psychic views?" he teased.

"Maybe then, but everyone's getting drunk. No one's worried about us. If they were, they'd have come hunting long before now."

He swept an arm beneath her knees and picked her up as if she weighed nothing. Her first instinct was to demand he put her down, but being cradled against his chest felt too damned good, so she wrapped her arms around him and held on.

Daide carried her out of the galley, along the back wall of the dining room, and through the door into the corridor. The glimpse she'd gotten of everyone eating, drinking, and laughing warmed her. They'd earned today, by God, and they were right to take advantage of it. She'd been worried the Kelpies would ruin things, but that was before Poseidon's bombshell.

"You can put me down, now," she said and let go of the magic shielding them from curious eyes.

"What if I don't want to?" He walked down a side corridor past the lab and kicked open a door that led to a small cabin. "I've taken a catnap or two here," he said. "It's how I know about it." He placed her on the bed and shut the door firmly before turning back to where she lay.

Daide bent and tugged at her boots, pulling them off one at a time. He ran his hands over her feet, rubbing the arches as he stripped off her stockings. When he reached for the fastening of her pants, she batted his hands away.

"What?" he teased. "Feet are all I get to look at?"

"No one's doing much looking. It's dark in here." Karin kindled a mage light, and it cast a bluish glow, making the cabin look like something out of a Grimm's fairy tale. "Take your boots off and lie next to me."

He bent to his own boots, toeing them off. While he did that, she tugged off her vest and slithered out of her long-underwear top. She'd given up on things like bras long before her stint in Ushuaia.

Daide glanced up from his boots and made a wonderfully male noise, somewhere between a growl and a purr. "Jesus." Breath whooshed from him. "You're gorgeous." He captured a breast in each hand, rubbing her nipples between thumb and forefinger.

Sensation cascaded through her, and her hips writhed, settling into their own rhythm. She made a grab for his cock but couldn't reach it. Her breath was coming fast now, and she had to fight to get words out. "Naked. I want you naked."

His lips parted in a lascivious grin. "Do you now? Purely for clinical observation purposes, right?"

"Purely." She grinned back and arched into his touch. No one had set eyes on her breasts for years, and she'd been afraid he'd find her lacking, particularly if he'd been used to women in their twenties and thirties.

He bent and took a nipple into his mouth, sucking hard. Her belly tightened, reminding her of the empty place between her legs. And the cock she had yet to lay eyes on. "Naked," she panted.

He raised his head from her breast. "Tell you what," he said, sounding breathless himself, "I'll let go, and we each get out of our clothes as fast as we can."

"What does the winner get?"

"We're both winners because we get each other."

A rush of feeling so profound it nearly brought tears followed his words, and she struggled with what to say to express how lucky she was to have him in her life. He straightened and shrugged out of his jacket. Next came his stretchy top.

"Better hurry." His dark eyes sparkled with merriment, but passion burned in their depths.

"Or what?" She undid her pants and pushed them down her hips, followed by her panties.

"Or I'll be forced to finish what you began."

He unzipped his trousers and slid them over his high, tight ass and down his legs. Karin surged forward and placed a hand over the tented-out front of his shorts right before she pushed them out of the way. His cock looked the way she'd imagined it from feeling him grow erect against her belly. Long, thick, perfect, it sprang from a mat of black hair.

She took a moment and gazed at him, enjoying the smooth expanse of bronze and the scattering of dark hair around his nipples. Muscles stretched over bone in a beauty that made it hard to stop staring at him.

"Do I pass?" he asked.

"By the goddess, you're exquisite," she managed around a narrow place in her throat.

"So are you." He ran a hand lightly down her belly, resting it atop the vee between her legs. She bucked into his touch, wanting everything all at the same time.

"Tell me what you'd like," he said as if he'd discerned her thoughts.

Rather than words, she repositioned herself and took him into her mouth. Running her tongue up and down his shaft, she explored the velvety head as she sucked and teased.

He threaded his hands into her hair and groaned. His nipples had formed peaks, just like hers, and every muscle was outlined in bas relief. Daide pulled out of her mouth. "I need to be inside you. We can save the fancy stuff for when I'm not so close to coming."

Karin tumbled onto the bunk on her belly and then rose to her hands and knees. She'd barely stabilized herself when she felt his cock between her legs, pushing for entrance. He entered her slowly, so slowly she wanted to scream at him to hurry, to fuck her hard and fast.

Instead, she let lust build. He reached around and took a breast in each hand, twirling her nipples. Moving a hand to her nub, he sank full length into her, rocking his cock back and forth as he rubbed the center of her sensation. Heat and need and desire spooled into a vortex that pulled her over the top. Orgasm cascaded through her as he worked her between his cock and his hand.

"That's right," he crooned near her ear. "Come for me, darling."

She'd moved beyond words to reply. As her climax subsided, she thrust back toward him, urging him to move. He withdrew and pushed back inside, his tempo increasing until he was driving into her. A second climax seeded itself from her first, building in her belly. When it crashed over her, she felt him release, white-hot gouts of semen splashing her. They ground their bodies together, draining every last spasm of passion before they fell on the narrow bunk in an untidy, gasping, panting heap.

Karin cuddled into him. It felt so good to be in a man's arms. She hadn't allowed herself to recognize how much she'd missed skin-to-skin contact. "Thank you," she murmured. "You were amazing."

"I love you." His words vibrated with emotion. "You're mine, now. Truly mine. We belong to each other."

The same fear of losing herself that she'd always harbored reared up at *mine* and *belong*, but she pushed it aside. She'd find a way to make this work. Find a way to shutter her fears that giving herself to a man, heart, body, and soul, would make her less than she was.

"Yes." Her wolf was back. *"You will."*

Daide pulled himself from her body and turned her so they faced each other. He cupped her face with his palm. "I'll never hurt you, Karin. I'll care for you, protect you."

She started to blunder through a half-assed explanation of the fears that had kept her single, but it felt too complicated. Instead, she asked, "Do you think we should rejoin the festivities?"

"No, but we could move to your cabin. Or mine. The bunks are bigger than this one."

She smiled and pushed her hips into his still-erect cock. "I take it you have plans?"

"Big ones. The night is young, and we've only just discovered one another."

Her smile grew. If she didn't watch it, he'd batter his way through the last of the walls around her heart. To her surprise, she didn't snatch up her clothes and run out of the room. Maybe the independence she'd valued more than any treasure was overrated after all.

16

UNINVITED MAGIC

*D*aide stood at the helm staring out the windows lining three walls of the bridge. It was his turn to stand watch, and Viktor had run across the hall to ask Ketha to make them a midnight snack—if she was still awake. Stars were scattered across the clear night sky, and a quarter moon sat above the horizon. Strange how simple things like the stars and moon never changed no matter what happened to the land stretching beneath them.

He smiled. He'd been doing a lot of that lately. In the week that had passed since he and Karin first made love, they'd been close to inseparable. Sleeping next to her, making love, learning even more about her moods and temperament, had deepened his attachment.

And his respect and awe.

She was a strong woman, competent and sure of herself, with a sharp, incisive intellect. The type of woman he'd always wanted but had never approached for fear of having to disclose too much of himself. She'd finally admitted why she'd never married, and it made perfect sense. In the era she came from, women gave up a lot when they tied themselves to a husband. She'd have become chattel, bound to live her life by the standards her partner set for her.

He'd been surprised Shifters had lived by the same archaic

standards as humans where the man ruled the roost, but apparently there hadn't been many differences.

He checked the instrumentation, pleased everything looked the way it should. They'd be at the Solomon Islands later tonight or tomorrow morning. The beauty of travel by ship was constant progress at between twelve and fourteen knots an hour, twenty-four seven. The seas had been smooth, and the weather temperate, although not as warm as Vik and Juan had expected.

Viktor strode back onto the bridge. "All's well, mate?" He carried a thermos in one hand and balanced a plate laden with biscuits and assorted other items in the other.

"Yup. Just checked. I thought Ketha was going to do a galley run."

"Eh, she's asleep. I hate to disturb her. She's been worried about something, but I can't pry it out of her." Viktor set the plate on a low table and fetched two cups, pouring steaming black coffee into them.

"Gracias." Daide took one, sipping gratefully at the hot, bitter brew.

Viktor dragged a stool over and munched on a biscuit spread with tinned preserves. "Do you know?" He arched a tawny brow.

"Know what?" Daide got up and took a biscuit of his own, slathering jam on it.

"What Ketha is worried about."

"Why would I?" Daide countered. "She's your wife."

Viktor cast a pointed look his way. "Because you and Karin are thicker than thieves. I figure I'll get to officiate at another wedding one of these days."

Daide bent over his biscuit, unsure whether to share Karin's confidences. After a week had passed without any further attacks or anything untoward happening, they'd kicked around the possibility her fears about Poseidon were baseless.

"I know that body posture. We don't keep secrets on ships, especially not from the captain." Viktor's words held harsh edges, and he moved his stool until he sat knee to knee with Daide.

"It's not keeping secrets if we don't actually know anything."

"Yeah, but Karin suspects something. I've worked with her long enough to recognize the signs. And it's a sure bet she's confided in you."

Daide took another bite of biscuit before placing it back in the plate. He licked jam off his fingers before resting his hand on the wheel. "You really should ask Karin. I'm not sure it's my place to—"

"I did ask her. She blew me off. And I put Ketha up to digging, but Karin wouldn't talk with her, either. Goddammit. If you have any information, no matter how trivial you think it is, I need to know. And pronto. Things have been going too well. Every instinct I have says we're headed for a new catastrophe."

"Like sailing off the edge of the world?"

"I'm not in the mood for jokes."

Daide let go of the wheel and wrapped his fingers around the warm ceramic mug. He was in a bind, one where he had to respond to Viktor, and he hoped Karin wouldn't be angry. He was organizing his thoughts, deciding what to say, when she trotted onto the bridge.

Smiling, she said, "I came by to see if you two needed anything before I turned in, but it appears you're all set."

"Excellent timing." Daide walked to her and gave her a quick hug. "Viktor wants to know about your, um, concerns."

She turned toward Viktor, a guileless expression on her face, and said, "I may have had a few, but they've faded. Probably not worth hashing through."

"Everything is worth *hashing through*." Viktor's terse comment sliced across the bridge leaving shards of annoyance in its wake. "What did you pick up on?"

"In the simplest terms, I fear Poseidon switched sides."

A rapid intake of breath proved Viktor hadn't entertained that idea, and his words clinched it. "Of all the possibilities I've considered, that one never made the list."

"I lack hard evidence," Karin went on. "The series of events unfolding around his appearance could be coincidental, but I doubt it."

"Was he behind the Kelpie attack?" Viktor drained his mug and got up to refill it from the thermos.

"Maybe," Karin replied carefully.

"Mmph. Well, he certainly did something to alienate the sea Shifters, but that happened during the Cataclysm."

"Not coming to your aid would alienate anyone," Daide cut in.

"Poseidon claimed he couldn't, that he and Amphitrite were locked in stasis somewhere," Viktor muttered.

"Yes, and I don't believe that story for a second," Karin said. "They're gods. Only another god could detain them against their will."

"If your theory is true," Viktor spoke slowly, "what do you suppose will happen next?"

Karin turned her hands palms upward. "Sorry. The crystal ball's been a bit dusty. That's more a question for Ketha with her seer ability."

Breath hissed from between Viktor's clenched teeth. "She's looked but says nothing materialized. Since I have no idea how her talent works, I wasn't sure what she meant."

A fine vertical line formed between Karin's brows, and Daide figured she hadn't liked what Viktor disclosed. "Funny, she hasn't mentioned it to any of the rest of us," Karin said.

"Probably because there was nothing to tell you." Viktor jumped in to defend his wife.

"No. You don't get it." Karin closed her teeth over her lower lip. "I have no idea how many times she's tried to scry the future. A single failure, or even two, doesn't mean much, but if you can't break through consistently, it suggests someone doesn't want us privy to what's out there. Damn it."

"What?" Daide asked.

"She should have come to one of us, requested assistance. Our magic is additive." Karin turned and headed for the door.

"Ketha's asleep," Viktor said. "Don't disturb her; she hasn't been sleeping well."

"I just bet she hasn't," Karin retorted.

Viktor squared his shoulders. "This is precisely why we don't hold secrets on ships. You shelved your fears—"

"For the best of reasons," Karin bristled and turned back around. "No need to get everyone upset over nothing. Besides, the newlyweds deserved a span of peace to enjoy one another."

"Better to be prepared over nothing than caught with our dicks out when another atrocity blindsides us," Viktor countered. "As to Juan, the ship is his first responsibility, as it is mine."

Daide didn't bother to point out Aura might not quite see things that way. "Maybe we could work on this in the morning," he suggested.

"We could, but I'm going to find Leif and maybe the lead whale Shifter. They may know more about Poseidon's role during the Cataclysm than they've told us." Karin stood tall, rolling her shoulder blades back. "At the very least, they're sure to be able to shed light on his character before the world turned to shit."

The air around her took on an incandescent quality that meant she'd leveraged magic. Daide poured more coffee into his mug and handed it to her. Even though he'd spent a decade as a Vampire and a few months as a Shifter, when she'd said she was going to roust the sea Shifters, he'd assumed she was going to walk to their cabins or determine if they were swimming alongside the ship. Instead, she'd leveraged telepathy.

The salt tang of the sea intensified. When Daide turned toward the back of the bridge, he wasn't surprised to see Leif and the lead whale Shifter. Both were naked, and water streamed off them, forming puddles where they stood.

"You rang?" Leif grinned and trotted to the plate of food. Scooping up a biscuit, he took a large bite.

The door leading into the corridor opened, and a sleepy-eyed Ketha with tousled hair trudged in. She was wrapped in a thick terrycloth robe. "Geez, no one could sleep with all this magic happening a couple of thin walls away. What's up? Why are we having a middle-of-the-night meeting?" Moving to the thermos, she shook it.

"Sorry," Daide said. "Karin took the last of it."

"It's okay. If I drink any, I'll never get back to sleep."

"You may not, anyway," Karin said. A sour note ran beneath her words. "Why didn't you tell one of us you'd attempted to scry the future and failed? How many times did you try?"

Ketha's golden eyes widened as she focused on Karin. "Um, well, let's see here. When did I begin reporting to you?"

Karin walked to her and draped an arm around her shoulders. "That's not it at all, and you know it. How many times, Ketha?"

"Too many," she admitted. "I was going to call a meeting tomorrow and bring it up. You beat me to the punch."

Karin scrunched her forehead into worried lines and looked from Leif to the whale. "What can you tell us about Poseidon?"

Leif's pleasant expression faded. "That old bastard? It might save time if you homed in on what you're looking for."

"Could he have switched sides?" Viktor asked.

Leif raked his wet hair behind his shoulders, where it continued to drip on the floor, and exchanged glances with the whale. "It's possible. What do you think?"

"I wouldn't put it past him," the whale muttered. "Far as I know, evil didn't seduce him before, and there are many fell creatures in the sea. Entities that may have made him juicy offers over the years."

"Could standing by while so many of your kin died have changed him?" Karin asked.

"Anything is possible." The whale repeated a variation of Leif's earlier statement

"Can either of you recall the sequence of events when Poseidon and Amphitrite found you and the other sea Shifters?" Karin asked.

"There was no *sequence of events*," Leif replied. "They simply materialized one day with no credible explanation about where they'd been or why they'd bothered to find us, now, when we were clearly dying."

"They did stammer through a few lame excuses about how they'd wanted to come far sooner, but couldn't," the whale cut in.

"Did they try to save you?" Ketha asked. She'd moved next to Viktor and laced her fingers with his.

"No. They said we were beyond what their magic could accomplish," the whale said. "I didn't think it was true, but I was too sick to argue with them."

"Which was precisely what they were counting on," Karin growled and set her mouth in a tight, thin line. "How long after they showed up did you end up aboard *Arkady?*"

Leif blew out a tense-sounding breath. "Not an easy question for a dolphin who was counting his life in days, but it wasn't much time. Not more than a few hours."

"So their story about racing to your side as soon as they could to offer succor was bullshit." Ketha screwed her mouth into an angry moue.

"My take on it," Leif said.

"Mine too," the whale echoed.

"They sure didn't stick around once we began working on you," Daide mumbled.

"It seemed odd at the time," Karin agreed.

"My impression as well," Ketha spoke up. "I thought sure they'd at least stop in to check on all of you, but we didn't actually see them after that until we invited them to the weddings."

"I heard from them," Leif reminded everyone. "They read me the riot act for that agreement with the Witches."

"I'm not liking how this is shaping up," Daide said.

"What can we do about it?" Ever the pragmatist, Viktor spun both hands in circles to encourage them to come up with solutions.

"Hard to solve problems that haven't shown their faces," Daide told him.

"Certainly is," Leif agreed.

"If we put our heads together with the other sea Shifters, maybe we can come up with patterns or some other evidence that might give us a clue where they'll strike next," the whale said.

Leif's nostrils flared as he inhaled. "I'm kicking myself."

"Why?" Daide asked.

"When Poseidon announced we were on our own if we kept sailing north, I was so grateful to have him out of our hair, I didn't look for motives on his part. I figured he was being the same selfish bastard who took his ball and went home if you didn't play the game his way."

"We don't know anything. Not for sure," Karin cautioned. "Although Ketha's news is unsettling."

"What news?" Leif turned his unusual, pale-blue eyes her way.

Ketha disentangled herself from where she'd been leaning against Viktor. "He"—she jerked her chin at her husband —"started nagging a few days ago. Said things were too quiet and asked me to look into the future. I tried but couldn't see a thing. It was rather like when I tried to scry the roots of the Cataclysm and got nowhere until the spell hiding the information faded."

"Surely you tried more than once," the whale said.

"Oh yeah. I've tried maybe a dozen times; the latest effort was earlier this evening. Always with the same result. A blank wall blocked my efforts."

"When were you planning to say something?" Leif asked.

Ketha rolled her eyes. "Stop. Karin just rebuked the crap out of me. Tomorrow. I was going to ask for assistance boosting my power tomorrow, but even if I can break through whatever's thwarting me, we still might not learn much beyond generalities."

"I understand," the whale said. "I've done my share of information gathering."

"I'd forgotten that." Leif turned to the whale. "Can you help her? Our magic is stronger than theirs."

"Be glad to," the whale said, "but why wait?"

"Why, indeed?" Ketha aimed her next words at Karin. "Your prophecy came true."

"Oh?" Karin stared at her friend. "Which one?"

"When you said sleep was over for the night. I'll be right back. I need my glass, and I'll throw some clothes on."

"Will you need the rest of us?" Viktor asked.

"Probably not," the whale Shifter said, "but you may as well remain in case I'm wrong. While we're waiting for Ketha, I'll run down to the locker and dress."

"I'm going to the galley to get a refill on that coffee," Karin said.

"Take the thermos," Viktor urged. "It holds four cups."

"I'll come with you." Daide followed Karin out of the bridge and down several flights.

They worked in a companionable silence until she mumbled something in Gaelic.

"What?" Daide asked.

"I don't like any of this, but beating Ketha over the head won't fix it. Even if she'd come to me or Aura or Zoe after her second failed attempt, there wouldn't have been much we could do beyond supporting her with additional magic to try again."

"But you don't expect it would have yielded anything different." He screwed a lid onto the thermos bottle.

"No. That blank wall she described?" At his nod, she went on, "It means someone very powerful magically doesn't want us to have any clues."

"Maybe the whale will make a difference." Daide was shooting in the dark, but he kept talking. "You've told me different magics are synergistic, and the sea Shifters' power is different from yours."

"Was different," Karin said and looked askance at him. "They sundered their arrangement with the Witches. It was why they were so strong."

"How come Leif just said their magic trumps yours, er ours?"

She smiled. "Good thing you remembered what you are. You'd have crushed your bondmate, and goddess knows it needs all the encouragement you can offer it. I don't know why Leif said that. Maybe he still believes it. Maybe he knows something I don't." She spread her hands in front of her. "Does it matter? We'll go back to the bridge and keep a close eye on what unfolds."

Daide snatched up a half-eaten pan of cornbread. "I'll bring this along."

"Love your optimism, but I have a feeling the next half hour will kill everyone's appetite."

They plodded up four sets of risers to bridge level. When they pushed the door open, Ketha and the whale had set up shop in front of the windows. The moon had made a full commitment to traversing the sky, and light streamed through the glass. Daide took it as a positive omen.

He laid the cornbread on the chart table and set the thermos next to it. Karin stood next to him and placed a finger over her lips. He nodded, understanding full well how important it was not to disturb the two Shifters.

They began to chant, and power shimmered around them, forming a glowing nimbus that changed color from white to blue to green, and then back to white. They stood so both of them could look into Ketha's mirror. An eight- by ten-inch oblong, it was set in an antique brass frame. He wanted to look too, but they were turned at an angle that made it impossible for anyone but them to see.

Leif stood next to Viktor. He wasn't dripping water any longer, but he looked worried, with a pinched expression around his eyes. Karin crooked a finger and walked closer, stopping near Leif. Daide stood next to her, alert and watchful, but not expecting much beyond one more failed attempt to see something in the scyring mirror.

He felt Karin summon power, saw it eddy around her, and smelled the wild, untamed scent unique to her. It always intensified when she called magic. Daide switched to his psychic view, the transition clumsier than he would have liked. Glowing lines transected the bridge. Ley lines, they depicted areas where power aggregated.

Karin began a low, urgent chant. He felt the vibration in his gut. Ketha pointed at something in the glass; the whale nodded, and both of them picked up the pace of their incantation. Maybe they'd almost broken through.

"You have to stop them." The coyote sounded frantic. *"Something's not right."*

"They'll be done soon." Daide tried to placate the coyote, but it howled mournfully.

Tension poured off Viktor. He never took his eyes off his wife, as if he was willing her to find her way through the psychic thicket that had stymied her previous efforts. Was his raven cawing warnings in the background alongside Daide's coyote?

If Daide hadn't dialed in his third eye, he'd never have noticed when the ley lines nearest Ketha and the whale began to vibrate. Black-tinged light bloomed along the lines, and the stench of ozone filled the bridge.

"Nooooo!" Karin shrieked and bolted toward Ketha and the whale with Leif right behind her yelling in Gaelic.

Daide had no idea what was happening, but figured it couldn't be good. A flaming border formed around Ketha and the whale, accompanied by a low, ominous booming sound.

Karin chanted furiously, heaving magic at the flames. They absorbed her magic and burned brighter, higher.

"Fuck! It's feeding off me," she shouted and withdrew her magic.

Leif reached through the fire and grabbed hold of the whale. Viktor grunted with strain as he did the same with Ketha. The skin on the backs of his hands turned red and then blistered, but he didn't let go. The stench of burning flesh rose. Karin grabbed Viktor's waist and helped pull. Daide latched onto Leif.

No matter how hard they jerked and struggled, they couldn't budge Ketha or the whale out of the circle. Breath rasped in Daide's throat as he inhaled smoke and ash. His heart thudded hard against his ribcage, and sweat dripped down his sides as he dug in his heels and exerted as much backward pressure as he could manage.

"Can't you leverage magic?" he shouted at Leif.

"No. It will ricochet."

The boom turned to a high-pitched shriek, and the fiery circle blasted upward like a miniature atomic explosion. When it cleared, Ketha and the whale were gone.

Viktor shrieked in German and clawed at the air.

Leif held out his charred arms to Karin. Pain carved lines into his face, and he held himself stiffly. Nodding, she wrapped his burnt flesh with glistening magical ropes.

Daide gripped Viktor's shoulders so hard it had to hurt, although maybe he couldn't feel anything beyond the pain of his burns. "Pull yourself together. Now." He made his voice stern, even though his heart hurt for his friend.

Viktor shook himself from head to toe and regarded Daide through anguished eyes, eyes that looked like he'd emerged from Hell.

Karin wrapped Viktor's hands and forearms in the same enchanted dressings she'd used on Leif. "At least we know more than we did," she growled.

"Indeed we do." Leif nodded solemnly.

"Was it Poseidon?" Daide asked.

"Not sure. I thought I caught sight of Amphitrite in the midst of a dense mist, but it might have been some other goddess." Karin narrowed her eyes. "I hope to hell we can raise some allies in the Solomons. We need reinforcements. Hell, I'd even take that Witch right now—if we'd brought her along."

"But we have to go after Ketha. Now." Viktor spoke like a dead man, his tone flat and without inflection.

"They're not anywhere we can get to." Compassion lit twin fires in the depths of Karin's copper eyes.

"What do you mean?" Viktor reached for her and groaned as the movement created pain.

"They're either on a borderworld or a long way from here in a place that's both desert and frozen at the same time. I caught glimpses before the portal banged shut. Only magic can bring them back, and it may well end up being theirs. Your burns will be healed in a few hours." She turned to Leif. "Yours too."

He inclined his head. "Thank you. We seem to be bound to heal one another's injuries. I will summon my kin."

"Have them gather here," Viktor said and walked to the PA system's speaker. "I'll wake everyone else."

"I can hold the mic button," Daide said. "We'll get her back, *amigo*."

Viktor didn't reply, but at least the frantic hysteria that had gripped him had apparently passed, and he was back in sea captain mode. Daide activated the PA system, and Viktor barked. "Everyone to the bridge now."

Karin and Leif walked to where they stood.

Viktor skewered them with his green-eyed gaze. "What are the odds? Don't sugarcoat this. I have to know."

"Not good," Karin said.

"Going after them isn't practical," Leif added. "First, we'd have to locate them, which would take far too long. I've only been to two borderworlds, and the trips were so arduous I never tried again. If it isn't a borderworld they're on, I didn't recognize the landscape."

"Frozen and a desert," Viktor repeated Karin's words. "Could be the high Arctic."

"Easier to get to," Leif said, "but we'd blow through a hell of a lot of magic, and that's where the gateway is. We might be walking into a trap."

Daide considered Leif's words. "If you could get back from a borderworld," he said slowly, "then maybe they can too."

"Maybe so," Leif agreed. "The whale is ancient and strong. If anyone can pull off an escape, it's him, and if they're in the Arctic, it's surrounded by ocean. Easy for him to don his whale form. Once he's in the sea, he'll be able to communicate with us."

A shadow crossed Viktor's face. "Would the whale leave Ketha alone?"

"If it was the only way to get them out of there, then yes," Leif replied. A grave light flickered in his eyes. "Try to have faith, raven Shifter."

"What choice do I have?" Bitterness lined Viktor's words. "It's all that's left."

17

ONE MORE BARGAIN

etha fell through blackness. When she tried to breathe, her lungs seized, and she understood she was plummeting through an airless void. She reached for her wolf.

"I'm here. Where would I go? We're bonded."

Tears leaked from her eyes, but a chill wind filled with scraps of grit dried them almost instantly. She shielded her face from the sandpaper scrape of gravel, but then the backs of her hands stung and burned. The whale? Was he here too? She moved her hands and narrowed her eyes, attempting to peer through the dense gloom surrounding her, but couldn't see a thing.

Her heart was pounding; adrenaline left a sour taste on her tongue. If there'd been air, she'd have forced some nice, deep breaths, but sucking fumes only intensified her panic.

Think. I have to think.

She'd been drawn through some kind of gateway, so presumably someone would be waiting for her at the other end.

Maybe not. Maybe this is their way of killing me. I'll die without oxygen, and damned quick.

She pulled up the neck of her sweater, burying her nose in its folds to capture any air molecules trapped within the garment. It worked. She didn't get much, but enough to mute her dread of suffocation.

"Cushion your descent," the wolf warned.

Ketha didn't waste energy questioning her bondmate. She drew magic, grateful her power hadn't been stripped along with her free will, and wrapped it around herself. Her end-over-end tumbling slowed, and her reflexive attempts to breathe yielded a small amount of oxygen. It answered one question. A destination lay ahead—one with a breathable atmosphere. It beat immediate death in the airless void.

"Good." The wolf was back. *"For a while there, I was afraid you'd given up."*

"Never."

A ferocious howl rose from her belly, reminding her how much she loved her wolf. The black yielded to gray, and cracked, rock-strewn ground rose up to meet her. She hit, bounced, and hit once more before lying still. The magical shielding around her had taken the brunt of the landing. If the wolf hadn't warned her, she might have broken a few bones.

Ketha loosed her protective magic and scrambled to her feet. It was cold, below zero, and wind drove small, sharp rocks into her legs. Rivers of ice traversed a plain that might have been in northern Russia or the Canadian Arctic. No trees. Nothing green.

Movement caught the edges of her vision, and the whale lumbered into view. "So, we're both here," he said. "I sensed you near while I fell."

She didn't bother to tell him she'd been too spun out about the lack of air to recognize his energy. A shiver racked her, and she wrapped her arms around her body, wishing for a hat and gloves. "Where are we?" She turned to face him.

"Two choices. A borderworld, which would be truly bad news..."

"Or?"

"We're on Wrangel Island, somewhere near the portal we're supposed to be closing."

"Why not Siberia? Or Baffin Island? Or a hundred other locations in the high Arctic?" she demanded. The cold, thin air hurt her lungs, but she was relieved to have something to breathe.

"Any of those are possible." He held out his arms. "Come closer. You're cold."

"And you're not?"

"Not the same way you are. I retain some of my whale physiology as a human."

Grateful for his warmth, she let him fold his arms around her. "Do you know how we can get out of here?"

"Depends. Can you teleport?"

"Only over very short distances," she replied. "Even if I could, it can't be that easy. Someone went to a lot of work to separate us from *Arkady*. I don't believe they'll allow us to waltz out of here."

The whale twisted his head from side to side as he scanned the barren landscape. "No greeting party," he pointed out.

"Maybe we beat them here." Ketha straightened. "If that's true, this might be our only chance to escape."

"If this is a borderworld, and the lack of air on our journey suggests it might be, escape will be very hard."

"The animals inhabit a borderworld," she pointed out. "Mages breached the boundaries; it's how Shifters came to be." An idea bloomed, and she turned her attention inward.

"Can you take us to your world?"

"Maybe," the wolf said.

Ketha knew her bondmate well. *"What's the catch?"*

"You have to travel in my form, and at the end of things, you may never find your human body again."

"I heard that," the whale said.

Ketha opened her mouth to ask what he thought about it when the ground began to undulate beneath their feet. Deep fissures formed amid cracking ice, and a low, menacing growl emerged from the wounded land.

"Choose now," her wolf said. *"No more time."*

"Listen to me." The whale gripped her arms. "Shift and leave this place. Your wolf will find Viktor's raven on the borderworld, and they'll come up with a way to return you to your rightful place."

Ketha swallowed back panic. Being a wolf forever wouldn't be all that bad if it weren't for Viktor, but she couldn't think about any of that. If she wasn't careful, longing for the only man she'd ever truly loved might break her, strip her of hope.

"Are you coming with me?" she asked

"No. I will teleport. If we're still on Earth, I'll find an ocean and swim."

"But, what if we're not?" Her gut twisted with apprehension.

A corner of his mouth turned downward. "Then I'll have to figure out something different. Hurry." He let go of her. "Your wolf is correct. We're almost out of time."

"Open fires and safe journeys." She invoked an old Shifter blessing.

"To you as well," the whale replied in a formal tone. "If fate is kind, we shall meet again."

Ketha felt her wolf raging within her.

"Take my form. Now!"

Ketha offered a hasty prayer to the goddess before ceding to her bondmate, trusting its wisdom. The noise of ripping fabric joined the malevolent crackling, booming cacophony that meant the ground was doing its damnedest to swallow them whole. At least she wasn't cold anymore. The wolf's coat and thick pads protected her from such things.

She took off at a dead run, leaping gaping holes opening all around her. Light flared as the wolf summoned its brand of magic, and, with a mighty leap, they sprang through an opening that formed above them.

KARIN WAS TOO KEYED up to stand still, so she paced in a tight circle.

Bleary-eyed people were still filing onto the bridge. All the sea Shifters were here. When she did a nose count, the only ones missing were Boris and Ted, and they pushed through the door wearing worried expressions.

Daide straightened from where he'd been bent over nautical charts. "We should reach the southernmost Solomon Island in about a quarter hour."

"I'd planned our course around it, but that could change," Juan said.

Karin stalked to the charts and studied a map of the islands. "Here." She stabbed a finger at the three southernmost islands. "Can we place the boat north of San Cristóbal and south of the other two?"

"Of course," Viktor said. "Those are Guadalcanal and Malaita."

"Good. I should be able to scan all three for sources of assistance from that vantage point."

"What exactly are you hoping to find?" Aura asked.

It was a reasonable question, but Karin didn't have any answers.

Aura drew her aside and switched to telepathy. *"Look. If you're shooting in the dark, maybe we should try something else."*

"Like what? Even combined, our magic isn't strong enough to reach the borderworlds. I was surprised when Leif said he'd visited a couple."

"Damn it." Aura's eyes sheened with tears. *"It's Ketha. We have to get her back."*

"You think I don't know that?" Karin reverted to normal speech to conserve her magic. "I'm heading out on deck. Maybe I'll be able to pick up on a source of power before we divert too far off course."

"No one has ever heeded our call. Even before the Cataclysm, our entreaties to the gods were pro-forma. None of us actually expected them to show up."

"Taking gods out of the equation, we're not the only respectable magic-wielders in the universe," Karin said.

"Damn near. Are you counting the Fae? Or maybe Witches or mages or—"

Without waiting for Aura to come up with more reasons to take imprudent risks, Karin slipped out the door and down the stairs. Behind her, Viktor's voice droned as he informed everyone about what had happened.

Karin bit her lower lip hard enough to hurt. She wanted Ketha and the whale shifter back too, but they had a task ahead of them. The fate of Earth depended on them reaching Wrangel Island. If they could save their companions without throwing their own lives away, they'd do it. If not, Ketha would have to find her own way back.

She was resourceful, and Karin had faith in her. Apparently, more confidence than Aura was feeling. Footsteps hurried after her, and she recognized Daide and Leif's energies. "Thought you might need to augment your magic," Leif said.

"Thanks."

"What did Aura want?" As usual, Daide's question cut to the meat of things.

"She's worried about Ketha."

"We all are," Daide said. "And about the whale Shifter."

"He's old and ingenious," Leif cut in. "If there's a way out of their predicament, he'll find it. Besides, we can't hunt them down. It's not practical. There are hundreds of borderworlds. It would take years to do a methodical search, and none of us has enough magic to accomplish such a thing."

"The high Arctic isn't much better," Karin said. "As I recall, it's thousands of islands with ocean and ice between them." She pushed out a door with the men behind her and breathed in the damp air. It wasn't as semi-tropical as she'd expected, but at least she didn't risk hypothermia if she didn't don a hat, gloves, and multiple layers every time she set foot outside.

Karin turned and faced the men. "I admit I had a Joan of Arc moment when I wanted to race after Ketha. Until I realized how foolhardy it would be. And how impossible."

"Then why are we hunting for an augmentation to our magic?" Daide asked.

"Choices," Leif answered for her. "The stronger we are, the better prepared. I suspect what transpired on the bridge was only the first salvo. A test to see if they could shanghai us, split us up."

"I should have recognized that possibility." Karin balled her hands into fists, frustrated by how easy it had been for the group of malevolent spirits—or whoever they were—to catch them flat-footed.

"Who's they?" Daide asked, aiming his question at her and Leif.

"The list of possible suspects is long," Karin replied. "Hard to know where to start."

"Better not to," Leif broke in.

"You're right, of course." Her hands hurt, but she didn't release her fists. She had to be more on the ball here. Needed to think, rather than reacting.

"You two are talking in riddles." Daide sounded exasperated.

"Names hold power," Karin explained.

"Yes, if you say them, it's the same as summoning their owners—providing they're looking for an easy way to access us," Leif added.

Karin swallowed a grunt. Evil had found them without any added help on their part. They'd been sloppy, not particularly vigilant. Ketha's failed scrying attempts had provided the underpinnings for a trap, one that had snapped shut.

"This isn't the time for questions," Daide said, "but how do you determine which deities or mythological characters to focus on? Each culture has its own. The batch I grew up with were mainly passed on through oral tradition. There are Greco-Roman gods. Norse gods. Celtic gods. A whole passel of Asian gods, although the Chinese and Japanese ones are—"

"Don't mean to cut you off," Karin said, "but I know what you're getting at. Each magical creature has an affinity for a particular pantheon. For Shifters, it's always been the Celts."

"How does that work, though?" Daide persisted. "Are Diana, Artemis, and Arianrhod the same?"

"I don't actually know," Karin replied. "They're all virgin huntresses who control the moon and tides. Beyond that, I've never questioned whether they're three manifestations of the same energy." She rolled the idea around and went on. "The Cataclysm appears to have broken the bonds tying magical beings to a particular place. We found Sirens in Antarctica, Kelpies in New Zealand. Seems to me if they could show up in those locations, we have to be ready for anything."

"When we broke away from the rest of you, we ended up with Poseidon." Leif shook his head. "I've often wondered why we didn't stick with Llyr and Manandan."

"Perhaps to distance yourselves from any of them after you took up with the Witches?" Karin suggested. "Hecate is their goddess, and she's a Greek."

"She's an odd one," Leif muttered. "Didn't she rule magic, witchcraft, the night, moon, ghosts, and necromancy?"

"All of the above." Karin walked to the railing and stared at the horizon. It was developing the pearlescent gray of the coming dawn. "I'm going to open my magic and see if anything resonates."

"Before you begin, what are we looking for?" Daide asked.

It was an important question, and Karin struggled to articulate a reply. "Several things. I want to home in on whether something wicked is hovering, waiting to strike again."

"What if they are?" Daide looked so earnest, she wanted to hug him. He was doing his damnedest to understand enough to help her.

"Then we ward the ship as best we can and keep right on sailing north," Leif replied.

"What about Ketha and the whale Shifter?"

"They'll have to find their own way back," Karin murmured, not bothering to add she'd come to that conclusion before she left the bridge. "We're wasting time. Let me do a quick scan."

"I'll open a channel to my magic. Yours will reach farther that way," Leif said.

Karin licked at dry lips. Leif was strong, but linking with him before had almost killed her. What if some residue from her last run-in with him remained and acted as a magnet?

She angled her gaze at Daide. "I'll join with you, borrow power from yours."

A pleased look flared in his eyes, turning them darker still. "Of course. I'll help any way I can."

"Probably a better deployment," Leif agreed. "I'll stand ready to bail you out if things turn sour." He gripped her upper arm hard. "Be conservative. No leaping before you look."

"Got it." Annoyance intruded, but she pushed it aside. She'd never liked being ordered to do anything, but Leif was right to clarify his expectations. They couldn't afford to lose any more Shifters.

Karin extended a hand to Daide to make it easier to access his magical center. A small shiver worked its way down her spine at his touch. It would be far too easy to fall headlong into their growing connection, so she reached for his coyote and her wolf.

"Are we all ready for this?"

Her wolf howled, the coyote yipped, and Daide murmured, "Just the four of us, eh?"

Karin sent a quick blast of magic outward in a 180-degree arc. Nothing pinged back at her beyond human and animal life forms.

"If Ketha and the whale return, we should stop here long enough to hunt," her wolf suggested, longing in its voice. Karin understood. The few hunts they'd gone on after they'd beaten the Cataclysm back had been an appetizer, and the wolf longed for more. So did she.

Flanked by both men, Karin moved to the other side of the bow and repeated her action. Something unusual flagged her attention, but it was too faint to interpret.

"Try again," Daide urged, so he must have sensed it too.

"Hold up," Leif said. "If we toss too much power around, we'll alert anything magical. Let me try this time. My energy has a very different feel from yours."

"We can trade off, but if something out there is edgy, being bombarded with two types of enchantment will make it run for the hills," Karin said.

"So will a double dose of your power," Leif argued.

"All right. We'll stand guard over you." Karin extended her magical net until it extended to both men.

"You'll have to tell me what to do," Daide said.

"Follow Karin's lead and you'll be fine." Leif squared his shoulders. "I'm ready."

Karin tracked the dolphin Shifter's power as it arced from him. It stuttered the same place hers had, and she made a field decision and probed with her own magic. Light exploded, showering them with bright bits of energy. Karin reeled in her magic as fast as she could, hoping the hooks she'd dug into Leif's power would drag him back with her.

"Take what you need from me." Daide poured his own brand of energy into her working, exerting backward pressure.

Another kaleidoscopic light show bloomed, accompanied by the piquant scents of greenery and fresh-cut flowers, things she hadn't sensed in years. Maybe it was the smell, but she grew bold. Lacing compulsion in with her words, she commanded, "Show yourself."

The lights eddied and shimmered. A tall, imposing woman emerged, floating upright in the air. Black hair shot with silver fell to her bare feet, and her eyes were an ever-moving collage of imagery. A crimson robe richly embroidered with runes was sashed in black and clung to her spare frame like a second skin.

Understanding slammed into Karin, and breath whooshed from her lungs. She bowed deeply. "Ceridwen. You honor me with your presence."

"Bow all ye like. It doesna excuse ye from disturbing my peace. I had to work to find a corner of the world where I wouldna be disturbed."

"It's an honor to lay eyes on you." Leif bowed so low his forehead hit knee level.

Ceridwen skewered Daide with her unnerving eyes. "Are ye not planning to offer obeisance to me as well, Shifter?" She angled her head to one side, and Daide flinched under her examination. "Aha! Ye were one of the dark ones, and until quite recently. Do ye miss drinking blood, Vampire?"

Karin stepped between them. "Pardon, goddess. He fought on our side to defeat the Cataclysm. In doing so, he earned the right to choose a Shifter bondmate."

Ceridwen waved a dismissive hand. "The rift that broke the world is scarcely defeated. It gathers dominion even as we stand here. Soon 'twill finish what it began."

Leif straightened. "Have you come to terms with that? You're just going to stand back and let it happen?"

The goddess drew her dark brows into a thick, disapproving line. "Show a wee bit of respect. Even if your kind abandoned my pantheon, once ye owed us allegiance."

"Are the rest of you here too?" Karin asked.

"Pft. No. We went separate ways after the world broke apart."

"But it didn't," Karin protested. "It's still here."

Ceridwen shrugged. "For now. Not for much longer. Ye might follow my lead and find a pleasant environment to wait things out."

Daide stepped away from Karin. "We're sailing north to close the gateway. Once that's done—"

The goddess dissolved into laughter. Harsh, derisive laughter that set Karin's teeth on edge and made her want to slap Ceridwen. "At least we're trying," she ground out. "You gave up."

Ceridwen tossed her head until her hair floated around her. "I recognized the futility of fighting back. There have been many ages since the dawn of time. This is the fifth. Another will rise from the ashes, but none of us will live to see it."

"Aren't you immortal?" Daide asked.

She shrugged. "In a manner of speaking. All of us remain as long as there are those who believe in us. Once that goes away, we fade into memory."

Karin sliced past her fear of annoying the goddess, who'd clearly abdicated from whatever role she'd played before the Cataclysm. "Are any others with power here?"

"Do you mean in these islands?"

"Yes."

"Why? What possible difference could it make?"

Karin decided she had little to lose by laying her cards face up. "We need help."

"Aye, that ye do. Closing the gateway is an impossible task, and—"

"We have more pressing concerns," Daide spoke up.

Karin cringed. He'd interrupted a goddess. Would she strike him dead for his impertinence?

"Let's hear them." Ceridwen crooked a long-nailed finger.

"Two of our companions were shanghaied. We need to find them."

"Ha. I saw that happen and wondered if they were willing participants."

"Do you know where they are?" Leif moved closer to Ceridwen. "One is a whale Shifter, and only five remain."

"I'm not daft, young man. I recognized what he was, him and the wolf Shifter with him. They were taken to the far north but didn't remain there long."

"Where are they now?" Leif repeated his question.

"Let's see." The goddess shut her eyes for a moment. When she opened them, she said, "Come close, dolphin. Read their fate in my eyes."

Karin crowded behind Leif and stared at pictures floating across the goddess's milky corneas. Ketha cavorted with other animals in her wolf's body. The whale was swimming.

Deep within, her wolf growled and then yipped.

"Aye, your bonded one knows," Ceridwen crooned. "Ask it."

"Ketha is in the animal's world," Karin's wolf said. Surprise ricocheted through its words.

"You're certain it's Ketha and not her wolf by itself?" Karin sought to clarify the impossible.

"Of course, I'm sure." Her wolf sounded surly.

"How'd she breach the borders of a land that is closed to us?" Karin asked

"I have no idea."

"The whale is swimming our way," Leif said, "but it's thousands of miles from here."

Ceridwen blinked, and the images cleared, replaced by others.

"Can you help them return to us?" Karin clasped her hands together in supplication.

"Perhaps, but I require a boon in return."

"And that would be?" Leif asked, clearly more familiar with the way deities operated than Karin.

"Stop a while. Visit with me. 'Tis been many a long year since subjects have venerated me." She took a step closer; magic shimmered around her. "Ye can regale me with your travels. In particular, I would hear from ye." She thumped Daide's chest. "How ye were turned by blood, and how ye rose beyond it."

Alarms rang in Karin's mind, and she understood if they took Ceridwen up on her offer, they'd never leave. The goddess would ensorcel them, tempt them with things no one could resist.

Did she dare bargain?

Leif saved her the trouble of figuring it out. He folded his arms across his chest and leveled his gaze at Ceridwen. "We will remain, but not for more than three days. Take it or leave it."

"Did no one teach ye respect?" The goddess stood toe to toe with Leif.

"They did, but you would hold us here forever, and that must not happen. Even if you believe we've set off on a hopeless undertaking, nevertheless we must try." He softened his tone. "Believe in us, Goddess. Very little has gone our way. My people are almost all dead. If anyone has reason to give up, it's me. We would appreciate your assistance restoring our companions to their rightful spots by our sides, but not if it costs us our ability to travel to the gateway."

Karin sucked in a breath and held it. Leif's words had been powerful, but would they be enough?

The goddess looked away. Long moments dripped past, and Karin expected her to shimmer into nothingness at any moment. When Ceridwen finally looked up, her eyes held sadness.

"I accept your terms, sea Shifter."

Leif sliced a fingernail through the ball of his thumb and offered his hand. Ceridwen looked surprised but did the same. They clasped hands, and their blood mingled and dripped onto the deck.

"Where shall we find you?" Leif asked.

"Yon island." She pointed. "I shall do what I can about the wolf and whale Shifters. Until then." Her form took on an insubstantial aspect.

Before she vanished entirely, Karin said, "Thank you," but the goddess didn't reply.

"What just happened?" Daide asked.

"I did the only thing I could think of to force her to keep her word," Leif said. "Even she can't wiggle out from under a blood bond."

"Beyond that, it appeared she agreed to help us in exchange for a few days of our time." Daide looked from Leif to Karin.

"She did." The aftermath of too much adrenaline left Karin shaky, energized and drained at the same time. "Come on. We should let Vik know immediately."

Daide wrapped an arm around her. "How's your hand?" he asked Leif.

"Fine. I've redirected magic to close the wound."

"What's wrong?" Daide probed. "You made the best bargain you could."

"She's a goddess. Old and canny. And I bound myself to her with blood. She'll have to honor her agreement, but there's no way of guessing what will happen in the few days I promised her." Leif trotted across the broad expanse of deck and vanished inside the ship.

"What do you know about Ceridwen?" Daide steered her toward the same door. "Only thing I recall is she stirs a cauldron."

"She's a Welsh medieval goddess," Karin began, grateful to have a task to center herself. "Stronger by day, she symbolizes change, rebirth, transformation…"

18

FIGHTING DIRTY

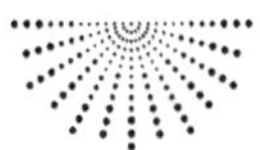

aide reached the bridge in time to hear Viktor bellow, "What do you mean she'll try to return Ketha? How'd she end up on the animals' world in the first place?"

"We don't know." Leif didn't bother to placate Viktor; he sounded tired and like he wanted to get on with finding out exactly what Ceridwen had in mind.

"There has to be more than what you've told me." Viktor advanced on Leif, green eyes narrowed and radiating danger. "Are Poseidon and Ceridwen in cahoots?"

Leif held his ground. "How would I know? Remember who your allies are." He didn't raise his voice, but his words were lined with steel.

Viktor stopped in his tracks, deflating like a balloon pricked by a pin. He dragged the heels of his hands down his face. "Jesus, mate. I'm sorry. I went a little nuts when Ketha was taken. I've moved past railing at fate, but I'm still a long way from myself."

"Understandable." Leif scanned the room and aimed his next words at the sea Shifters. "I entered into a blood pact with the goddess. It was the only way to ensure she wouldn't hold us here

227

forever." His nostrils flared. "You must talk among yourselves and select your next alpha in case I'm no longer able to fill that role."

"But why?" one of the whales asked. "You bargained for our freedom."

"Blood gives her power over me." Leif spread his fingers wide. "I'm not planning on falling prey to her machinations, but I'd be worse than a fool not to recognize how strong she is."

A female dolphin stepped forward. "We won't let her have you."

Leif leveled his gaze at her. "You will not put yourself at risk. No matter how things unfold. Is that understood?"

"Is that an order?" she countered.

"Yes. From your alpha," he replied.

"I've engaged a new course to put us in position to launch Zodiacs for Malaita Island," Juan said from where he stood next to the wheel.

"There are humans there, animals too," Karin spoke up.

"Anything magical beyond Ceridwen?" Aura asked.

Daide started to say no, but then remembered how evasive Ceridwen had been. She'd responded to Karin's question with one of her own, asking what possible difference others with magic would make.

"Well?" Aura pressed.

"Ceridwen hedged," Daide replied. "Makes me think she's hiding something."

Karin made a sound somewhere between a grunt and a snort. "The gods have never shared much of anything with those like us. No reason for them to start now."

"So we might acquire assistance from unexpected quarters," a whale said.

Leif shook his head. "Don't count on it. If there are other magic-wielders, Ceridwen established dominion over them long since. She's always had to be at the top of the heap." He cracked a bitter grin. "Wonder if she still has that kettle of hers."

"Och, and 'twas always a sore point," Zoe muttered. "Whatever you do, don't mention boiled babies."

"Huh?" Daide glanced at Karin. "That never came up in the two-minute tutorial while we walked up the stairs."

"Because I couldn't cover everything and only hit the high points," Karin retorted. "Zoe, you brought it up."

"Aye, that I did. Ceridwen was originally a Witch. One of her children, a boy, was ugly, misshapen, and dumb as a block of wood. Ceridwen hunted far and wide for a special mixture of herbs and flowers for her cauldron. The blend had to boil for a year and a day. At the end of that time, three drops would impart wisdom and poetic inspiration that she hoped would transform her son into a bard. More than three drops was a fatal poison."

Zoe stopped to take a measured breath. "To shorten the telling, the boy stirring the pot ended up with the three drops by mistake, and Ceridwen chased him for months. In some tellings, she ate him. In others, she threw him into the kettle. Regardless, one sure way to fall into her ill graces is to crack jokes about boiled babies."

"How'd she change from a Witch into a goddess?" Recco asked.

"Ready to drop anchor," Juan broke in and added, "Perhaps you could ask her since we'll be there soon."

"Not a particularly good idea, either," Karin mumbled.

Daide drew her aside. "I'm getting the impression you'd rather remain aboard *Arkady*."

"True enough, but it's not an option. The ones she hasn't met can do that, but we can't."

"Gangway in a quarter hour," Viktor said in clear dismissal.

"What do you want us to do?" Boris asked.

"Us as in the nine humans aboard?" Viktor clarified. At Boris's nod, he went on. "Up to you, but you might be safer remaining on the ship."

"Do you suppose she'd notice if we took the raft in to shore for an opportunity to wander around a bit?" Ted spoke up. "It's warmer here, and we might find greens."

"Karin indicated there were other people," Boris said. "Perhaps some might want to come with us. We still need crew."

"That we do," Juan agreed. "Our two-hour watch system is working, but we're spread quite thin."

"Some of this we'll have to play by ear," Viktor said. "Get moving so you'll be ready when the rafts are."

"A couple of you meet me down by the anchor." Juan strode out of the bridge.

"We could do that," Daide said to Karin.

"We could," she agreed and followed the path Juan had taken.

Three flights down, they walked into a colorful dawn. The sky was riddled with shades of red and pink where the sun hid behind thick clouds. Juan had most of the heavy lifting done by the time they joined him. He trained his hazel gaze on them.

"Any relationship between the Witches who parlayed with the sea Shifters and Ceridwen?"

Daide felt like someone had kicked him in the guts. He hadn't seen the connection, but of course there had to be one.

"Maybe." Karin sounded as if she'd bitten through a handful of nails.

"If there is," Daide said, "we have to make certain Leif is never alone with her."

"Easier said than done, particularly since he entered into a blood pact with her," Karin observed. "He's beyond independent, and she's a wily one. She can wave a hand and order us to leave. Or hypnotize us with those odd eyes of hers. Look." She straightened from where she'd been bent over the anchor housing. "Let's wait until we're on the island. We'll know a hell of a lot more about potential allies—and enemies—than we do right now."

"What can we do to get the rafts ready?" Daide asked. Having a concrete task was suddenly very appealing.

"If the humans remain here, we'll only need one raft since I'm certain our sea kin will swim," Juan replied. "If you want to go center a raft in the sling, be my guest."

"Fourteen will be a tight fit," Daide noted.

"I expect some of us will stay with *Arkady*," Karin said. "Moira will likely take to her vulture form." She addressed her next words to Juan. "Will it grow warmer as the day wears on?"

He shrugged. "I doubt it. We had perpetual winter in Ushuaia courtesy of the Cataclysm. From what we've encountered so far, my guess is the weather patterns altered worldwide."

"I'll meet you at the gangway," she told Daide and hurried to a nearby door.

"I'm done here. I'll help with the Zodiac," Juan said, selecting an outside staircase leading up one level.

Daide trotted after him. "What are you expecting to find here—beyond Ceridwen?"

"After South Georgia and McMurdo, I've trimmed my expectations, *amigo*." Juan flipped a raft upright, and Daide went to work arranging the sling.

"I've never been here before, so anything you know would be helpful."

Juan creased his brow as he thought. "Geographically, it reminds me of South Georgia, long and narrow with a mountainous interior. Like many of these South Pacific islands, the people were tapped as slaves for years, mostly by Australia, but by Fiji too. The island was a British protectorate for a while, but they've been a free nation since the late 1970s. If we're lucky, there will be sweet potatoes and taro root since they grow without much tending."

The clouds overhead had shaded to a dull gray, and they spat rain. Daide pulled a hood over his head.

"Good idea. It's always wet here." Juan mirrored his actions. "Used to be warm and wet. Do you have any sense about how likely we are to see Ketha again?"

"None. From the history I was taught, we can't get into the animals' borderworld, which might argue she can't leave."

"But she's in her wolf form. The animals come and go. I asked my bondmate to try to find out what happened."

"Any word yet?"

Juan shook his head.

"My coyote left on its own without any prodding from me. It's not back, either. Raft's ready."

"Let's get it into the water." Juan tossed a life jacket Daide's way.

He hung it over one arm, planning to don it later, and lowered the raft with Juan in it. Once he'd retrieved the sling, he slipped back inside, planning to find Karin and do a better job dressing for wet weather.

He stopped by his cabin first and located a light pair of waterproof pants to layer over his trousers. He tossed a few items into a duffel and wondered if they should bring medical supplies. He'd kick it around with Karin, but was almost certain she'd say yes.

A few quick steps brought him to her cabin about the time a low, keening wail reverberated through the air. Not bothering to knock, Daide pushed the door open. Karin had clapped her hand over her mouth to stifle further sounds. Leif had an arm around her, and so did Aura.

Daide fought a jab of jealousy. What was Leif doing? Had his original suppositions about the sea Shifter's interest in Karin been more accurate than he'd believed.

"Shut the door," Aura said, her voice terse.

He complied, kicking the door shut. "What happened?"

Karin dragged herself clear of both Aura and Leif. "My wolf just returned from the animals' world. In order to ensure Ketha's safety, her wolf locked her in its form. It's how they ended up where they are."

"So?" Daide didn't understand. "Her wolf can come to us, and they can reverse whatever it did."

"Doesn't work like that," Aura said, still sounding grim.

"Sorry to be dense, but you have to say more." Daide glanced from one to the other, avoiding Leif's direct stare. Maybe the sea Shifter would make a more suitable mate for Karin. They were better matched magically, and they shared a knowledge base Daide was just tapping the surface of… He shut that line of thought off fast.

"Ketha can't join us," Leif spoke slowly. "For the wolf to move out of the borderworld requires its human as a drawing factor."

"There may be a way to overturn the magic," Karin said.

"Not without severing her bond with her wolf," Aura cut in.

"Nothing we can do about any of it right now." Leif crossed the cabin in two long strides. "I'll see you on the island. I'm swimming with my kin." The door shut behind his departing form.

"Who's going to talk with Viktor?" Daide asked. It had to be done, but he didn't relish being the bearer of bad news.

"He already knows," Karin replied. "My wolf made certain to inform his raven."

Daide gripped Karin's arm. "Can you bring your bag along?"

The confusion and pain in her copper eyes cleared. "My medical supplies?" At his nod, she added, "I'd planned on it."

"Good. I'll see you in the raft. I'm going up to the bridge to do what I can for Vik." Daide wanted to hug her, but maybe it wouldn't be welcome. Not after she'd been in Leif's arms. Wishing to hell he knew more, that a Shifter rule book existed in written form, he turned on his heel and bolted from the cabin and up three flights of stairs.

He pushed onto the bridge, not sure what to expect. Viktor stood at the wheel, tight-lipped. The remainder of the bridge was empty. "We'll get her back." Daide crossed to where Viktor was.

He turned anguished green eyes on Daide. "I need her back, even if it's in wolf form. I'll figure out how to come to terms with it."

"Maybe Ceridwen can break the enchantment." Daide aimed for hopeful. Aura had said it wasn't possible, but magic seemed like a fluid entity, one which could be bent to suit the user's needs.

Viktor looked away. "If my bondmate is correct, and I have no reason to believe it's not, severing the current arrangement will also break her bond with her wolf."

"Even if it's true, why can't they simply re-bond?"

"I wish to hell I knew more. I'm so new to this, I still understand more about being a Vampire than I do being a Shifter."

"Funny, or maybe not, but I was thinking the same thing." Daide dropped a hand on Viktor's shoulder. "Hang onto hope, *amigo*. Not because it's all that's left, but because you truly believe things will work out. Are you coming ashore?"

Viktor nodded. "Yeah. A couple of the McMurdo folk will be here shortly to watch over the ship."

"See you on the Zodiac."

Viktor's mouth twisted into a bitter expression, as if he'd bitten into something sour. "Thanks for checking up on me."

"*De nada.* You'd do the same for me."

"Yeah, but it's my job."

Daide moved until he stood right in front of Viktor. "Maybe so, but you'd also do it because you care." Without waiting for Viktor to contradict him, Daide sprinted out the side door, the one leading to the warren of outdoor stairways.

Rain pelted him, and he pulled his hood up again. He needed to sit down with Karin, ask her point-blank about Leif and if she was having second thoughts. When he replayed their intimate moments, he didn't see how she could be, though. Their lovemaking had grown progressively more ardent as they'd become more familiar with one another's bodies.

Thinking about her, the muscled planes of her body with softness in all the right places, created a familiar ache in his groin. He craved her. Having her hadn't made the slightest dent in his desire. If anything, it was sharper and more urgent than it had been before he'd tasted and touched and plumbed her.

He pushed the sexual heat aside, and his worries along with it. He'd need all his faculties front and center once they landed on Malaita's beaches. Who the hell knew what they'd find. Humans might be out for blood. And it was a sure bet they'd find others with magic, otherwise Ceridwen would have denied their existence and been done with things.

He pushed his shoulders back and closed his jaws with a snap. Would the unknown magic-wielders be friend or foe? If his past experiences were any bellwether, he voted for the foe category and hoped against hope there wouldn't be any Vampires. Killing the master Vamp back in Invercargill should have been the end of them, but, according to Karin, none of the old rules applied in a post-Cataclysm world.

His reflections galvanized him into ducking back inside the ship and grabbing both rifles and the iron saber from their third-deck locker. He scrabbled for shells, filling his pockets, and hustled to the gangway. Juan was already at the bottom with the Zodiac, and it was filling quickly.

Awkward with the three weapons, he made his way down the wobbly gangway steps. Juan nodded his approval and extended a hand to take first the rifles and then the saber. "Thanks. You saved one of us a trip back inside. Thought about these while I was moving the raft into position."

"They were an afterthought for me as well," Daide said. Stepping into the raft, he settled in its bottom since the pontoons were crowded with bodies.

"The sea Shifters left a few minutes ago," Karin informed him. "If there's trouble, they'll let us know."

"Are you expecting things to blow up in our faces immediately?" Recco asked. He sat next to Zoe in the craft's stern.

"Nay. 'Tis never so convenient as all that," Zoe replied. "Ceridwen will want us well inland—where retreat to the beach will take time and planning—afore she springs any mischief."

"Am I the last?" Daide asked.

"Yup." Juan opened the throttle and eased the raft away from the ship. "If we're expecting trouble—and it appears we're at least apprehensive enough for it to be a discussion point—perhaps a few of us should remain with the raft."

"What were the humans from *Arkady* planning?" Zoe asked.

"Vik is bringing them in a second raft," Juan said. "It's why we didn't need to wait for him."

"We should leave them one of the weapons," Daide said.

"Good idea. I'll let Vik know." Juan pulled a radio out of an inner pocket.

Daide hoped it was a weatherproof model since the rain had done nothing but grow worse.

After a terse exchange, Juan dropped the radio back inside his coat. "You all heard that. They're about ten minutes behind us, and we're going to wait for them and hand off the Remington and shells. You did bring shells?" He aimed his question at Daide.

"Of course. Do we have a plan once we land?"

"I've given that a lot of thought," Aura said. "Since we're here at Ceridwen's summons, I say we wait for her rather than slogging through wet jungle tracking her with magic."

"What if she doesn't show up?" Juan asked.

"The chances of that are zero," Karin replied, sounding grim. "So far, it's all quiet from Leif. I've been expecting to hear from him. I'm sure they've shifted by now, and—" She broke off and pointed at an expanse of white sand. "Yes. There they are, milling about."

Juan whipped a pair of binoculars from another of his many pockets and held them to his face. "Drumroll, please," he announced. "Not much of a wait for the greeting party."

Daide made a grab for the binoculars and adjusted them so he could see. Ceridwen strolled toward the sea Shifters, accompanied by two women who were almost as tall as she was. Where the goddess was garbed in the robe she'd worn earlier, the two other women were naked. One had dark hair, the other blonde; their tresses fell to their knees, obscuring their bodies.

"Who the hell are they?" he muttered.

"Witches, who else?" Karin sounded rattled. "It appears Ceridwen has retreated to her roots."

"Will they know about the ones we killed?" Recco put out a hand, and Daide slapped the binoculars into them.

"Probably," Aura replied. "Nothing for it but to let this play out. Witches are clannish. For all we know, this batch hated the crew we did away with. They're as likely to thank us as slit our throats."

"That was metaphorical, right?" Juan spoke up.

"Not really. They fight dirty. The trick to dealing with them is to strike fast and hard." Aura narrowed her eyes. "If they were a threat, we'd have heard from Leif and the other sea Shifters."

"Maybe, or they might be playing along so as not to alert Ceridwen. She'd intercept any type of telepathic communication." Karin's words were as warm as a death knell.

"Let's get this over with," Juan said, mirroring Daide's thoughts.

It was always easier to face something than worry about it, and he cleared his thoughts so he'd be ready for whatever the Witch-goddess threw their way.

19

LIES, LIES, AND MORE LIES

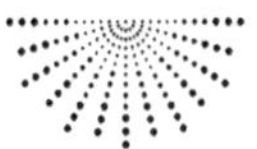

*K*arin ground her teeth. The news about Ketha had rattled her. She'd never heard of such a thing happening before, where the human half of the Shifter bond was locked within the animal.

"It was the only way to save her," Karin's wolf said, clearly front and center in her mind.

"I already figured that out." Karin's response was testier than she'd intended it to be, so she added, *"Sorry. Not much I can do about that problem until Ketha's wolf shows up. What are your thoughts about Ceridwen and the Witches?"*

"Whales and dolphins beware."

"Could you say more?" Karin chewed her lower lip, grateful no one was trying to talk with her. They'd be on the beach very soon. The goddess and her sidekicks were clearly waiting for them. So were the sea Shifters. Leif's silence was disturbing, but she might be reading too much into it.

"Because of their last bargain with Witches, the sea folk will be vulnerable."

Karin had suspected as much. Traces of the pathways linking the sea Shifters to Witch coercion remained. If they looked, this group of Witches would sense the weakness and exploit it. Witches were like that. They never missed a trick, not if they could turn it to their advantage.

The raft's bottom scraped against sand. Juan took his time exiting the craft, anchor rope in hand, and yet more time locating a place to secure the Zodiac. He was stalling, waiting for Viktor's Zodiac to appear. No one else said much of anything. Ceridwen stood about fifty feet away and presumably would be privy to words flowing among them.

"Need help?" Leif ran lightly toward them, his bare feet leaving footprints in the wet sand.

"We're good," Juan said. "Waiting for Vik."

The dolphin Shifter's eyes widened as he took in the weapons scattered across the bottom of the raft.

Karin wanted to at least warn him to be careful, but he probably already knew.

Ceridwen closed from behind him. "Guns?" She snorted. "What an archaic concept. Are ye planning a wild pig hunt?"

"Now there's an idea." Juan smiled disarmingly and extended a hand. "Fresh meat would be welcome. I'm Juan Torres."

Ceridwen scanned the raft's occupants while ignoring Juan's outstretched hand. "Fascinating. Three of ye were Vampires, and for a considerable span of time, it appears."

The sound of the second Zodiac's motor grew louder. Karin spoke over it. "A fourth is in the approaching boat." She clambered over the pontoon and slogged through surf and onto the beach. "They came through when we needed them."

"Vampires?" The goddess curled her lip in disdain. "Whatever would ye require them for?" A cunning gleam lit her image-laden eyes. "Och, I understand. They're exceptional bedwarmers. Indefatigable, as I recall, and the addition of blood ritual adds spice—"

"If you and I are going to get along"—Karin took a chance and spoke over the goddess—"I'm requesting you quit right there. The

Cataclysm was formed by a Shifter spell gone bad, but Vamps were part of it too, which explains why we required their particular brand of magic."

"What kind of Shifter spell?" the blonde Witch asked from a few feet away.

"They never did command enough magic to be more than be a nuisance," the dark-haired Witch muttered.

Karin ignored the insult. "A small, secret group of Shifters decided to do away with Vampirism once and for all, but they needed something to entice their prey. They lied and told Vamps they'd teach them how to change form. Had the spell run to its conclusion, it would have wiped Vampirism off the map. Some would have reverted to human; those found worthy of the bond would have turned into Shifters."

"Fascinating." Ceridwen leaned forward. "First time I've heard details. What happened?"

"A Vamp caught wind of the deception and bedded a Shifter. It derailed the spell and broke the world."

Ceridwen fisted a hand and punched the air in front of her. "I knew it had to be something like that. It held the stink of loose magic gone awry."

"Sure and we looked for a way out." Zoe moved until she stood next to Karin. "Our seer, the one in the animals' borderworld, finally broke through. 'Tis when we finally learned the truth about what had occurred. When she told us we'd have to join forces with Vampires to fight the perverted enchantment, we all rebelled, but in the end, we agreed. 'Twas that or die from bad air and water."

"Ye do realize ye altered evil's grip on Earth, but ye dinna come close to doing away with it?" The goddess raised one dark brow.

"Aye, that point has become abundantly clear." Zoe tossed her head.

Aura joined them. "We're here at your behest," she told Ceridwen, pointedly ignoring the Witches. "What did you have in mind when you issued the invitation?"

Karin cringed. She wouldn't have been quite so direct, but it might be best to get to the crux of the goddess's motives, at least the surface lies meant to disarm their concerns. Behind her, the second raft's hull scraped as it ran aground. The muted hum of voices meant weapons were changing hands.

Viktor's unmistakable energy approached quickly. He planted himself between Karin and the goddess. "Can you get my wife back?"

Karin edged sideways to keep an eye on Ceridwen—and the Witches.

"Ye're not one to waste time, raven Shifter." The goddess raked him from head to toe with her gaze, and probably with her magic as well.

"Can you?" Viktor asked again. "Because if you can't, there's no point in us being here."

Power flared from the goddess, creating a glowing nimbus around her. "I struck a bargain—sealed with blood. Ye have no choice but to remain."

"I'm not who you bargained with." Viktor's expression hardened. "Part of that agreement was you'd attempt to—"

"Attempt, not guarantee," she cut in, her voice harsh and grating. "What era did ye spring from to show so little veneration for those like me?"

"One that didn't believe in magic." He skinned his lips back from his teeth.

"Ye were a Vampire. How could ye not be steeped in the dark arts?"

"Easy. I was human first. Never warmed to the transformation."

Leif squared his shoulders and faced the goddess and Witches. "What of my whale?"

"It's swimming." Ceridwen shrugged. "Ye'll see it again someday."

"Not good enough," Leif countered. "We need him with us when we attack the gateway. In truth"—he took a step closer—"we could use your help as well. When did you decide to check out? To abandon the world you once cared for?"

"Enough." The blonde Witch snapped her fingers beneath Leif's nose. Magic sparked, but it bounced off the dolphin Shifter.

He sneered. "You'll have to do better than that if you expect to immobilize me."

Surprise flickered from the Witch, but she snuffed it out fast.

Ceridwen shot a pointed glance her way, and the Witch shuffled backward. "Take this as a sign of my goodwill," she purred, and power surged around her, crackling with strength. The air filled with the scents of herbs and young animals.

Daide dropped his hands onto Karin's shoulders from behind, enveloping her in determination. "What's Ceridwen up to?" He spoke low into her ear.

His nearness warmed her; so did his concern. "Not sure." Cautiously, she opened a magical channel between them. Better to have it and not need it than the other way around.

Colors flashed and flared around Ceridwen. While the goddess spun her casting, Karin extended her magic until all the Shifters were loosely linked. One of the Witches figured out what she was up to. Her shrewd dark eyes traveled from Ceridwen to the Shifters and back again as if she were gauging the impact of disturbing the goddess.

Karin could imagine the gist of her thoughts. If she bothered Ceridwen mid-spell, the goddess would be furious. If she kept her mouth shut and the Shifters' amalgamated magic spawned chaos, it would be her fault.

Karin locked gazes with her. *"We mean no harm."*

"Like you'd tell me if you did?" the Witch retorted.

Karin scented the air and the magical vortex swirling around the goddess. If she was any judge, whatever Ceridwen was up to would manifest soon. No one, not even a god, could maintain that output of magic for very long. She debated asking the Witch who else was on this island, but it might be a long reply—or none at all. Worse, more than short bursts of telepathy might divert Ceridwen's single-minded concentration. If a spell that powerful boomeranged, it could blow up the island.

Magic pressed in from all sides, and Karin's muscles tensed. Something was approaching. Had Ceridwen summoned another god or perhaps a demon? She'd said what she was creating was a sign of her goodwill. Had she been lying? Could she even lie outright? Karin didn't believe so. The gods could hedge and lie by omission and inference, but—

Wind whistled out of nowhere, echoing as the vortex pulsed. Motion caught her attention as Viktor shouldered the Remington. His green eyes held a wild, unfocused edge. *"Viktor!"* She aimed her mind voice directly at him. *"Not yet."*

A raven cawed ferociously in her mind, and she took it as an affirmation he wouldn't shoot the goddess. At least not yet. Silver-and-iron-laced bullets might harm her, but Karin had a feeling they'd only piss her off.

Her mouth flooded with blood from where she'd bitten through her lip. Magic pummeled her from all sides, the air so crammed with it, every breath got its hooks into her. If this kept up much longer, she'd pass into the netherworld where magic ruled. She'd been there before, but she'd controlled the spell. Who knew what an involuntary jaunt might mean?

Her wolf howled and howled again. The sound ripped through her. Daide held on, digging his fingers into her upper arms. The pressure had a stabilizing effect, and she started weaving their combined power into a ward. Karin had moved beyond giving a rat's ass if it offended the goddess.

Ceridwen swayed with the cadence of her spell. She was chanting now, and the cavalcade of imagery across her milky corneas spun so fast it was nothing but a blur.

Her bondmate's howls gave way to one word. *"Ketha."*

Karin sent magic spilling outward, seeking her friend. She whooped and jerked from Daide's grip just as a black-and-gray timber wolf sprang from the jaws of the vortex, landing on the wet sand.

Viktor dropped the rifle and fell to his knees. The wolf bounded into his arms, licking his face for all it was worth. He murmured in German, smoothing Ketha's fur, and she whined softly, nuzzling his neck.

The oppressive noise, electric buzzing, and mélange of scents ceased abruptly. Ceridwen shook her hair back over her shoulders. "Enough for one day. Now that you're convinced of my intentions, follow me."

The Witches flanked her. Power buzzed as they communicated telepathically, no doubt telling the goddess everything, including how Viktor had her in his rifle's sights.

Karin hurried to where Viktor cradled the wolf in his arms and placed a hand on the animal's head. If this problem had a cure, she'd find it, no matter how difficult or how long it took."

"I agreed to this," Ketha's voice eddied in her mind. *"It was the only way. We didn't have time to come up with anything else."*

"Offer my thanks to your bondmate for keeping you safe," Karin said formally. Something like a cattle prod sent an electric shock up her spine. She shot upright to find Ceridwen staring at her.

"Ye can visit with your returned companion once we reach our destination."

Karin bowed low. "Thank you, goddess, for the return of our seer."

Ceridwen grunted. "At least one of ye has manners." Turning on her heel, she set a quick pace angling away from the soggy beach.

"I suppose we have to follow her," Aura muttered.

"Her and those crappy Witches," Zoe said.

Viktor rolled to his feet and nodded at Boris, who'd come close enough to snap up the Remington. Ketha walked by Viktor's side, her tail pluming. Karin knew how she felt. Escaping the animals' borderworld had been the first step. Ketha wouldn't rest until she'd figured out how to separate from her bondmate, and Karin vowed to stand by her every step of the way.

Before they could do anything, though, they had to placate Ceridwen and get off this island.

As if he'd been inside her head, Daide said, "We'll figure this out. At least we have Ketha back. Any idea what we're walking into?"

"None. Ceridwen's had a lot of years to carve out a comfortable niche, though. And this is her turf."

Karin took a quick minute to turn around. No one remained with either raft. Four humans from *Arkady* ranged up and down the beach. Boris, Ted, and two of the McMurdo scientists. They had the iron saber and the Remington. From time to time, they bent and picked up something, probably varieties of shellfish.

If she'd been correct about sensing humans on this island, they weren't in any rush to show themselves.

Recco gripped the Ruger guide gun; no one had told him to leave it behind. It was as prepared as they were likely to be. Leif joined them, walking shoulder to shoulder with Daide. "Other Witches are here." He said it as if he was talking about house cats or the weather.

"How many?" Daide asked.

Leif shrugged. "I haven't wanted to deploy too much power. When Ceridwen was deep into her spell, I used it as a smokescreen and dug a little."

"Find anything else?" Karin chewed her sore lower lip.

"Odd energies."

"Odd, how?" Karin pressed. Who knew how long a walk it was until the trap snapped shut?

"I checked twice. Felt like the faerie folk to me, along with some Fae."

"'Twould make sense," Zoe said from behind them. "When Ceridwen was at the height of her power, both ranged far and wide in Wales."

"Whose side are they on?" Daide cut to the chase.

"Their own," Karin replied tersely.

"Aye. If they came with Ceridwen, 'twas to further their agenda, not hers," Zoe agreed.

A mist rose around them, silver and frothy. Scents accompanied it, sharp and piquant. Karin was trying to identify them when Zoe said, "Och, 'tis a recreation of the Highlands. Heather and gorse and fog so thick you can taste the sea."

Karin gave the swirling silver vapor an experimental shove. It pushed back, but she'd expected as much. "We've entered a one-way channel," she said, not caring if Ceridwen overheard her. "Don't fight it, or goddess only knows what will happen."

"We'll see about that." Daide's words were fierce, but when he made a staunch effort to turn around, the mist formed an impenetrable shield holding him facing forward. Coyote outrage burst from him in a long, pealing series of high-pitched yips.

"It's illusion," Aura growled. She halted and stared into the gray fog eddying above them.

"Nay!" Zoe caught her arm. "Sure and I've never seen aught like this afore, but I've read the legends. Leif mentioned Fae. This has the feel of their workings. They could help us—unless we alienate them by ripping through their enchantment with magic of our own."

Aura exhaled noisily and plodded forward. "Damned if we do, eh?" she muttered.

"Aye, and damned if we don't." Zoe patted her shoulder. "Wonder what Ceridwen promised to get them to build this pathway for her?"

"It won't be long before we come to the end of it," Karin said. "Maybe then we'll know more. An illusion like this is a real power hog."

"Is it possible it's here to confuse us?" Daide asked. "Make us think we can't find our way back to the beach?"

Karin wished it were so simple. Should she give voice to what she was nearly sure was happening?

One of the whales spoke up, saving her the trouble of deciding. "By Poseidon's balls, this isn't just a path, it's a gateway."

"Huh?" Viktor asked. "To where?"

Next to him, Ketha howled mournfully. Being reduced to telepathy for speech must be damn near killing her.

"A borderworld," Karin said dully. "Somehow, and I have no idea precisely how Ceridwen finessed it, she persuaded the Fae to create a channel between Malaita Island and one of the other worlds. She's used this path so often, it opens—and closes—at her bidding, without much magical fanfare."

"If it didn't, we would have hesitated before following her," Aura cut in. "Had second thoughts and like as not fought back if she exerted force."

"No shit." Karin spat the words, knowing full well if the goddess had cast obvious magic to conjure a magical, glowing, fog-shrouded portal, none of them would have set foot in it. Not willingly, anyway.

"If we're entering another dimension, how will we return?" Recco asked.

"Good question, *amigo*, but this isn't *Star Wars*. Should we be paying attention so we can recreate whatever this is?" Daide spread his arms wide. When he lowered them, he draped one across Karin's shoulders.

He felt good. Solid. She was tempted to lean her head against his shoulder and go with the flow, but it was what the goddess wanted. "Watch it." Karin raised her voice to make certain everyone would hear. "Compulsion is woven in with this working. So's something to make us not care."

Deep within, her wolf snarled, a harsh, bitten-off growl that chilled Karin, iced her to her soul. *"What is it?"*

"No matter how hard I argue, you must not shift."

"Why?" Karin had been considering shifting as an option to get them out of this mess.

After another strangled-sounding whuff, the wolf managed,

"Ketha. Example. She knows." A pain-filled shriek followed the words, as if her bondmate had walked over hot knives.

Panic twisted Karin's guts into a knot. In two centuries, she'd never known her bondmate to fight for words. "Ketha." Karin didn't bother with telepathy. The wolf would hear her either way. A brisk woof confirmed her assumption, and she asked. "What kind of example are you? Why would my wolf warn me against shifting?"

A series of woofs rose from the wolf as if it approved of her questions.

"Christ!" Ketha replied, sounding disgusted. *"If you hadn't asked, I'd never have thought to say anything. Ceridwen dissected the mechanism holding me within my bondmate's form. It's why she took so long returning me. I wondered what she was about when she shot power through my wolf over and over, but that must be it."*

"Excellent news," Viktor broke in. "Means she can undo it."

"Och, and 'twould be a two-way street," burst from Zoe.

Understanding swept through Karin in a hot, bitter tide, and she sent warm thanks inward to her bondmate for the effort it had expended alerting her. "Listen up, everyone." The mist wouldn't allow her to turn around, so she spoke as loud as she could. "You must not shift, no matter what happens."

"Why not?" a whale yelled from a long way behind her.

"The goddess knows how to lock you into your animal form. Once you're no longer human, her blood bond with Leif is nullified."

"Nullified won't matter if we're forced into being whales on dry land," the whale Shifter retorted. "Our weight will crush our lungs."

Karin moved forward, the only direction available, until she was next to Ketha's wolf. "Are you all right? My bondmate paid a price for warning me."

Ketha's laughter, grim and bitter, flickered through Karin's mind. *"Yeah, my wolf is fine, but only because I'm standing between it and the goddess. Her power is impressive, but not bottomless."*

The mist thinned, and the smells of the Highlands intensified. "Wherever we're going, we're almost there," Karin yelled.

"Be vigilant," Leif cut in. "She'll engage every trick she can to get you to trust her, but if you fall for any of them, she'll be able to use you to bind all of us here."

"If it's a borderworld, aren't we stuck until she releases us?" Juan broke a long silence.

"Not necessarily," Aura said. "We could—"

"Quiet!" Karin ordered before Aura launched into an explanation. She had no idea what was in the mountain cat Shifter's mind, neither did she want to offer the goddess any advantage.

"Thanks," Aura mumbled. "Complacency is woven in with all her other spells. Loosens the tongue—and my wits."

Speaking of wits, Karin made a grab for hers. So long as one of them was alert, maybe they could avert disaster and find a way back to *Arkady*.

20

FAE, FAERIES, AND WITCHES

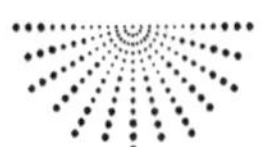

*D*aide had dropped into surveillance mode back on the beach. Watching closely and gathering data had been a hallmark of his professional life. It shunted him to a detached, observational place where he could think clearly. While he hadn't expected Ceridwen to deal fairly with them, he'd been shocked and infuriated when Karin made it clear the goddess planned to use their bond animals to snare them.

We don't know that. Not for sure, he reminded himself, yet the evidence pointed in that direction, and he'd be an idiot not to prepare for it.

He focused his attention inward. *"You caught all that, right?"*

"Of course. I hear everything you say." The coyote's tone was testy.

"Sorry. Didn't mean to imply otherwise." Daide sent warm thoughts along with his words.

"I'm sorry as well. The best strategy is for all of us bond animals to retreat to our borderworld."

"Why?" Daide wanted his coyote next to him in the upcoming battle.

"You're weak." The coyote didn't mince words. *"I can force you to shift. Once you do, you'll be vulnerable to the bleak one's power."*

Daide winced at the truth in his bondmate's statement. *"I can see why you'd want to retreat, but what about the women's animals? They've all been bonded for a long time."*

"Doesn't matter. If we're pressed, we can force you into our form." The coyote yipped, harsh and strident. *"I will tell the others, the older, wiser ones. If they agree, we will depart for a while."*

The gray fog around Daide had thinned to almost nothing, but he still couldn't see through to what lay on the other side. Karin had run ahead to where Ketha trotted at Viktor's side. He lengthened his stride to catch up with her, intent on communicating what just happened.

He slotted a hand beneath her elbow. She looked askance at him and flashed a quick half-smile. "Good work," she said. "Having the animals leave is so obvious, I should have come up with it immediately."

"See? Complacency has us in its crosshairs." Aura gritted her teeth. "We have to question everything."

"Why didn't it impact me?" Daide raised one eyebrow.

"Maybe she wants the men lively and chipper," Karin muttered. "Not lost in zombie-land."

"I don't care for the sound of that," Daide said.

"Yeah, me either," Viktor cut in. "Do you have any idea why she shanghaied us?"

Aura shrugged. "She was bored? No men to fuck? No one to venerate her?"

"Aye, there 'tis." Zoe jumped on Aura's ideas. "Not the fucking, but the goddess worship."

"You might be onto something." Karin creased her forehead in thought. "When we raised her from *Arkady's* deck she said something like 'All of us remain as long as there are those who believe in us. Once that goes away, we fade into memory.'"

"If that's true, she must be hanging on by her fingernails," Aura mumbled.

"Look!" Daide pointed at a vista spreading before them.

The mists had parted, revealing something he'd only seen on television and the Internet. A green, verdant land marked with hills, barrows, and standing stones stretched to the horizon. Bubbling brooks fed a good-sized lake rimmed with tussock grass. It wasn't raining here. Fluffy clouds swam across a deep-blue sky. On a nearby hill, a castle stood, complete with turrets, spires, an outer wall, and towers. When he stared closer, he even saw a moat and a drawbridge.

"Christ on a fucking crutch," Viktor snarled, followed by a flood of cursing in German.

"Do you suppose a dragon guards the moat?" Juan asked.

Daide narrowed his eyes, attempting to alter his perspective, but the landscape didn't change. "I'm not sure what I'm asking here, but is any of this real?"

"Real enough," Karin replied, but even she sounded unsettled, and it gave him pause.

Zoe snorted laughter. "If 'twas truly real, 'twould be pouring. Apparently, Ceridwen built this world to her specifications, and she was as sick of the rain in the U.K. as the rest of us who've lived in that part of the world."

"Now there's a conversational opener," Aura said acidly.

"Aye, sure and I'll keep it in mind," Zoe retorted.

The creak of wood and iron chains reached Daide as the drawbridge moved slowly downward. He closed his other arm around Karin, wanting to shield her from whatever would emerge from the castle courtyard.

She leaned into him before breaking loose. "Thanks for the thought, but we may have to fight. I can't do that if you're hanging onto me."

"Can you find your way back?"

She shot an incredulous look his way. "You're not telling me to leave?"

He gripped her upper arm. "I want you to be safe. More than anything."

The forbidding lines of her face softened. "Doesn't work that way."

"I will protect you. Even if you don't want me to." He leveled his gaze at her.

Karin laid a hand over his before extricating herself from his grip. "How about we protect each other? And everyone else too. Before today is over, we'll need everyone's gifts and wish we had access to more still."

"Damn it, Karin. I love you."

"I love you too."

Emotion clotted in his throat. She'd finally said the words out loud, and he wanted to pick her up and bully his way through whatever spell held them captive on this alien world. Once they were free, he'd spirit her back to *Arkady*, strip her naked, and lick and kiss every single inch of her—

Ketha barked once, shrill and sharp. A warning bark that ripped Daide's attention back to the drawbridge. Garbed in the same robes as before, Ceridwen walked across it, taking her time. Five Witches flanked her, two on each side and one behind. He recognized the ones from earlier, but they'd been joined by one more blonde and two redheads. All of them were naked except for colorful lengths of fabric sashed about their waists. Perky, bouncing breasts fed into the sexual fantasy he'd spun about Karin.

Daide pushed desire aside, bolting it behind what he hoped were bombproof gates. Karin loved him. No matter what seduction gambits the Witches offered, he'd rise above all of them. Leif may have succumbed, but he wouldn't. He hadn't been a willing participant in a trade offering sex for power. It might be enough to allow him to resist if a Witch—or god forbid, Ceridwen—came on to him.

Leif had said there were other Witches. Daide was relieved to see only five. After their last go round in Invercargill, he'd expected more. The intoxicating scent of the Highlands intensified, and the ground stretching between them and the castle undulated.

Daide squeezed his eyes shut, certain he was hallucinating. When he opened them, the earth was still heaving, rippling, and creating swells where flat ground had been a few moments before.

"What the fuck is going on?" Recco lurched toward the unsettled ground until Zoe latched a hand around his arm.

"We're about to meet the Fae and faeries who constructed the channel from Malaita to here," Zoe said.

Questions bounced from one side of Daide's head to the other. He knew less than nothing about faeries, and the sum total of his knowledge about Fae was they came in dark and light varieties. The air took on a glistening, shimmery aspect, and beings popped from a series of gleaming gateways. They all glowed as if lit from within, but that was where any similarities ended. A dozen looked the way he'd always envisioned faeries, tiny with quick-beating wings and wands and clouds of hair in pastel shades.

Next to them, regal beings stood. They had to be Fae. All were robed in gold and silver with jeweled circlets around their brows. Mostly blond, a few had silver hair. Perhaps twenty of them in all, but Daide was too fascinated by the alluring magic billowing from them to do anything as prosaic as counting. He felt as if he'd dropped into one of the old tales he'd read as a boy; disbelief vied with wanting the moment to last forever.

One of the silver-haired Fae floated to where Ceridwen had finished crossing the drawbridge. "Have ye lost your mind?" he demanded, anger evident in his straight back and the taut set of his shoulders.

"I've brought visitors," she responded. Power oozed from her, thick as honey and as sweet and cloying.

"Aye. Nothing wrong with my eyes," the Fae shot back. "Ye had no business bringing humans here. 'Tis our world. Ye promised sanctuary once we built the illusions for ye."

"So that was the inducement," Karin muttered.

"Och, but they're not humans." Ceridwen lingered over the last word. "I've brought Shifters. Magical beings to entertain us."

A low, hissing growl emerged from the other Fae, and they turned as a group to face the plain where Daide and the others stood. "Why do they hate us?" Daide asked Zoe, assuming if anyone had the answer, it would be her.

"Not us, but the Celts. They trapped the Fae within the hills and barrows of the Highlands."

"The distrust is more by inference," Karin added. "We allied ourselves with the Celts, and the friend of my enemy—"

"Is my enemy as well," Aura finished for her.

"Ceridwen must have freed them," Daide mumbled, thinking out loud.

"Aye, and made promises in exchange for labor," Zoe agreed.

"Have your sanctuary," Ceridwen was saying. "I tell ye, they're merely visiting."

"Send. Them. Back." The Fae stood tall and crossed his arms over his chest.

"Or?" Ceridwen skewered him with the full force of her gaze.

"What we created, we can destroy," the Fae replied.

"But it's your home too." Ceridwen smiled with a mouthful of teeth and zero warmth.

"We created a separate pathway out of here."

"Aye, and 'tis sealed to ye," a second Fae who'd joined the first spoke up. This one was female with clouds of fair hair.

The buzzing of wings grew louder as the faeries closed on Daide and the others from *Arkady*. Their faces were screwed into fury, and small arrows rained from bows clutched in their chubby, upraised hands.

Karin stepped between the flying horde and the rest of them. Raising her hands, she spoke in old Gaelic. Daide would have asked his bondmate to translate, but true to his word, the coyote was gone.

"She's greeting them," Aura said. "Telling them what an honor it is to lay eyes on them." A surprised look flickered across her green eyes as Karin continued speaking. "I had no idea she'd met them as a young woman."

"Aye, or that she frolicked with them at moonlight revelries," Zoe added. "I was about to join her, but she's doing fine without my assistance."

Daide curled his hands into fists, battling helplessness. He wanted to do something, goddammit, not stand around useless as tits on a boar. Without taking the time to engage in his usual pro-and-con arguments, he strode to Karin's side. Facing the faeries, he bowed low and was greeted by hisses and a flood of the small arrows. They stung where they pricked him.

A faery with green hair and bare breasts flew so close Daide felt the breeze from her wings. "Ye're mine now," the cherub announced.

"No. I'm hers." Daide pointed at Karin.

"Not anymore." The faery sounded pleased with herself. "I shot ye." She flew in figure eights around Daide's head, whooping and squealing until the temptation to swat her out of the sky was hard to resist.

KARIN HAD BEEN SPLITTING her awareness between the tableau playing out between Ceridwen and the two Fae and the faeries—until Daide showed up. Reluctantly, she turned her full attention on the faeries and tried for a compromise. "He doesn't know your customs," she informed the faeries, sticking with Old Gaelic.

"He's mine," the green faery crowed. "Mine. I shot him fair and square."

"Doesn't count if he didn't understand what it meant." A crimson-haired male faced off in front of her.

"Does too count."

"What can I trade for him?" Karin tried another tack. Faeries loved to bargain.

"English," Daide said, sounding nonplussed. "If you're deciding my future, I need to understand."

The green-haired faery fluttered to the ground, her miniature bare feet leaving prints in the damp grass. "How is it ye doona speak the one true tongue?" she inquired and placed her hands on her hips as she stared up at him.

"Because I'm from Argentina."

"Where is that?" the faery demanded.

"Across the shiny sea and many leagues to the south." Karin switched to English.

"How many?" The faery tilted her chin up.

"Ten thousand," Daide answered.

The cherub held up both hands. "Here's ten," she announced. "How many is a thousand?"

Daide crouched so he was nearer her level. He flashed his fingers open and closed and said, "If you do this ten times, you've counted to a hundred. Nine hundred more, and you've reached a thousand..."

The faery shook her head. "It's enough. Ye come from too far away. I relinquish my claim."

Karin squatted too and extended her fingers. "Thank you, fair one. I promise I shall take good care of our mate."

The faery batted her wings until she was airborne and planted three kisses on Karin. One on each cheek and another on her forehead. Karin grinned despite herself. "Let's hope you don't have the dryad's gift."

"Even if I do, and I'm not admitting one way or the other"—the faery waggled a finger beneath Karin's nose—"I've barely made a dent in your two hundred sixty-eight years." Laughing merrily, the cherub joined her companions.

Karin rolled her eyes. If Daide had any doubt about her precise age, the faery had just obliterated them.

"Thank God that's done with," Viktor said. "Things are heating up down there." He angled his gaze to Ceridwen, the Witches, and the Fae. Where there'd been two Fae, now ten lined up against the goddess and her minions.

Karin aimed her words at the faery who'd claimed Daide. Lowering her voice to a conspiratorial whisper, she said, "I hear there's another way out of here back to the island. Do you know where we can find it, so I can keep our mate out of harm's way?"

The faeries buzzed and hummed as they debated her question. Karin recalled they had their own, secret language, separate from Gaelic. Magic swelled from where the Fae stood toe to toe with Ceridwen, along with raised voices. One of the Fae made a slicing motion, and lightning forked from his fingertips. A Witch shrieked and clutched at her throat before crumpling to the ground. The other Witches turned as a unit and dashed across the drawbridge.

"Goddess save me from Witches," Aura growled. "Faithless sluts, one and all."

Karin snorted derisively. Ceridwen had been a Witch. If anyone was familiar with their perfidy, it should be her. Chains creaked and clanked as the Witches raised the drawbridge.

"Serves her right," Aura said.

"Aye, better to trust a scorpion than a Witch," Zoe chimed in.

Karin eyed the faeries. She needed them to hurry while Ceridwen was engaged in arguing with the Fae. Fury blasted from the goddess until the air around her developed a reddish tinge. In this mood, she was likely to mow down everything in her path.

The crimson-haired cherub who'd told Greenie she couldn't have Daide whistled once, shrill and piercing. Karin took it as a summons and said, "Follow him."

"How do we know where he's taking us?" Aura ran after her.

"Do you want to remain here?" Karin countered.

She had to project confidence, but was she leading them into something worse than where they were? She'd forgotten how childlike the faery folk were until Greenie had begun counting on her fingers. Fae were the ones who delighted in playing nasty tricks on humans. Faeries had never harbored any fondness for the Fae, but put up with them in exchange for protection from the Celts and others.

Sick of their internecine squabbling, the Celts had taken the lot of them—Fae and faeries alike—and imprisoned them beneath the Highlands early in the twentieth century.

Mist rose, eddying about them, and the Scottish Highlands disappeared. So did the argument unfolding in front of the castle. The trip back to the beach was fast. Far quicker than their journey the other way.

"Where'd they go?" Daide turned in a 360-degree circle, clearly hunting for the faery folk.

"Back to their dens on the borderworld, if I were to guess," Zoe said.

"If I were them, I'd hide too," Aura spoke up.

"Ceridwen will be furious." Leif emerged from the silver-gray fog with everyone else strung out behind him. "We need to get out of here."

"What about your missing whale Shifter?" Karin asked.

"He's closer to Wrangel Island than we are," Leif replied. "When I hear from him, and I will, I'll wish him good hunting and tell him we'll meet him in good time."

Karin did a nose count. All of them were accounted for except for Viktor and Ketha. She fumed, anxious to leave. "What happened to Vik and Ketha?"

"They were right behind me," a whale replied.

Karin bit back a tart rejoinder that she'd asked where they were now, not a few minutes before. Shitting all over the whale, who'd only tried to be helpful, would be a mistake.

"Come on," Juan said. "We can pile into the Zodiac and motor back to this part of the beach so we're in position to leave when they show up."

"We'll shift and be in the sea," Leif said. Power shimmered as the dolphins and whales ran into the surf. Once they got deep enough, their magic grew brighter still as they took their sea forms.

Karin ran back along the wet sand, calling for Ketha and Viktor with her mind voice, but neither answered. The second Zodiac was still in place, so the humans from *Arkady* hadn't left yet, either.

"There you are," Boris cried and bolted their way from the other direction.

"Jesus. You fucking vanished," one of the McMurdo scientists yelled. "We searched and searched when we were ready to leave. Just to make certain you were all right…" His voice ran down, and he gulped air.

Karin glanced in the rafts. A smallish wild pig had been dressed out and lay in the bottom of one along with bunches of taro root and sweet potatoes. If she hadn't been so worried about Ketha, she'd have been thrilled at the prospect of food that wasn't powdered, freeze-dried, or canned.

"Go back to the boat," Juan ordered.

"What are you going to do?" Boris asked and readied the raft with the pig.

"Wait for Vik and Ketha," Juan replied. "Now get moving."

"Do you need this?" Boris raised the Remington.

"I don't believe so," Juan replied.

"You'll tell us everything, right?" The McMurdo scientist had finally caught his breath and vaulted over the pontoons and into the Zodiac.

"Most of it," Karin reassured him and watched the raft edge away from the beach. Once it hit deeper water, Boris swung the bow around and opened the throttle.

"Damn it. This is my fault," Daide said. "If I hadn't played Sir Galahad, we'd have been able to focus on Ceridwen and the Fae." He looked away. "I'm sorry. I wanted to save you, not make your job harder."

"In a backhanded way, you did save me and all the rest of us." Karin climbed into the Zodiac. She'd been touched when Daide crouched next to the faery, explaining arithmetic to her.

"How?" He slogged through surf with the anchor rope, tossing it over the stern before he scrambled aboard.

"When the green faery claimed you and you were kind to her, they began to trust us, not view us as Ceridwen's guests. They've always hated her and her kind. And they abhor Witches."

"Everyone hates Witches," Zoe muttered.

"If it weren't for the Cataclysm, I doubt Ceridwen could have enticed the Fae or the faeries to do anything for her," Aura said.

"Isn't that the truth." Karin shielded her eyes with a hand and scanned the beach. "I don't understand how Vik and Ketha could have gotten stuck in that pathway. It was short, clear of illusions."

"If they're not back shortly, I'm going after them," Daide announced.

Karin was impressed. Even though his magic was raw and untrained, one step up from an unknown element, he had spirit and determination—and courage.

They floated about a hundred feet offshore, staring through rain that hadn't let up. The day was mostly spent, which meant they'd spent hours on the borderworld, but time passed differently on each of them. The sea Shifters' energy fanned out fifty yards behind them as everyone waited.

"There's Vik!" Juan pulled the ignition rope. The engine sputtered to life, and they headed for shore.

"Ketha!" Karin screeched in mind speech.

"Coming!" echoed back to her.

Rather than facing them, Viktor hovered near the spot they'd emerged from the faeries' track to the borderworld. Juan ran the raft onto the sand and leapt over the pontoons.

"Where's Ketha? For that fact, where were you?" Juan yelled.

Before Juan reached Viktor, he opened his arms and Ketha, a very human Ketha, burst out of the ether. Rather than appearing relieved and happy, she grabbed one of his outstretched arms and dragged him toward the raft.

"Hurry," she cried.

Karin didn't have to dig too deep to understand why. "Join your power to mine," she exhorted and threw her magical well wide open.

Sure enough, malevolent energy hurtled toward Viktor, Ketha, and Juan, but from the direction of the original portal. Made sense. The Fae had told Ceridwen their escape route was closed to her.

The goddess burst into sight, her long silver-and-black hair curling around her head like a nest of snakes. She pelted toward them but then switched course. Clearly intent on catching them before they reached the ship, she headed for the sea.

Ketha threw herself into the raft, followed by Juan and Viktor, who gunned the engine. For a moment, the propeller churned up sand from the ocean bottom, but it freed itself, and they sped toward *Arkady*.

"How'd you manage the transformation?" Karin eyed Ketha.

"Long story," Ketha replied. "If we're lucky, we'll live long enough for you to hear it."

Karin gathered power from the others. She let it simmer and build until she couldn't hold it any longer. Ceridwen skimmed over the surface of the sea, intent on doing maximum damage. Wind skinned her hair back from her face, and her timeless features were twisted into a rictus of rage and hate.

"Leif!" Karin called.

"We're here."

"Keep the path between the Zodiac and Ceridwen clear."

"Understood." His telepathy was tense. Perhaps he and the sea Shifters had something in mind, but didn't want to tip off the goddess.

Unsure if she commanded enough magic to dissuade the angry goddess, Karin took careful aim and hit Ceridwen with the full force of their combined power. The goddess shrieked in pain and outrage. Rather than holding her position on the water's surface, she sank a few feet, floundering.

Waves from whale tails hitting the ocean's surface crashed over her, but she fought past them.

"Damn! She'll track us to the ends of the earth," Daide muttered as Ceridwen clawed her way upright once again.

Lightning bolts shot from the goddess's upraised hands, striking all around the raft. One of the pontoons sizzled as it deflated.

"We can lose two or three more air cells," Juan said tersely. "More than that, and we'll sink."

"I'll ward the raft," Ketha screeched.

Karin had established battle lines and couldn't back down now, so she gathered another volley and heaved it at the goddess. Without Ketha's magic, they were weaker, but Ceridwen still flinched when she was hit. Four more salvos and they'd nearly reached *Arkady*. Fortunately, the water was smooth. If Ceridwen had known more about ships, she'd have sent twenty-foot swells to make it impossible for them to board.

Undeterred, the goddess was closing on them. Karin gauged the distance, wanting the goddess closer before she struck again. She hadn't conserved their combined magic, and not much was left. Leif and his pod were moving nearer. If Ceridwen was aware of them, she didn't give any indication.

Boris stood at the bottom of the gangway. Not bothering with anything as elegant as tying off the raft, he held onto the rope while the Zodiac emptied until Karin, Daide, Viktor, and Ketha were the only ones left aboard.

"Hurry," Boris urged.

"One more blast." Karin was so wiped out she could barely talk. She marshaled her power, wishing her wolf was there to help.

"We'll take over," Leif said. *"Move inside to safety."*

"Thanks, but I have to see this through," she told him.

The air thrummed with another brand of power, and she groaned. Now wasn't the time to deal with another enemy. Not when she was about to fall on her face. Daide wrapped an arm around her shoulders, feeding power into her. "We've got this," he said.

"If not," she mumbled, "you're the best thing that's ever happened to me."

"Ye canna run from us," a menacing voice boomed out of nowhere.

Karin whipped her head around in time to see a phalanx of Fae advancing on Ceridwen. "Och, leave off. Ye're my subjects." The goddess waved a dismissive hand, but the Fae kept right on coming, skimming the water's surface.

"In your dreams, Witch." A blond Fae hastened toward her.

"Aye, we'd never offer allegiance to one such as ye." A second Fae joined the first. "At best, 'twas a convenient alliance. No more. No less."

The silver-haired Fae who'd first accosted Ceridwen floated a few feet from Karin. "Go." He jerked his chin northward. "Close the gateway. Restore our world."

"How'd you know about that?" Karin sputtered, too exhausted to find a subtle way to ask.

"Ceridwen has a big mouth. Now, go."

Behind him, Ceridwen shrieked epithets in old Gaelic.

The Fae kept talking. "Doona hold concerns about her. She'll bother ye no more."

"Are you certain?" Leif had swum close to the Fae.

"Aye, sea Shifter. We doona require your aid, but we thank ye for offering."

The air turned liquid, electric with power. Shades of silver, violet, and blue turned into a horseshoe-shaped opening that inhaled the Fae and Ceridwen along with them. It vanished so fast, Karin blinked. Had she hallucinated the whole thing?

Daide tightened his hold on her. Good thing because she slumped against him as consciousness fled.

HOPE WINS AFTER ALL

$\mathcal{D}$aide swept an arm beneath Karin's knees and carried her up the gangway. Viktor and Ketha trudged behind him. Juan and Recco were bent over the anchor housing. "I assume we're leaving?" Juan glanced over one shoulder at Viktor.

"Good guess, mate. I'll hit the bridge and set a course."

"I'll join you once I'm done here. Zoe and Aura are whipping up something for a late supper," Juan said and got to his feet.

"Maybe an hour before it's ready?" Daide asked.

"Yeah. Is she all right?" Recco strode to where Daide stood with Karin cradled protectively against his chest.

"She will be." He offered a crooked smile. "She's like a damn Valkyrie. Doesn't know when to quit."

The air thickened with the salty tang of sea Shifter power, and Leif shimmered into view, water sluicing off his naked form. "Dinner in an hour?"

Juan nodded. "Love to see all of you inside."

"We'll be there. I'll let everyone know." Striding to the rail, Leif dove cleanly back into the ocean.

Karin wriggled in Daide's arms and cracked one eye open. "Maybe I only wanted a free ride up the stairs."

"Using me for my muscles, eh?"

"I'll never tell." She opened the other eye and winked.

Daide pulled her closer. "You can use me for whatever you need, wench. I'll always be here for you."

"Best watch it. I'll hold you to those words." Love flowed from her in waves, and he soaked them up.

Ketha stopped where they stood and smoothed tangles away from Karin's face. "Thanks for waiting for us."

"No thanks needed. No. Wait. Scratch that. I want to hear everything. How you ended up back in your human form. Where your wolf is. Why it took you so long to show up on the beach. All of it."

Ketha laughed. "Same old pushy bitch. Except not quite so old anymore. That faery did a number on you."

"Maybe it's a good thing she stopped at three kisses?" Karin arched a brow, and Daide noticed they'd darkened, as had her hair. Where it had been snow-white, now thick dark streaks ran through it, and it was continuing to alter as she lay in his arms.

"How about a shower and clean clothes?" Daide asked. She'd always be beautiful to him, but words like that required privacy.

Karin thrashed in his arms. "Put me down. I can walk."

He shook his head. "Not a chance. You'll get a thorough examination, madam physician. Otherwise, I wouldn't be practicing good medicine."

"Be sure not to miss anything." Recco punched him in the arm and took off for the inside of the ship.

"See you at supper, mates." Viktor started up an outside stairwell with Ketha beside him.

Daide shouldered through a door and down the corridor leading to their cabins. They'd been spending most of their time in hers since it was larger, so he stopped in front of it and sent a jot of magic to open the door. He walked through and kicked it shut. Anticipation about being alone with her kindled a fire that raced along his nerves like quicksilver. Laying her gently on her bed, he ran his hands down the length of her body.

She made a sound suspiciously like a giggle. "If you're going to palpate for injuries, the place you should be looking is where my magic lives."

It was too good an invitation to bypass, so he dropped a hand atop the vee between her legs. "You must mean here."

The giggle turned into a laugh, and she gripped his hand with hers, holding it in place. "Since we're showering anyway…"

"We may as well make it worthwhile?" He levered her boots off.

"Something like that." She flipped a clump of hair in front of her eyes, studying the darkening strands. "Son of a bitch. Ketha wasn't kidding."

"I love you. What color your hair is doesn't matter a whit."

"Someone taught you well."

"I mean it. I'm enchanted and humbled by your mind and your power and your courage. Those are the things that last. The things that matter."

He stripped off her socks and went to work unzipping her jacket and sliding it off her shoulders. "What was that about faeries and dryads and kisses?" Bending, he kissed her nose.

Karin pushed to a sit and tugged her top over her head, followed by the layer beneath. "Sure you want to talk?" Her copper eyes glittered with heat, and her naked breasts, tipped with pebbled nipples, stole his breath.

Before he fell into the lust-laden magic they created together, he said, "Quick version, please."

"Fair enough. Kisses from tree spirits—dryads—make you younger. No one's certain how many years one kiss equals. It seems to vary depending on how strong magic runs in the one who kissed you."

"So, the green faery was a dryad?"

"No, but they're related in the magical world. Sheesh. Before I know it, you'll be asking for magical genealogy charts." She glanced at his still fully clad form. "Get those clothes off. Now."

"Is that a technique you used on your patients?" He grinned.

"Nope. They were naked by the time I got into the exam room. At least the part I needed to look at was. Clothes?"

Daide toed his boots off, followed by damp socks. He hated to put even a centimeter more distance between them, but in the interest of expediency, he stood to zip out of his upper layers. Heat from Karin's gaze seared him as he removed enough clothes to bare his torso.

"By the goddess, you are one gorgeous man," she murmured and went to work unfastening her pants and sliding them down her legs.

Daide pushed his trousers aside, working them over a full-blown erection. His shorts followed them, and he stepped out of the pile of clothing.

"You're stunning." He let his gaze slide from her face to her shoulders to her breasts and downward.

"Are you only planning on looking?"

"Maybe. What'd you have in mind?" he teased through a throat thick with lust and need.

She ran her fingertips down her breasts and stomach until she reached the spiky mat of tight curls guarding the entrance to her body. Daide's heart slammed against his chest, and his breath came fast. His cock grew even harder, although he didn't see how it was possible.

When she began to rub herself, arching her back and moaning softly, he surged between her legs, pushing them wider apart. Batting her hand aside, he replaced it with his cock, swirling the head in long circles from her nub to the opening to her vault and back again.

Her fluids mingled with his as they tantalized one another. He longed to plunge into her, deep and fast. She wanted him there, but they were building desire. She lifted her legs, wrapping them around his hips, and pinched her nipples. Beneath him, her hips bucked and her body writhed.

"What do you want?"

He almost couldn't get the words out. He also didn't know if he could resist until she begged him to fuck her. They'd played this game before. Sometimes, she folded first. Sometimes, he did. His cock shuddered in the hand he had wrapped around it.

Her back arched, and she thrashed her head from side to side. "Now." She groaned low in her throat.

Stoked he'd won, Daide said, "What was that?"

Karin's copper eyes flashed open, liquid with wanting him. "Do me."

He wasn't strong enough to resist, or maybe she'd seeded her words with compulsion. Didn't matter. He lined his cock up with her hot, slick opening and buried himself to the hilt. Heat surrounded him, tantalizing, enticing, impossible to withstand. He withdrew and heaved into her, every nerve alive with the contact.

Her vault quivered around him, and he slid his hands beneath her, cupping her ass and increasing the contact between her nub and his pubic bone. She ground herself against him; he pushed back, and she dissolved around him in a flood of heat. Her nipples were copper points and her chest and stomach mottled with a lovely rose color.

Daide breathed, holding himself back until he made her come again. Once her spasms faded, he dragged his cock from her body and barked, "Turn over."

"Damn if you didn't sound like a coyote." Karin smiled, soft and languid, and flipped onto her hands and knees.

The view of her sex framed with dark curls heated his blood to molten, and he thrust back into her. Reaching around, he found her swollen nub and rubbed it fast and hard while he plumbed her. He lost himself in sex with Karin. Transported to another plane where sensation ruled, he gave in to it.

His balls snugged against his body, more than ready, but he rode a ragged edge until her vault gripped his shaft in rhythmic contractions. One more thrust and he let go of any semblance of control. Semen jetted from him in pleasure so intense he never wanted it to end.

Gasping, panting, grinding their bodies together, they ended up in a tangled heap on her bunk. "I'd love to stay here for hours, have another go at that hunky body of yours"—Karin wriggled out from under him—"but if we don't hurry, we'll miss dinner."

"I could make us plates." He stroked her back, loving the feel of her skin beneath his fingertips.

"But then we'd miss hearing about Ketha. We'd find out eventually, but aren't you curious?"

He was. Events had happened so fast once they'd spied Viktor on the beach, he hadn't had an opportunity to think about much beyond first surviving and then making love with the woman who meant everything to him.

"Come on." She jumped off the bunk and crooked a finger. "If you hurry, I'll wash your back."

"Now, there's an offer." He hurried after her into the bathroom. "How about my dick? Will you wash it too?"

"Don't tempt me, or we'll never get to dinner." She flipped on the taps.

He closed the bathroom door to keep both heat and water inside.

A QUARTER HOUR LATER, they trotted smartly out of her cabin and down one flight to the dining room. Karin's hair, almost completely black now, streamed down her back in damp curls. He held the door for her and followed her into a room rich with the scents of food and drink.

"There you are." Ketha rose and smiled. "Grab yourself some supper. I was waiting for you before I began."

Daide shouldered into the galley, holding the door for Karin. She loaded plates for them, and he poured glasses of a credible red wine.

They'd located several crates of Cabernet, Shiraz, and Merlot in Invercargill, wines that tended to improve with age.

"Ready?" she asked. "It was good of Ketha to wait for us, since we're late."

"We're like newlyweds," he countered. "Everyone expects us to be late."

Karin snorted and grinned. "Is that a roundabout marriage proposal?"

He set the wine down and crossed to her, placing his hands on her shoulders. "No, it's a direct one. Will you be my wife?"

Her grin shaded to a shy smile. "I'd be honored. We need to get moving, though. I bet everyone's dog tired and just waiting on Ketha before they fall on their faces in bed."

"Sure. I'll grab us some utensils."

Happiness swept through him until his heart cracked open with it. Karin, his Karin, had promised herself to him. He dropped forks and knives into a pocket, snapped up the wine, and followed her to a pair of empty seats along one wall.

Ketha straightened from where she'd been lounging against Viktor. "I'll be as brief as I can," she began. "Everyone is tired, including me. When I watched Karin bartering with the green faery, it reminded me how much faeries love a good bargain. I conferred with my wolf, and we came up with a plan."

She took a sip from a glass Viktor offered her and went on. "Our plan was contingent upon the faery folk wanting to return to the Highlands. It's always been their home, and they'd never have ended up Ceridwen's minions under normal circumstances.

"Turns out that hunch was spot on. They jumped at a chance to go home. Not only did it get them out from beneath Ceridwen's thumb, but the Fae as well. The reason the faeries knew the location of the second pathway was because they were the ones who constructed it."

Ketha rolled her eyes. "The Fae are famous for taking full credit when what they actually did was act as overseers."

"You're wandering, sweetie," Aura said from a seat nearby.

"So I am. In truth, it's a wonder I can string two words together, let alone something as complex as what happened."

"I'm not trying to steal your thunder"—Viktor cast a loving glance at his wife—"but I was there too."

"Be my guest." Ketha smiled warmly.

"We had the makings of a bargain." Viktor picked up the threads of their tale. "The faeries wanted to return home, and we needed a way to separate Ketha from her wolf." He paused, glancing around the room.

From nearby, Juan muttered, "Sailors love spinning yarns."

Aura elbowed him to silence.

"I'm not as clear on this next part," Viktor went on, "so any of you Shifters jump in if I blunder too badly. Turns out the borderworlds are arranged in something akin to spokes on a wheel. Once you're on one, it's not nearly as challenging to get to another as it is to return to Earth."

"My wolf agreed to escort the faeries back to the Highlands," Ketha said. "Provided they stopped in the animals' world long enough for my wolf's magic to recharge."

"But it had to be free to do so," Viktor chimed in.

Daide inhaled briskly. "Smooth," he whispered to Karin.

"It would certainly have motivated the faeries to lure Ketha from the wolf," Karin agreed, also in whispers.

"We've pretty much covered it," Ketha said. "Turns out the faeries were able to break the enchantment holding me within my wolf easily. Didn't even have to think about it, which makes me believe such a thing has happened before.

"Once I was human, my wolf herded them through a gateway of its making to the animals' borderworld."

"Has it returned?" Karin asked.

Ketha tilted her head, probably scanning the place her bondmate dwelt. "No. Wait a minute. It just did. Hang on."

Wonder blossomed on Ketha's face. Daide leaned forward,

anxious to hear how the wolf's journey had gone.

"Exceptional news!" Ketha danced a jig in place. "They're back in the Highlands, but they offered to help when we face off against the dark portal on Wrangel Island."

"Wonderful news!" Leif fist pumped the air from where he and the other sea Shifters sat.

"How will they reach us?" Viktor asked.

"How else?" Ketha smiled broadly. "The bond animals will escort them when the time comes."

Daide's coyote yipped, announcing its return and sounding pleased with itself. *"You did a good day's work,"* Daide told it.

"Not only good. Inspired. Superb. Dazzling." More yips punctuated its series of superlatives, and Daide laughed.

"What?" Karin turned her gaze his way.

"My bondmate feeling its oats."

"My wolf's singing the same song, but they deserve all the glory on this one."

"They do, indeed." Daide laced his fingers with hers.

"Anyway, it's why we didn't show up with the rest of you," Viktor said.

"Sorry we didn't tell anyone, but things unfolded fast," Ketha added. "One of those last minute, desperate gambits where once you've grabbed greased lightning, all you can do is hang on."

"I'm headed back to the bridge," Viktor said. "I hate leaving it unmanned. Same watch schedule is in play, so I'm planning on one of you joining me as soon as you're done eating."

"That would be me." Ted waved from the far side of the room. "I'm on it, captain, sir."

"You'd better be." Viktor narrowed his green eyes. "Keelhauled at dawn if you fail to show." Laughing, he strode out of the room.

"Bet he would have liked sailing in the 1800s," Daide said.

"You have no idea," Juan called from one table over. He directed his next words at Ted. "Never found any humans on Malaita, huh?"

Ted shook his head. "If they were there, they remained well-hidden."

"Probably in their best interest. I bet Ceridwen shanghaied a few before they went to ground," Aura spoke up.

Daide turned to his meal, eating methodically. The fresh pork was succulent, and he savored it. "What do you think?" he asked Karin.

"About?" She drained what was left of her wine.

He shrugged. "Any of this."

Her expression turned serious. "We got lucky. Again."

"It's happened a lot."

"It has," she agreed. "So many times, I'm beginning to think we have help."

"What do you mean?"

"Earth wants to survive, to endure. When we beat back the Cataclysm in Ushuaia, it must have noticed, as did whatever gods and goddesses are tasked with caring for it."

Daide rolled the idea around. He'd never been religious or even particularly spiritual, but the concept of divine assistance—no matter how it manifested—was appealing to him.

He tapped her glass. "Would you like a refill?"

"Sure, if we're going to be here for a while."

Daide got up and took both empty glasses into the galley. Recco was there, doing the same thing.

"You're looking unusually happy," Recco observed.

"Karin agreed to be my wife." When he said wife, joy bubbled through him in a hot rush of delight.

Recco broke into a grin. "But that's wonderful news." Before Daide could intuit what he was about—or stop him—Recco dashed to the galley door, swung it open, and yelled, "Hey, everyone. Daide and Karin are getting married."

Hoots, whistles, and shouts of congratulations and best wishes rose from the dining room. Daide's face heated. "Christ, Recco. You didn't have to do that."

"Oh but I did. By the time you got around to letting people know, we'd have been sailing past Russia. I get to be best man, right?"

"Who else?"

"That's my *amigo*." Recco sauntered out of the galley, almost as pleased with himself as Daide's coyote had been.

Daide grabbed the wine tumblers and pushed through a crowd that had gathered around Karin. Catching her eye, he mouthed, "Sorry."

"It's okay," she mouthed back.

He passed her glass to Aura, who gave it to Ketha, who handed it off to Karin.

"A toast!" Ketha raised her clear, fine voice.

"Toast. Toast," echoed through the room.

"Here's to Karin and Daide," she said. "And to all of us. As long as we believe in ourselves, we'll prevail."

"Karin and Daide," and "Prevail," traveled around the room as glasses clinked together.

"We may not drink"—Leif was on his feet—"but we share your sentiments. I have nothing but hope for our future."

Applause rose, swelling through the dining room.

Daide gazed at the sea of merry faces. These people were his family. The tribe he'd been cheated out of as a child. And Karin would be his wife. No matter what the future held, he'd make the most out of every single moment.

Karin joined him, standing by his side. "You're looking thoughtful."

"Just happy, darling."

"Me too." Karin tapped her glass against his. "To us."

"To us." He drank deep right before he wrapped her in his arms and kissed her.

~

You've reached the end of *Betrayed*. Please leave a review. Doesn't have to be fancy. A line or two will do. Reviews help so much. Thanks in advance!

Read on for a sample of *Redeemed*, last of the Bitter Harvest books.

ABOUT THE AUTHOR

Ann Gimpel is a USA Today bestselling author. A lifelong aficionado of the unusual, she began writing speculative fiction a few years ago. Since then her short fiction has appeared in several webzines and anthologies. Her longer books run the gamut from urban fantasy to paranormal romance. Once upon a time, she nurtured clients. Now she nurtures dark, gritty fantasy stories that push hard against reality. When she's not writing, she's in the backcountry getting down and dirty with her camera. She's published over fifty books to date, with several more planned for 2018 and beyond. A husband, grown children, grandchildren, and wolf hybrids round out her family.

Keep up with her at www.anngimpel.com or http://anngimpel.blogspot.com

If you enjoyed what you read, get in line for special offers and pre-release special reads. Newsletter Signup!

BOOK DESCRIPTION: REDEEMED

Alpha for the few remaining Sea Shifters, Leif's been playing fast and loose with death for years. Plagued by a poisoned ocean, treacherous sea gods, illness, and bad bargains, he's learned to roll with the punches. Setting ancient antagonism aside, he joined a group of land Shifters, pledging both his help and that of his pod.

A vulture shifter, Moira embraces her life on *Arkady*, a small polar cruise ship. She faces problems—ones that may kill all of them—but at least she's free. No more sneaking around hiding from Vampires and not having enough magic to shift, courtesy of short rations and toxic air.

Leif yearns for Moira, but Sea Shifters don't mate with their land cousins—ever. Besides, they have their hands more than full. Not only is there no time for love, there's barely space to breathe as they wend their way through a volatile obstacle field littered with demons, hostile gods, and ancient horrors bent on their destruction.

REDEEMED, CHAPTER ONE MAGIC UNDER FIRE

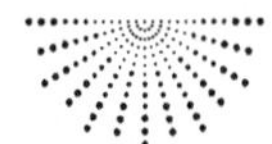

*L*eif swam lazily next to *Arkady* with his dolphin pod spread around him. He could have moved twice as fast as the ship, and then some, but he couldn't keep up that pace all day, every day. Four of five whales paddled nearby. They'd rendezvous with the fifth when they were closer to the Siberian Arctic. Two-and-a-half days had passed since Ketha's transformation back to her human body, and they'd just crossed the equator. Normally temperate, the central Pacific was far colder than he'd expected, but it went along with the weather as a whole being chilly and unsettled. Nothing like Antarctica or New Zealand, but different enough for him to suspect Earth would never fully recover from the Cataclysm's onslaught.

Times like these, though, when he cut cleanly through water that was clear of toxins the Cataclysm had pumped out for ten years, the simple joy of movement filled him with hope.

And then reality intruded.

They were so few. Fourteen sea Shifters. Fifteen land Shifters. Nine humans. An unknown number of the fair folk had promised their aid, but who knew how long their memories were? Poseidon, god of the seas, had ordered him and his sea Shifters to halt their northward journey. Leif defied him, a decision cutting them off from a potential source of aid. He slapped the water with his tail. In his secret places he was nearly certain his liege had switched sides, but he had no proof. Only instincts honed over his five-hundred-year lifespan.

Leif had stopped trusting Poseidon long before his surprising edict to turn the ship around. The sea god, along with his consort, Amphitrite, had stood by and done nothing while nearly all the sea Shifters died, victims of poison spread by the Cataclysm. Nothing much worse than the song of a dying whale. Multiply it by a thousand or more, and his soul was permanently riddled by sorrow.

Perhaps whale dirges were the lynchpin that had been Poseidon's undoing. If he'd opened his magic to darkness, evil may have blotted out the haunting laments.

Leif was nearly dead himself when the land Shifters aboard *Arkady* had reached out to them. They had no idea how desperate their plight was, but once they found out, two veterinarians had worked like hell to cure the parasitic infestations choking the life out of them.

Leif exhaled in a shower of salty water. He felt better than he had in a very long time. The crippling pain that used to soak up all his attention was gone, and he felt like cavorting in the surf. If he'd been in his human body, he'd have shaken his head. Being in the water at all was an indulgence, but he'd herded his group into the sea to take a break from endless battle planning going on throughout the ship.

They were at least two weeks away from Wrangel Island, their objective in the Arctic, but he agreed with Viktor, *Arkady*'s captain and a raven Shifter, that they needed to leverage every advantage they could.

"What do you think will happen next?" Lewis, another dolphin Shifter, swam close enough to talk. Their vocal chords were close enough to human, they didn't require telepathy to communicate.

"After we reach the Arctic?" Leif focused one laterally placed eye on the other dolphin.

Lewis sputtered around a mouthful of briny foam. "You actually believe whoever's masterminding this isn't going to strike long before we get that far?"

Leif's small, artificial window of peace frittered to nothing. "If the ship's journey to date is any indication, I'm surprised we haven't run into some other atrocity. What's it been? Nearly three days since we left the Solomons. Three days of harmony, tranquility, goodwill—"

Lewis batted him with a flipper. "Spare me your cynicism." He shook himself and water flew everywhere. "I'm apprehensive. I like to have backup plans."

"Rather difficult to finesse when we have no idea what will crawl out of the ether next," Leif countered. "I don't expect any more Kelpies, but beyond that, the field is wide open. For all we know, the Cataclysm spawned some new breed of monster we have yet to meet."

"Aren't you Mr. Cheerful?"

"You're who brought this up," Leif countered. "You are right about one thing, though. Playtime is over. Spread the word, and I'll see everyone back on the ship."

"If I spend too much more time in my human body, my skin will shrivel," Lewis groused.

Leif didn't answer. Hundreds of years ago, sea Shifters and their land kin had played by the same rules. Land Shifters always had an easier time hiding their dual natures, though. Far simpler to conceal themselves in a forest, turn into a wolf—or a coyote or a bird—and join a local pack than it was to swim into the ocean and shift in plain sight of boats and fishermen. The rise of the church meant his kind faced persecution. Torture. Hangings. Burnings. So they'd taken to the sea for greater and greater chunks of time.

When the Cataclysm hit, many hadn't shifted to their human forms in decades. And then there'd been their ill-conceived bargain with Witches to augment their magic in exchange for stud service. Who'd have guessed it would turn into a death sentence for the Shifter unlucky enough to be picked as a sperm donor?

"I thought you said play time was over." Lewis prodded him with a flipper.

"It is. I got lost thinking about how we ended up like we did."

"Not much value in that. It's a bloody miracle any of us survived." Magic turned the air around him shimmery and iridescent.

Leif summoned his own power and shifted right along with the other dolphin. They ended up dripping water on the broad quarterdeck. Viktor kept the surface clean enough to eat from, but he'd never complained about their sloppy transition from sea to ship. The damp, marine air glowed and pulsed as the other dolphins and four whales shucked their ocean-going bodies.

All the dolphins had names beginning with "L" for convenience. Their dolphin names would have been impossible for humans to pronounce. At the time Leif proposed that small concession—since they had a better chance passing for human if they didn't lapse into sea speech—the whales told him to stuff it. A corner of his mouth twitched. That little episode occurred at least a century before the Cataclysm. He'd always thought it strange none of the whales wrestled him for the alpha position, but none ever had.

"We were hoping for a few more hours in the water." One of the whales pushed past a pair of dolphins and planted himself in front of Leif. He stood at least six inches taller and was impossibly broad. Fair hair was already beginning to curl as water dribbled down his body.

"Maybe we can catch some surf time tomorrow." Leif latched onto the whale's dark-eyed gaze, staring him down.

The whale twisted water out of his thick locks. "This has the stink of a meeting. Where and when?"

"You're assuming the one taking place round the clock on the bridge ended," Lynda broke in. Another dolphin shifter, dark hair eddied around her framing high cheekbones and violet eyes.

"The bridge is as good a guess as any location," Leif concurred. "Say half an hour?"

The whoosh of wings caught the edges of his sensitive hearing. He looked up in time to see a good-sized, black vulture swoop from one of the upper decks. It dive-bombed their group, cawing like a mad thing.

Lynda snorted laughter. "She gets to play. It's good for us."

The vulture made another pass, flying low and veering off scant moments before impact. Leif made a grab for her, but she tossed her tail as she made a ninety-degree turn. "Moira!" he called.

Who else? she countered in telepathy. Unlike him, her vocal chords weren't conducive to speech when in shifted form.

Ketha bustled out one of Arkady's many doors and onto the broad, flat deck that took up a portion of Deck Three. Dark hair shot with red and gold hung loose to her waist and she shielded golden eyes—a throwback to her wolf bondmate—with one hand.

"Goddammit, Moira! Get down here."

Still shrieking with delight, the vulture obligingly veered hard left and headed straight for Ketha, landing on her shoulder and digging in her talons for balance.

"Ouch!" Ketha thumped the flat of her hand across the bird's talons, but Moira didn't uncurl so much as one of them.

Sensing a story lay behind Moira's appearance, Leif aimed his words at Ketha. "What happened?"

"We were deep in tarot spreads, or the other women were. I was working with my glass trying to get it to give me something but the past."

The tarot was contradictory, Moira said, clacking her beak a time or two for emphasis.

Ketha angled her head and eyed the vulture. "Patience never was your strong suit."

Never claimed it was. Another beak clack.

"Anyway," Ketha went on. "One minute Moira was at a table with Tessa and Zoe. The next, she jumped to her feet and bolted from the room. Right after that, I heard her yapping in vulturese, so I'm betting her clothes are in a heap on the floor somewhere."

"When what you're doing isn't working," the vulture inserted in a sing-songy tone, *"do something different. Sitting on my ass for another three hours begging the cards to cooperate isn't my style."*

Leif smothered the smile that hovered in the background. He liked Moira. She was outspoken and gutsy. Beyond that, her acres of dark hair and liquid dark eyes were lovely, as was her delicately-boned face sprinkled with a dusting of freckles. Her lush lips were always rosy, and she had a way of licking them that made him want to replace her tongue with his own. Medium height, he'd spent surreptitious moments taking in the curves of her breasts, hips, and ass. She had a fine ass, high and round and made for a man's hands to grab.

His cock began to swell, and he cut off his line of thought fast before his arousal became noticeable. He angled a cascade of his long, thick hair to provide better cover for his nether regions, but no amount of hair could conceal a full-blown erection if his unruly appendage got totally out of hand.

Ketha drew her mouth into a frustrated line and made another effort to displace Moira's talons, with no success. "How about making dinner? Is that more up your alley? It would free Aura and Zoe to waste more time with the cards."

"Sure. I'll lose myself in the galley. Probably for the best. Maybe the cards decided to cooperate after my negative energy left." Still cawing, the bird launched hard off Ketha's shoulder.

She stifled a yelp and rubbed the place the bird had been. "How can a bunch of feathers and hollow bones weigh so much?"

"I heard that!" Moira punctuated her words with a hearty squawk.

One of the whales approached Ketha and inclined his head. "I am not as skilled at scrying as the whale waiting for us in northern waters, but what happened when you tried to coax a vision out of your mirror?"

Ketha drew her brows together and exhaled raggedly. "It's different than before the wickedness that yanked me and the whale Shifter out of *Arkady*. Then I ran up against a blank wall. This time, when I tell the mirror to show me the future, something that's already happened pops up."

"Not good," the whale muttered. "It's a time inversion."

Alarms tolled in Leif's mind and he switched to his third eye, the one allowing him to view the world from a psychic perspective. Glowing bisecting lines formed. Some vertical. Some horizontal. Ley lines, they carried the world's magic, concentrating it in key locations. He stared at them, assessing their integrity, and bit back a startled exclamation.

"What?" Several voices, including Ketha's, asked almost in unison.

He held up both hands, fingers spread in front of him. "Do. Not. Panic." Leveling his gaze at everyone, he repeated, "Do. Not. Panic," knowing the injunction was aimed at himself as much as anyone.

Lynda rolled her eyes and made come along motions with one hand. "Fine, oh fearless alpha. What did you find?"

He shuffled through palatable explanations, but couldn't come up with anything, so he stood straighter and muttered, "Magic is weaker here than it was last time I looked at the ley lines."

"How much weaker?" Ketha demanded, followed by, "Never mind. I'll look myself."

"I don't know how much weaker," Leif answered, but she'd shut her earth eyes and was deep in her own assessment. "These things aren't easy to quantify. It's a sure bet, though, that if our magic isn't as effective, neither is theirs."

"I wouldn't be so sure about that," one of the whales said

"I agree," Lewis broke in. "I never believed the dark ones sucked power from the same trough as us."

"You make us sound like pigs," Leif protested.

Lewis shrugged. "Sorry if my analogy offended you. It's not the point, though. If something has laid siege to our power, you can bet an ugly surprise is right around the corner."

Ketha opened worried-looking eyes. "You won't remember Rowana. She died before we met up with you, but she discovered small chewed places at the convergence of some of the lines. It looks to me like whatever started that destruction is still working on it, and it's finally had an effect on how much magic is available for us to tap into."

"Probably why the tarot wasn't cooperating. Or your scrying," Leif said.

"Exactly what I'm thinking. Crap. We do not need anything extra to stumble over. I'm going back upstairs. I'll tell the women to conserve their efforts. Only one tarot spread at a time. While they're working on that, I won't do anything with my glass."

Leif nodded and glanced around the grim-faced group. "A staged approach may help. If there's only so much magic, rationing it so it only has to do one thing at a time should maximize its utility."

Ketha ran across the deck, vanishing inside the ship.

"Turns out us coming out of the water when we did was prophetic," a whale muttered.

"Yeah. I wish I could disagree, but it rings true for me," Lynda said. "I'm headed for the clothes locker. See all of you upstairs."

"Before you leave," Leif called after her, "have any of you checked the ley lines lately? Last time I looked might have been New Zealand, and I'd like a more recent comparison if anyone has one."

I drew power from them during the Kelpie attack," a whale said. "Didn't notice much of anything other than the augmentation I needed was there for me."

Leif glanced at a sea of shaking heads. "Thanks for trying. See you in a little bit."

It wasn't cold, but a shudder tracked down his body, his earlier arousal forgotten. Who could be sabotaging their magic? The damaged ley lines couldn't be accidental, and whoever was behind the problem had clearly been chipping away at them for a long time. Months from the sound of things.

He hunkered beneath a bulkhead near the door his pod had taken as they filed inside. Five minutes would give him time to think. Besides, with everyone crowded around their clothing locker, he wouldn't be able to get close to it anyway.

He catalogued what he knew, which wasn't very damn much. The assault on their magic had been subtle, so subtle it had mostly gone unnoticed until today. Rowana, the eagle Shifter he'd never met, may have sounded a muted alarm, but the other women hadn't been worried enough to check the lines regularly.

Balling one hand into a fist, he brought it down on the deck. Pain had a stabilizing effect, forcing him to narrow his roiling thoughts. The way they were bouncing around, he'd never make sense of anything, let alone figure out what he needed to do next.

One fact smacked him squarely between the eyes. It would take a hell of a lot of magic to erode the ley lines—even more to do it so delicately as to go mostly unnoticed.

Could Poseidon possibly be behind such an undertaking?

Leif played the possibility through his mind, but it seemed remote. Poseidon had magic to burn, but it was an in-your-face type of power. The sea god had never been a cloak and dagger type, mostly because he lacked the incisive elegance required for subterfuge. When he'd gone after the Kelpie, staff swinging, it epitomized his approach to most everything. Hit fast and hard and ask the tough questions afterward.

If there was an afterward.

If not Poseidon, then who?

Leif slumped lower, resting his naked butt cheeks on the deck. When the answer came, it was so obvious he cringed. Amphitrite. In her own way, she was far stronger than her consort, and her magic held both grace and refinement. She was more than capable of taking a chink here and there out of the ley lines, siphoning power to augment her own while leaving less for Shifters and others who relied on the lines for their ability.

Soon after Leif entered into the bargain with the Witches that was almost his undoing, Poseidon had cuffed him, cussed him out, and called him things far worse than stupid without offering to cast even one spell to aid the sea Shifters so they could nullify their pact.

Furious at his liege's patronizing condescension, Leif had hurtled out of the royal dwelling intent on losing himself in the sea. He'd no sooner found his dolphin form when Amphitrite joined him. Nereids swam next to her, sending glowing contrails through the sea's murky surface.

He ground his teeth together, the memory of that day still engraved in his memory. The queen of the sea had apologized for her consort, but once she was done, she'd invited Leif to share her bed. Nonplussed, he'd blundered through a refusal. He hadn't totally given up on Poseidon coming to his senses and aiding the sea Shifters. Sleeping with his wife would certainly put the kibosh on any possibility of assistance.

With a knowing smile on her ageless face, Amphitrite said her invitation was open-ended, and she'd encouraged him to give it some thought. The Nereids had flashed breasts and tails his way before the whole convoy disappeared as quickly as they'd arrived.

Fury swept through him. Had Amphitrite been skimming power even then? Or was this something new? A little trick she began experimenting with after the Cataclysm struck?

He raked his wet hair out of his face. If it was Amphitrite, he had an idea. One that would send a nasty magical shockwave boomeranging back in her face the next time she had the temerity to dabble in what didn't belong to her.

"Magic belongs to all of us."

His dolphin's voice reverberating through his mind shocked Leif, and he shot to his feet. "You never talk with me when I'm human. And you're using English. I had no idea you spoke anything but our sea tongue."

A low chuckle tickled the corners of his consciousness. *"How could I not know your human language after sharing your mind for centuries? When we spent most of our time in my body, there was no need to speak during the rare occasions you were human, but we seem to have reached a turning point."*

Leif sent warm thoughts swimming inward. "I agree about magic belonging to us all, but what would you have me do to stymie her?"

"If you set a trap, it will snap shut no matter who's meddling. Right?"

"Maybe. If it's someone from the darker side of things, it might roll off them without much effect, but it should protect the ley lines from further degradation."

"It might be enough." The dolphin paused. *"We must do everything we can to ensure Poseidon and Amphitrite survive. Our power is rooted in theirs, and if they fail…"*

The dolphin stopped there, but it didn't have to say any more. Leif understood. Suddenly, the task stretching before him grew far more complex. Cutting the sea gods off at the knees wasn't an option. No. Somehow, he had to convince them to return to their proper roles. Protection, rather than exacting what they needed without a thought to their subjects.

Weariness crashed over him as he made his way inside. The lower corridor was empty, and he dressed fast. The sooner he laid his thoughts out for the others to pick apart, the sooner they could come up with a plan.

Regardless, they had to move fast, before magic to summon even the simplest of castings ran through their fingers like sand through an hourglass.

www.ingramcontent.com/pod-product-compliance
Lightning Source LLC
Chambersburg PA
CBHW071233190726
48292CB00007B/2268